Kane swung his starboard...

He cut a course that would head him directly for the landing craft instead of the sailboat. He shouted over the drone of the diesel engine to the four-man crew, "Brace yourselves! I'm going to ram!"

Cries of terror burst from the men aboard the Mag boat. A man with a copperhead abruptly sprang up and dived over the far side when he realized what Kane intended to do. The man at the wheel screamed at him to veer off. The crew added their own panic-shrill voices to his screams. They knew if their boat sank, their armor, as lightweight as it was, would still be an impediment in the water.

The rest of the man's shout was overwhelmed by the impact of the turtle-boat ramming the landing boat. The prow of the vessel shattered, planks wrenching, groaning and tearing in splinters twice as long as a man.

Other titles in this series:

JAMES AXLER

OUTLANDERS®

PURGATORY ROAD

THE
IMPERATOR
WARS
BOOK 3

A GOLD EAGLE BOOK FROM

WORLDWIDE®

TORONTO • NEW YORK • LONDON
AMSTERDAM • PARIS • SYDNEY • HAMBURG
STOCKHOLM • ATHENS • TOKYO • MILAN
MADRID • WARSAW • BUDAPEST • AUCKLAND

Once again—let's make this one for Melissa.
And once again, she knows why.

First edition May 2001
ISBN 0-373-63830-2

PURGATORY ROAD

Special thanks to Mark Ellis for his contribution to the
Outlanders concept, developed for Gold Eagle Books.

Copyright © 2001 by Worldwide Library.

There is fear in the night and death in the clouds
for the sculpted dead frozen in their shrouds;
Imprisoned in black purgatorial vales.
                                        —Justin Geoffery

The Road to Outlands—
From Secret Government Files to the Future

Almost two hundred years after the global holocaust, Kane, a former Magistrate of Cobaltville, often thought the world had been lucky to survive at all after a nuclear device detonated in the Russian embassy in Washington, D.C. The aftermath—forever known as skydark—reshaped continents and turned civilization into ashes.

Nearly depopulated, America became the Deathlands—poisoned by radiation, home to chaos and mutated life forms. Feudal rule reappeared in the form of baronies, while remote outposts clung to a brutish existence.

What eventually helped shape this wasteland were the redoubts, the secret preholocaust military installations with stores of weapons, and the home of gateways, the locational matter-transfer facilities. Some of the redoubts hid clues that had once fed wild theories of government cover-ups and alien visitations.

Rearmed from redoubt stockpiles, the barons consolidated their power and reclaimed technology for the villes. Their power, supported by some invisible authority, extended beyond their fortified walls to what was now called the Outlands. It was here that the rootstock of humanity survived, living with hellzones and chemical storms, hounded by Magistrates.

In the villes, rigid laws were enforced—to atone for the sins of the past and prepare the way for a better future. That was the barons' public credo and their right-to-rule.

Kane, along with friend and fellow Magistrate Grant, had upheld that claim until a fateful Outlands expedition. A displaced piece of technology...a question to a keeper of the archives...a vague clue about alien masters—and their world shifted radically. Suddenly, Brigid Baptiste, the archivist, faced summary execution, and

Grant a quick termination. For Kane there was forgiveness if he pledged his unquestioning allegiance to Baron Cobalt and his unknown masters and abandoned his friends.

But that allegiance would make him support a mysterious and alien power and deny loyalty and friends. Then what else was there?

Kane had been brought up solely to serve the ville. Brigid's only link with her family was her mother's red-gold hair, green eyes and supple form. Grant's clues to his lineage were his ebony skin and powerful physique. But Domi, she of the white hair, was an Outlander pressed into sexual servitude in Cobaltville. She at least knew her roots and was a reminder to the exiles that the outcasts belonged in the human family.

Parents, friends, community—the very rootedness of humanity was denied. With no continuity, there was no forward momentum to the future. And that was the crux—when Kane began to wonder if there *was* a future.

For Kane, it wouldn't do. So the only way was out—way, way out.

After their escape, they found shelter at the forgotten Cerberus redoubt headed by Lakesh, a scientist, Cobaltville's head archivist, and secret opponent of the barons.

With their past turned into a lie, their future threatened, only one thing was left to give meaning to the outcasts. The hunger for freedom, the will to resist the hostile influences. And perhaps, by opposing, end them.

Chapter 1

Shoki's slippered feet were silent against the polished cedar floor. Grant caught only a whisper of sound, a glimpse of a flitting shadow. He rolled away, flinging himself clear as the samurai hurtled through the air, driving down with his *naginata*. The curved blade buried itself in the edge of the tub, inches from Grant's right arm.

In that peculiar slowing of time perception in combat, Grant saw everything at once. Shoki's face was twisted with savage anger. Shizuka was pressed against the wall of the tub, her eyes wide in shock. The flame of the lantern flickered in the breeze wafting in through the open door.

While Grant's mind registered each detail of the attack, his body instinctively reacted. As Shoki tried to free his blade from the tub, Grant drove his right fist at the point of the samurai's chin.

The idea was to break his adversary's neck with one blow, but Shoki released the long handle of the *naginata* and rolled with the blow. He staggered half the length of the room, but managed to retain his balance. Grant coiled the muscles in his legs and bounded forward, his broad bare chest colliding violently with that of the Japanese man.

Arms windmilling, Shoki catapulted backward through the rear wall, taking lath work and oiled paper squares with him in a loud, clattering crash. The air was nearly driven from his lungs, but he came to his feet again, kicking and tearing his way through the wreckage to renew the attack. Shizuka shouted shrill words at him, but the man paid her no attention.

Grant felt a flash of grudging admiration for the man's courage. Although he was barely five and half a feet tall, Shoki showed no fear of the big black man. Grant stood six feet four in his bare feet and was exceptionally broad through the chest and shoulders. The scars of past battles were easily discernible on his naked body. Gray sprinkled his short-cropped hair, and a fierce, downsweeping mustache was jet-black against the coffee-brown of his skin.

Shoki launched a straight-leg kick at Grant's exposed genitals, but he turned sideways and the foot landed on his upper thigh, not his groin. Still, the impact hurt, and in response, he hooked a punishing right fist into the samurai's ribs. He heard the crunch of bone, and the Japanese staggered back with a grunt of pained surprise.

Grant moved after him, not wanting to let the man regain his balance or find a new weapon. Shoki kicked out at his groin again, and then at his kneecaps. Grant sidestepped the first kick, but the second one landed on his shin, peeling the flesh up over the bone.

"You little prick!" Grant growled between clenched teeth. Angrily, he kicked out himself, but Shoki dived aside. His dive brought him back to the tub, where he closed his hands around the handle of his *naginata*.

He wrenched the blade loose from the wood, but Grant leaped on him like a black panther. His right hand encircled Shoki's wrist, and he wound his left arm around the man's neck. He drove his knee into the base of the samurai's spine, and Shoki screamed in pain. At the same time the samurai slammed the blunt butt end of his weapon hard into Grant's lower belly.

Air left Grant's lungs in an agonized grunt and his grip loosened. Shoki wriggled free and spun, raising the *naginata* for an overhead blow that would split Grant's skull like a melon.

Shizuka chose that instant to vault over the edge of the tub, water trailing from her naked body. Both of her feet struck Shoki between his shoulder blades, and he stumbled forward, his back arched. The blade hissed down and chopped into the floor barely a finger's width from the tip of Grant's big toe.

Shoki pulled it free and began circling his adversary slowly. "Stay back," Grant growled to Shizuka.

He couldn't afford to have his attention divided.

One wrong move, one misstep and he was dead—
or at the very least, grievously wounded by a cas-
trating scythelike sweep of the *naginata*. Shoki
showed no interest in Shizuka, despite her nudity.

She obeyed Grant's command, but her small,
beautifully shaped mouth compressed in a tight
white line. Shaking her tumble of glossy black hair
from her smoothly contoured face, she slitted her
dark, almond-shaped eyes as she watched the two
men. They glittered with a fierce light. Her complexion, normally a pale gold with accents of roses
and milk, was the color of ashes. Her small breasts
heaved with emotion.

When Shoki feinted, pretending to slash at
Grant's groin, the big man took the feint and cursed
himself an instant later when the samurai shifted in
midmotion and hacked at this throat. Grant ducked,
but he felt the passage of the blade over his head,
so close he wouldn't have been surprised if it shaved
off a few twists of his hair.

From between clenched teeth, Shoki hissed, *"Hir-
etsukan!"*

Grant didn't know what it meant, but he assumed
it wasn't an endearment. Shoki crab-stepped forward, trying a different tactic, whipping the blunt
end of the *naginata* toward Grant's throat. Lifting
his hands, he crossed his wrists and caught the end
of the wooden shaft between them. Grasping it
tightly, he pivoted and yanked the weapon from
Shoki's grasp. He howled as the pole slid through

his hands, inflicting painful friction burns on both palms.

He tossed it aside and advanced on the samurai, half expecting him to flee. Instead he leaped forward, bending at the waist. He extended his leg straight out, and the sole of his foot thudded solidly into Grant's midsection. Air left his lungs in a loud whoof and he stumbled, off balance. Shoki followed through with his leap, chopping with the edge of his hand at the base of Grant's neck.

Although his hand rebounded from the thick ropes of muscle there, the impact caused little pinwheels to ignite behind Grant's eyes. Before they stopped whirling, Shoki secured a stranglehold.

Fingers like flexible iron bands locked around Grant's throat, the thumbs pressing against his larynx. A grin of triumph and exertion creased Shoki's face as Grant growled from deep in his chest. The samurai had a great deal of experience in hand-to-hand fighting, but he hadn't ever pitted himself against someone like Grant.

He brought up his forearms and knocked away the samurai's hands. At the same time, he drove a knee into Shoki's groin and, as he doubled over, folding in the direction of the pain, Grant brought his right fist down like a pile driver on the back of the man's neck. His face hit the floor first, followed a second later by his knees, then the rest of his body.

Grant stood over him, panting and massaging his hand. He had broken a few knuckles before, and he was pretty sure he had done it again. Shizuka came to his side, her dark eyes wide with worry and a flickering gleam of anger. "Are you all right?"

He shook his aching right hand and said, "You'd think after all this time I'd have learned to hit the soft parts."

Shizuka didn't laugh. She bent and wrestled Shoki onto his back. He wasn't a pretty sight. One eye was swollen shut, and his mouth and nostrils leaked blood. A couple of teeth lay on the floor, floating in a little puddle of crimson. She jerked open his robe, lifted his left arm and pointed to a tiny black figure tattooed in his armpit.

"A Black Dragon!" she spit. "I knew he was hotheaded, but I never dreamed he would—"

From somewhere in the vicinity of the palace, three gunshots cracked, sounding like firecrackers going off under a tin can. Wordlessly, Grant and Shizuka threw on their clothes. He didn't express his disappointment to the woman that a second bout of lovemaking was unlikely to be scheduled in the near future. He hadn't expected to spend the aftermath of the first bout fighting for his life against a fanatic. All in all, it had been a hell of a way to end his long celibate streak.

She took less time dressing than he did, and he simply stuffed his feet into his boots without putting on socks or lacing them up. Carrying the *naginata,* Grant followed Shizuka out of the bathhouse. They didn't leave its shadow, because Shizuka suddenly went to one knee and gestured for Grant to do the same. They hazarded a quick look around a sculpted corner hedge.

In the gathering gloom, they saw many dark figures flitting across the lawn, moving in on the rear wall of the castle. "What the hell is going on?" he whispered into her ear.

"The Black Dragons are staging a coup," she responded angrily. "I don't know if they intend to overthrow Lord Takaun or merely bend him to their will, but the Tigers of Heaven can't allow either one to happen."

Grimly, Grant said, "If you can take me to where you stored our weapons, I think we may able to tip the scales in your favor."

She shook her head in frustration. "The room is all the way on the other side of the fortress. It would be the miracle of miracles if we could reach it undetected."

Another cracking gunshot split the sunset. Grant craned his neck to see around the corner of the bathhouse. "Somebody's got a working blaster in there," he murmured. "One guess who."

Shizuka regarded him a searching stare. "Kane-san?"

He smiled bleakly. "He'd be my first choice."

Sounding scandalized, Shizuka demanded in a fierce whisper, "You mean he smuggled a firearm into the palace?"

"Yeah. I wish I'd thought of that."

Shizuka's rejoinder clogged in her throat as one more snapping report sounded. This one was followed by howls of pain. They eased closer and saw a man reeling across the lawn, clutching at his shoulder. Through an open gate surged the Tigers of Heaven, their armor glinting in the sunset.

From almost every shadowed point on the lawn between the bathhouse and the castle rushed a horde of black-garbed and hooded figures wielding swords and lances. They struck the Tigers from both flanks, pushing them toward the rear of the fortress. A resounding roar arose from the ranks of the Black Dragons: "Banzai, banzai!"

There was almost no room to maneuver, and the *katanas* of the Black Dragons penetrated chinks in the Tigers' armor and sank deep into eyes through the slits in the visors. Screams blended in with the clash of steel on steel. The gloom lit up with little flares as blue sparks flew from impact points.

Grant could only pick out the Black Dragons in the swarm of figures by their ebony kimonos. He saw that most of them wore wide headbands, which Shizuka called *hachimaki*. The foreparts were augmented by strips of chain mail, and he guessed they wore chain mail beneath their robes. He recollected how Lord Takaun had described the Black Dragons earlier in the day.

According to the daimyo, their roots stretched back three or more centuries to the last days of Japan's old feudal system. A group of *soshi*, disenfranchised and rabidly xenophobic samurai, formed an underground organization to fight the spread of Western influence. In reality, they were terrorists and later they became Japan's pioneers of organized crime.

The Black Dragon society was revived in New Edo, hiding in plain sight, since most of them were recruited from the ranks of the samurai trainees. They wanted no commerce or contact with the mainland at all, and they were particularly incensed when Grant, Kane and Brigid arrived on the island.

Because he feared alienating the samurai, Lord Takaun didn't take action against the Dragons. He claimed that even offering hospitality to the three outlanders was risking a rebellion, perhaps even a coup. Bitterly, Grant realized the daimyo's fears were grounded in reality.

Then, over the clash and clamor of battle, a new sound floated in on the warm sea breeze. It was the brazen tolling of a bell. It rang in a three-one pattern and then repeated. Shizuka stiffened and stood, wheeling to face the direction of the tolling.

Grant tugged at her hand. "Get down, goddammit! They'll see you."

Shizuka struggled, wresting away from his grip. "No," she said in a strained, hoarse whisper. "The watchman—he's ringing the signal for *raikou!*"

"Who's that?" Grant demanded.

Her voice trembling, her eyes suddenly wide and

wild with terror, Shizuka cried, "Not who—a what. *Invasion!*"

Before he could ask her any further questions, Shizuka lunged from the concealment of the shadowed hedges and sprinted barefoot toward the battling mass of Tigers and Dragons. She shouted stridently as she ran. *"Teisen! Raikou!"*

The brassy gongs of the bell continued ringing in the same rhythm, but the clangor of sword meeting sword commingled with the clatter of pole arms, and completely drowned out the tolling. Biting back a curse, Grant started after Shizuka. His unlaced boots wobbled on his feet, and after stumbling and nearly falling in the first couple of yards, he kicked out of them without breaking stride.

Since he had fought a Black Dragon unarmed and stark naked, he figured facing a horde of blade-wielding men in his bare feet wasn't much of a risk. He had exposed appendages far more tender—and important—to the *naginata* than his toes. He cast a single glance toward the high cliff rising on the far side of the bay, where he could barely make out the watchtower. He was fairly certain of the identities of the invaders, but without confirmation from the watchman, he could only speculate. Still, one word burned in his mind: Magistrates.

The fortress of New Edo's daimyo, Lord Takaun, loomed above the battlefield like a gigantic, dispassionate spectator. Its many windows, balconies and ornately carved frames overlooked gardened terraces. The support columns were made of lengths of thick bamboo, bent into unusual shapes. The curving roof arches and interlocking shingles all seemed to be made of lacquered wood.

Only a few of the shuttered windows showed any light, and Grant wondered if the Black Dragons had already occupied the castle and taken Takaun prisoner. As he drew closer to the battle, he saw that most of the Tigers of Heaven weren't in full armor. Apparently, they had been roused only minutes before the attack.

Shizuka circled the milling edge of combat, screaming at the top of her voice.

A black-kimonoed man broke from the swarm of battle and plunged toward her, *katana* held over his head. A keening cry of battle madness burst from his snarling mouth. The Black Dragon was completely engulfed by blood fever. Grant recognized the symptoms—the man probably would've decapitated his grandmother if she got in his way.

Grant hefted the *naginata* by its long handle, but knew it was ill-suited for use as a javelin. He tried to increase the length of his stride, forcing more speed into his pumping legs. Even as he did so, he realized he wouldn't reach Shizuka before the crazed samurai did.

The curved sword blade in the man's hands slashed down in a stroke that would have split Shizuka's skull had it connected. But she was a samurai, too, and a lightning-swift sliding sidestep shifted her head and body away from the descending *katana*'s razor edge.

The Black Dragon recovered his balance instantly, pivoting on the balls of his feet, bringing his sword around for a disemboweling cut. Scarlet suddenly bloomed on the man's forehead, right above his left eyebrow. Pain and disbelief twisted his face as he staggered backward. His arms flopped bonelessly, and the flared sleeves of his kimono flapped like the wings of an ungainly bird. He fell heavily almost at Grant's feet. The sound of the gunshot, overwhelmed by the clash of swordplay, was like a distant handclap.

Reaching Shizuka, Grant insinuated himself between her petite body and the combatants. As he bent for the fallen *katana,* she impatiently elbowed him aside, stooped and plucked up the sword in two smooth motions. He quashed the impulse to swear at her, forcibly, reminding himself that as delicate as Shizuka appeared, she was still a Tiger of Heaven and far more deadly with a *katana* than he could ever hope to be.

Holding the sword in a double-fisted cross grip, she hissed between clenched teeth, "*Usagiuma!* Jackasses! Fools!"

Grant spotted at least three men among the Dragons who appeared to be wearing wicker baskets over their heads. That choice of headgear struck him as more than foolish—it seemed suicidal. Pointing them out to Shizuka, he asked, "What the hell is with those hats?"

Tersely, Shizuka answered, "They are called *tengai*. They're made out of woven reeds, but there are openings in front of the eyes. They're derived from the *komoso* sect, and the men wearing them are Black Dragon ringleaders, keeping their faces hidden even from their followers."

A stealthy movement on the far side of the courtyard caught Grant's attention. He saw Kane running in a half crouch toward him, holding a *katana* in one hand, not an autoblaster as he expected. Shizuka may not have been happy to learn he'd smuggled in a pistol against the express orders of Lord Takaun, but he doubted she'd upbraid him now.

Kane managed to join Shizuka and Grant without being attacked either by a Dragon or a Tiger. He breathed heavily, his gray-blue eyes burning from the high planes of his face. A shade over six feet tall and rangy of build, he carried most of his muscle mass in his shoulders and chest above a slim waist, which lent him a marked resemblance to a wolf. His longish dark hair held sun-touched highlights. His skin, usually tanned, was still somewhat pale from two weeks of imprisonment in Area 51. He wore a khaki shirt and whipcord trousers. Like Grant, he was barefoot, but unlike him he was unshaved.

"Where's Brigid?" Grant demanded.

Kane hooked a thumb over his shoulder toward

the palace. "Back there. She's going to try and find our weapons."

"I thought you were heeled."

"Baptiste has the blaster." He gestured with his sword toward the head-shot Black Dragon. "She picked him off."

Grant's eyebrows rose, but he kept his comments regarding Brigid's improved marksmanship to himself. Still, he was impressed. It had been a long shot for a handblaster.

Kane tilted his head toward the cliff. "What's the story with that damn bell?"

Clenching her small fists so tightly the knuckles stood out like ivory knobs, Shizuka said, "It's the signal for an invasion. The watchman's code indicates at least one ship."

Kane nodded bleakly, grimly. "A shipload of Mags sent from Baron Snakefish."

Grant's response was equally grim. "That's a safe bet."

A voice bellowed, rising above the din. *"Uragirimono!"*

They recognized it as the voice of Kiyomasa. An instant later, the armored form of the Tiger captain charged through the archway, mounted on a huge black stallion. Froth flew from the animal's mouth as Kiyomasa spurred it into the mob of battling men.

The Tigers made way for him, parting before the horse like the waters of the sea. A couple were too slow and were bowled off their feet. Kiyomasa wasn't wearing a helmet, and by the fading sunlight, they saw how his full-fleshed face was locked in a mask of bare-toothed, homicidal ferocity. With his sharp hooked nose set between and below heavy eyebrows and slitted eyes, he resembled a bird of prey. A thin mustache drooped at the corners of his mouth.

Captain Kiyomasa was armed with two swords, a long *katana* and a shorter *tanto*. The flickering, mirror-bright lengths of steel cut a crimson swath through the Black Dragons. The blades whirled, rose and fell. At each stroke, the swords cleaved through skull, sliced through flesh and severed limbs. Blood sprayed in a scarlet mist, its scent driving Kiyomasa's war horse mad. Neighing shrilly, it reared, forelegs lashing out. Steel-shod hooves slammed a Dragon to the ground with crushed ribs.

The formation of black-clad Dragons wavered, and then began to break apart. The rebellious samurai spread out across the rolling lawn, retreating from the twin blades of Kiyomasa. A voice shouted, and though neither Kane nor Grant understood the words, they knew it was an order for the Black Dragons to stand fast and close up ranks.

Bowstrings twanged and a flight of arrows hissed through the air. Kiyomasa jerked in his saddle, clutching at a feathered shaft that sprouted by magic from his breastplate. His horse screamed as a sharp barb gashed its left flank. The shouts of consternation turned into cries of triumph and the Black Dragons regrouped, moving in again toward the Tigers of Heaven.

Then a thunderclap and a lightning flash erupted in their midst.

Chapter 2

Padding soundlessly on the balls of her bare feet, Brigid Baptiste crept down the corridor, walled on one side by lacquered wooden panels and on the other by squares of opaque, oiled paper. She moved as swiftly as she could, even though her metacarpal bones began to ache.

Although stealth was a consideration, walking in such a fashion also kept her from tripping on the hem of her sky-blue kimono. She had hiked it up and recinched the sash, but it still dragged on the floor.

The dwindling light cast an eerie glow against the opaque paper window shutters and did little to mute the clash, clamor and screams of battle just outside the palace walls. Brigid held the little Colt Mustang in a double-handed grip, leading with the short barrel as she crept down the corridor.

She tried to visualize the layout of the sprawling fortress, accessing her eidetic memory for the most likely location of a storeroom or arsenal. Upon arrival at New Edo that morning, they hadn't been taken on a tour of Takaun's castle, but what she had seen of it was impressed indelibly in her memory.

Brigid was a tall woman, long limbed and full breasted, but she moved down the hallway with the grace of a dancer. Her red-gold mane of hair lay in heavy mounds on her shoulders and against her upper back. Even in the muted light, her big, feline-slanted eyes glittered with the color of emeralds.

From around the corner ahead of her, Brigid heard scurrying, as of swift, shuffling feet. Coming to a halt, she pressed her back against the wall, her finger curling around the autoblaster's trigger. Within a couple of seconds, a woman came around the corner, her feet sliding quickly on the polished floor.

Beneath glossy, piled-high hair that was held in place by long, blunt-tipped needles, her face was whitened by powder and her cheeks were brightly rouged. She was richly dressed in many layers of smoothly woven and embroidered silk. Despite the dim illumination, Brigid recognized her as Yoshika, Shizuka's sister, who had chosen the path of a geisha rather than that of a warrior.

Unlike other members of the geisha class, Yoshika didn't keep her eyes cast downward as she shuffled along. When Brigid stepped out into her path, the girl was startled but didn't seem particularly frightened.

"What are you doing in this part of the castle?" she asked in a high, quavery whisper. "If the Black Dragons discover you—"

She broke off, apparently too horrified by the prospect of the fate awaiting Brigid to even utter it.

Brigid wasn't surprised by Yoshika's facility with English. Upon their first meeting with Shizuka and the Tigers of Heaven, the female samurai told them how English had developed into a second language in Japan, akin to a trade or commerce dialect.

Curtly, Brigid said, "Take me to where our weapons are stored."

Yoshika's brightly painted eyelids fluttered in shock. "I cannot do that. It would be against the orders of the daimyo."

"Then take me to Takaun himself."

"I cannot do that, either. I don't know where he is."

Screams wafted in, hitting high notes of pain and fury. Yoshika flinched at the sound. Brigid latched on to her elbow and turned her around. "You're going to take me to either the daimyo or my weapons. Choose one."

Yoshika resisted for a moment. Even with her piled-high hair, she was still a half-head shorter than Brigid. She allowed Brigid to pull her down the corridor. "I will take you to the storeroom. That is the most likely place to find your weapons."

As they went down the hallway, Brigid was struck by the absence of guards, attendants and retainers. Although she couldn't claim she possessed even a fraction of Kane's uncanny sixth sense—his self-described "point-man's" sense—her flesh prickled with apprehension. She felt extremely vulnerable and exposed creeping along the shadowed corridors in her bare feet, wearing only a thin kimono.

She was also acutely aware that the clip of the Colt Mustang was four rounds short of a full load. Three of them had been expended on a pair of Black Dragons who had attacked her and Kane. The fourth she'd used to pick off a man who menaced Shizuka, but she didn't feel particularly proud of the long-range shot. She disliked shooting the unsuspecting man from cover, even though fully aware the man wouldn't have had a microsecond's hesitation about doing the same to her. But she liked less being plunged into the center of a palace coup.

Yoshika turned to the left. The corridor narrowed, bending sharply several times. They passed several closed door panels, but Brigid heard no sound from behind any of them, so she didn't bother to see where they might lead. She guessed they were in a far wing of the fortress.

Yoshika glanced up at her. "Close now," she said in a breathy whisper.

The girl's behavior certainly didn't seem in keeping with a shy geisha whose pampered life at court was torn asunder by revolution. Brigid tried to quell a rising wave of suspicion, telling herself she distrusted Yoshika because she reminded her of the treacherous Beth-Li Rouch.

When they reached an intersection, Brigid pulled Yoshika to a halt. "Where is everyone?"

In a voice so faint, so low that Brigid had to strain

to hear her, the girl answered, "Taking part in the war, in hiding. I don't know." She wetted her rouged lips with the tip of her tongue. "I think the House of Mashashige dies tonight."

Brigid made no reply as Yoshika moved on again. Swiftly, she replayed the thumbnail history Kiyomasa had provided about the House of Mashashige and the settlement of New Edo.

In the century preceding the nukecaust, the skydark, Japan had made one last attempt to revive its martial philosophy, the Bushido, or the way of the warrior. This attempt earned Japan the questionable distinction of being the first country to suffer from the effects of nuclear weapons. So at the end of World War II, the island nation put aside its weapons, its deification of samurai as folk heroes and its exaltation of a noble death. Instead, it focused on technology and, ironically enough, harnessing atomic power to make a safe and nearly eternal energy source. By the end of the twentieth century, the land of the rising sun was the premier economic power in the Pacific Basin.

On January 20, 2001, the day of the nukecaust, a chain reaction triggered not only meltdowns but explosions in Japan's nuclear reactors. Those in turn sparked volcanic eruptions and earthquakes of such magnitude, all of the smaller islands around Nippon sank without a trace. Northern Honshu, the largest province, was inundated by tsunamis, tidal waves a thousand feet high, according to legend.

All that remained of the land of the rising sun was a mountainous island, barely 150 miles long and no more than seventy miles wide at its broadest point. By the time survivors crept out of shelters and climbed down from mountain peaks, almost none of the technology that had made the country a world economic power remained intact.

But since the Japanese were an extraordinarily industrious race, they rebuilt their nation with the little they could salvage from the ruins. The first postskydark generation wrung its living from the sea, as had their ancestors centuries before.

The old feudal system was revived as an extreme reaction to the Westernization of Japan before the nukecaust. The new society was a return to the old ways of shoguns, samurai and peasants.

The peasants were put to work utilizing what little resources remained on the island. Many of the old skills had been lost, and so the industries that sprang up on the coastal areas pumped pollutants and toxins into both the sea and the air.

When a shogun by the name of Mashashige attempted to reverse this poisoning of Nippon, and end growing civil unrest by peaceful means, he was violently opposed by his own brother. Open warfare broke out, and the slaughter decimated both factions. Although Lord Mashashige was gone, his memory and name lived on in his clan, the House of Mashashige.

In the century following this disastrous coup, a

new group came to prominence. The House of Ashikaga had once been the power in the land until overthrown by Mashashige. Comprised of heretic lords who came to prominence during the anarchy following the war between brothers, the House of Ashikaga was an uncultured clan who appealed to merchants, not nobles or warriors. By good fortune, cunning and cruelty, incredible even in a land of cruelty, they rose to wield unparalleled power. They swore to restore order and prosperity to Nippon as a basis to rally forces to them. Only the House of Mashashige refused their support.

It didn't take long before the Ashikaga clan proved its devotion was less to restoring order to Nippon than to destroying the House of Mashashige, wiping its seed from the face of the earth. To achieve such an end, the Ashikaga clan employed assassins, religious cults and even private armies ruled by self-appointed warlords who served equally self-appointed god kings. These factions often fought among themselves, and so the edge of the sword ruled the country. Death had no meaning, no honor.

Due to these internecine conflicts, the country was in a state of civil war with the lords and landowners choosing sides or straddling the fence, while paying lip service until they saw which way the stick would float. Many of them were disillusioned by the rule of the House of Ashikaga.

The daimyo of the House of Mashashige, Lord

Takaun, made one last attempt to not only reclaim his clan's power but also to restore some semblance of order and dignity to his country. He failed, and the House of Ashikaga wouldn't give him a second chance, vowing to exterminate the Mashashige clan to the last of the line.

Lord Takaun had no choice but to flee into exile. Taking with him as many family members, retainers, advisers and samurai as a small fleet of ships could hold, he set sail into the Cific. Their destination was the island chain once known as the Hawaiians.

But the heavens broke open with the unchained fury of a typhoon. The storm drove the little fleet far off course. The ships had no choice but to make landfall on the first halfway habitable piece of dry ground they came across.

This turned out to be a richly forested isle, the tip of a larger landmass that had been submerged during the nukecaust. Evidently, it had slowly risen from the waters over the past two centuries, and supported a wide variety of animal and vegetable life. Lord Takaun decreed it would support theirs, as well. The exiles from Nippon claimed it as their own and named it New Edo, after the imperial city of feudal Japan.

Of course there were many problems to overcome during the first few years of colonization. Demons and monsters haunted the craggy coves and inland forests. They had a malevolent intelligence and would creep into the camp at night to urinate in the well water or defecate in the gardens. More than one samurai was slain during that time, their heads taken.

But the House of Mashashige didn't just persevere, it thrived, hacking out first a settlement then an entire city from the wilderness. And now, more than eight years later, a new empire arose, but one that kept its existence a secret from the inhabitants of the Western Isles. As Brigid, Kane and Grant had reason to know, many of the isles were overrun by pirates and Asian criminal organizations known as Tongs.

New Edo gave these a wide berth but established a friendly relationship with a coastal ville called Port Morninglight. The little island empire traded with them for several years, until it was wiped out by a force of Magistrates dispatched by Baron Cobalt. Captain Kiyomasa and a contingent tracked the Mags, and their paths intersected with that of the outlanders who were engaged in the same enterprise.

Yoshika stopped in front of a *shoji,* a long sliding door without the usual grid pattern of lath work and oiled paper squares. Head bowed, she said, "In here."

Brigid reached out for the frame, then paused. She gestured with the short barrel of the Colt Mustang. "You do it."

Yoshika said nothing as she carefully pulled at the door, sliding it aside on its narrow floor track. For a moment, Brigid wondered why it wasn't locked, then she assumed no palace attendant or retainer would dare to steal from the daimyo.

The room on the other side of the door was large, with a higher ceiling than Brigid expected. From the roof beams glowed candles in accordion-like paper lanterns. They shed a suffuse illumination over multishelved cabinets twice Yoshika's height, which lined the walls and formed narrow aisles. Big wicker baskets, some of them brimming with grains of rice, were arranged in such a way as to form even narrower walkways. Heaps of piled clothing, long pole arms and even scabbarded swords lay scattered in orderly profusion around the room.

Glancing from one tall cabinet to another, Brigid couldn't discern the shapes on the shelves. She turned toward Yoshika. ''Where are they?''

Yoshika didn't respond in words. She seemed to be preoccupied patting her hair back in place. Brigid caught only a glimpse of the geisha's hand darting from her hair and toward her face. A year's worth of near misses sparked an instinctive leap back before her conscious mind fully registered the thin blade in the girl's hand. The knife left her fingers, passing so close to Brigid's cheek she thought she felt the wind of its passage.

Brigid raised her pistol, but Yoshika grabbed the elbow and wrist of her right arm and twisted as though she were wringing out a wet towel. The fingers of one hand dug into the wing of muscle at her armpit. The girl's grip was astonishingly strong and

painful, and needles of pain lanced through her arm.
Brigid's hand opened and the Colt Mustang fell to
the floor.

Yoshika shifted her hold, trying to get Brigid into
a hammerlock and force her facedown on the floor.
She seemed to know exactly what she was doing.
Brigid gritted her teeth and went in the direction
Yoshika was trying to push her. She had received a
few lessons in down-and-dirty martial arts from both
Grant and Kane, and by not resisting the girl's hold,
she managed to wriggle out of her grip.

Yoshika's hands lashed out, sharp little lacquered
fingernails seeking her eyes. Brigid slapped them
aside and sprang backward, out of reach of the geisha's shorter arms. As she squeezed between a pair
of baskets, she dug her hand into the rice and
scooped up a fistful, flinging the tiny grains into
Yoshika's painted face.

The girl lifted her hands to ward off the cloud of
stinging particles, and as she did so, Brigid leaped
at her, getting behind her and sliding an arm around
her throat. To her surprise, the delicate-appearing
Yoshika didn't cry out. Instead, she leaned heavily
into Brigid as she tried to cinch down the chokehold.
At the same time, she jammed a tiny foot behind
Brigid's heel and threw her entire weight against the
taller woman. Brigid stumbled and released her grip,
not wanting to fall with Yoshika atop her.

She grabbed the edge of a free-standing cabinet
to maintain her balance and felt it sway ever so

slightly. Yoshika didn't press forward. She spun, bounding for a corner where a pair of crossed *katanas* stood. Brigid rushed after her, silently cursing the flapping hem of her kimono as it threatened to snag her toes.

Yoshika reached the corner a full second before the longer-legged Brigid. Closing her dainty fist around the handle of a sword, Yoshika snatched it up and swung it in a fast back arc, obviously hoping Brigid's momentum would carry her right into its edge.

She managed to duck and the blade only ruffled her hair. She heard the other *katana* fall to the floor with a distinctly nonmetallic clatter. Grabbing it, Brigid was perplexed for an instant by its light weight, then understood both weapons were *boken*, wooden practice swords.

The still silent Yoshika danced away as Brigid rose to her full height, then chopped at her. Brigid parried the blow, and the two wooden blades met with a sound like tree limbs being knocked together. She tried to riposte, but the geisha weaved gracefully away.

Deciding it was time to break the silence, Brigid demanded angrily, "What's this about, Yoshika? Are you part of this? Are you with the Black Dragons?"

A small, almost abashed smile tugged at the corners of Yoshika's baby-pursed lips. "You might say that, *gaijin*."

Transferring the *boken* to her right hand, Yoshika shrugged out of her kimono and stood in a sleeveless cotton shift that left her legs bare to the upper thigh. She raised her left arm. Barely visible in the dim light, Brigid could just make out the tiny black tattoo of a black dragon imprinted below the girl's armpit.

"You're a Black Dragon yourself," Brigid grated.

Yoshika nodded. "My sister joined the Tigers, and I joined the Dragons."

"That's taking sibling rivalry to an extreme, wouldn't you say?"

Yoshika's eyes narrowed. "It has nothing to do with that. It has to do with tradition, family honor. My sister turned her back on who we were and our house."

Comprehension dawned in Brigid's mind. "You're of the Ashikaga clan."

Yoshika nodded. "Shizuka hid our family connections from the daimyo so she could advance in the Tigers of Heaven."

"And you used yours to advance in the Black Dragons." As she spoke, Brigid shifted sideways, getting away from the corner.

Yoshika took a half step forward. "Something like that, gaijin. But I have no time to explain it fully."

Yoshika and Brigid circled each other. Brigid gave ground, moving backward between the wicker baskets. She tried to drive away the memories of the devastating performance of swordsmanship she'd seen the Tigers of Heaven display against the Magistrates. Fear would only slow her reflexes, make her clumsy and overcautious.

Yoshika slid her right foot forward, then lunged, aiming a blow for her head. Brigid blocked the cut, slipped sideways between two baskets and struck for Yoshika's arm. An expert twist of the *boken* blocked Yoshika's cut, and she backed away uncertainly, her eyes flickering briefly with respect for the gaijin woman's speed. Sweat beaded her brow, cutting runnels through the thick face powder. Apparently, she had expected to win instantly.

Brigid knew she had scored only a brief respite. Over the past year and a half, she had been involved in any number of life-threatening situations, and she still didn't know if she'd survived them through luck, divine intervention or simply the proper management and application of skills to circumstances. Although she had taken pains to develop survival and fighting skills, they were still undeveloped in many areas, and fencing was one of them.

Not too long before, when dueling with the deranged Otto Skorzeny, he had inflicted a serious injury to her skull. Now she found herself almost unconsciously overprotecting the left side of her head. After a couple of *boken* exchanges, Yoshika noticed how defensive she became whenever the wooden blade came near that part of her head.

Brown eyes glittering, Yoshika rushed Brigid with her wooden sword held high and her body entirely exposed. Brigid tried for a swift thrust, but she realized too late the geisha's maneuver had been a feint. The girl pivoted at the waist and simultaneously she swung her sword in a sideways slash at Brigid's head.

Rather than trying to block the blow, Brigid let herself fall forward beneath it, though she landed unceremoniously on her stomach. Yoshika hadn't expected such an undignified defensive move, and the momentum of her blow caused her to stagger.

Pushing up with her elbows and toes, Brigid swiftly regained her feet, silently enduring the painful throb in her breasts. By the time she was erect, Yoshika had recovered her balance and lunged to the attack again. She barely parried a blow, and Yoshika hammered at her aggressively.

All Brigid could do was duck, weave and deflect as best she could. Still, three blows penetrated her guard and struck her shoulder, ribs and arm. If the sword blade had been steel instead of wood, she knew she would have been killed, or at the very least, permanently maimed.

Brigid couldn't withdraw further into the room. She tried to block Yoshika's thrusts and slashes, but despite the relatively light weight of the *boken*, her muscles were protesting the strain put upon them. Taking a deep breath, she went on the offensive, flailing at Yoshika in a flurry of sword strokes.

Yoshika met the attack by hacking wildly, her *boken* engaging Brigid's sword with bold cross strokes and furious thrusts.

Brigid kept her sword from being knocked out of her hands as the two women circled each other, the blades striking together with an almost continuous clatter. However, her longer reach drove Yoshika backward.

The geisha didn't care for a forced retreat. She closed in on her opponent, body to body, blades crossed and locked. For a long second they stood eye to eye with each other. Yoshika drove her head forward between the two *boken,* trying to blind Brigid with the long blunt needles in her hair.

Brigid leaned back, pushing off from her, but Yoshika pressed her advantage, hammering away with her *boken* as if to beat Brigid to her knees. Brigid blocked and parried, but didn't try a countermove. Her arms began to lose all feeling, the muscles turning to mud, the strength seeping away. A fireball of agony burned in her shoulder socket where Yoshika had earlier dug her fingers. Placing both hands beneath the circular cross guard, she tried to knock the *boken* aside long enough for her to get into an open area.

Yoshika suddenly swatted out with a kick. Her dainty foot glanced off Brigid's hip, and in a blur of motion she hooked the girl's heel with the edge of her sword and gave an upward push.

Yoshika started to fall, but in a lightninglike explosion of reflexes and sinews, she turned the fall into an gymnastic back flip. She landed gracefully in a crouch. At the same time, she launched a blow with the wooden *katana* toward Brigid's unguarded legs.

With animal quickness, Brigid sprang away from the blade, but she wasn't quite quick enough. The weapon whacked against a clump of ganglia behind Brigid's left knee. Yoshika knew exactly where to strike.

As her leg went momentarily weak beneath her, Brigid lunged to the right, dragging her leg like a sack of bird shot, wondering where the hell her Colt Mustang might be.

Yoshika rose to her feet, her eyes flashing in the gloom, her teeth gritted in a snarl or a mocking grin. She spun the *boken* by the handle in her right hand, then swept the blade at her. Brigid ducked the first swipe and stepped inside the backswing. She jabbed the point of her sword into the pit of Yoshika's belly and, as the geisha involuntarily bent in the direction of the pain, slapped her across the face with the flat of the wooden blade. Yoshika rocked back on her heels, blood springing from her delicate nostrils.

Snorting crimson droplets, Yoshika came boring in, swinging wildly. Brigid dodged, spun and stepped back, letting the *boken* go over her head or whip past her torso. Balancing on the ball of her left foot, Brigid threw her long right leg up and around in a crescent kick of the type Kane had taught her.

The side of her foot caught the smaller Yoshika solidly on the point of her rounded chin.

The geisha staggered to one side and came to a bone-jarring halt against a twelve-foot-tall, freestanding cabinet. The shelves held a number of odds and ends. The entire cabinet case teetered and fell. Glass jangled and ceramic jars and pots shattered. Still, Yoshika managed to keep her footing.

Dragging her bare arm across her bloody face, Yoshika came at Brigid again. The two women circled each other once more. Yoshika made a number of feints, lunges and thrusts with the *boken,* but Brigid avoided them all.

They danced around the big chamber, and both felt their strength draining. Breathing in whispering gasps, Yoshika tried to maneuver Brigid into a corner. Her knees wobbled.

"Give it up," Brigid said, wishing her voice didn't sound so hoarse and strained. "This isn't your field. You're an entertainer."

Yoshika husked out a snarl and lunged forward, swinging the *boken* in a humming half circle. Stepping back, Brigid's heel caught on a shard of broken glass. Instinctively recoiling from the pain, she half stumbled. The edge of the wooden blade smashed into Brigid's right side, crunching against bone. As she staggered backward, she felt pain radiating from her rib cage through her torso. She would have fallen, if not for catching herself on the tall cabinet. It tilted slightly beneath her weight.

Gasping for air, Brigid put her back against it. Hampered on her left by a big grain basket and faced with Yoshika's *boken*, her only path of retreat lay on her right. She feinted in that direction, and Yoshika bounded in to block her. Holding the handle with both hands, she brought the *boken* down over her adversary's head.

Brigid shifted to the left and the blade crashed into a shelf, causing small items on it to jump and fall to the floor. As she flung herself to the side, slamming clumsily against the wicker container, she dropped her sword.

Yoshika lunged, and Brigid ducked a vicious roundhouse from her *katana*. The force of her unconnected blow turned Yoshika around completely, and Brigid swept the geisha's feet out from under her with her right leg. As Yoshika sat heavily on the floor, Brigid hooked the corner of the cabinet with her fingers and heaved with all her strength.

The freestanding case tottered, and Brigid kicked herself backward, going over the top of the basket in an uncoordinated somersault. The cabinet swayed, and small items fell from the shelves, clattering to the floor, pelting Yoshika.

The geisha raised an arm and her lips parted, but only a high-pitched keening wail issued from them as the heavy case crashed down atop her. Even over the grate of wood against wood, the snap and splintering of bones came plainly.

Kneading her sore midriff and probing her ribs

for fractures, Brigid climbed to her feet. Rubbing the back of her left knee, she limped toward the door, looking for her Colt Mustang. At the sound of a low groan, she turned.

Yoshika stirred, feebly pushing herself up with an elbow, grunting with the exertion and the pain. Only the girl's head and left arm were visible beneath the heavy case, but she swiped the *boken* at Brigid's ankles when she came near. Contemptuously, she kicked the wooden blade away. Blood glistened from a shallow gash on the crown of her head, and she breathed with difficulty. She had enough breath to bare blood-filmed teeth and husk out, "A trick. I should've expected no less from a gaijin."

"You started it," Brigid stated coldly. "Don't blame me for finishing it."

Yoshika set her teeth on a groan and her eyelids fluttered.

In a flat voice, Brigid asked, "Do you want me to help you or not?

Yoshika shook her head, attempting to curl her lips in a smirk. She coughed, a fine spray of bright crimson froth bursting from her mouth. Brigid guessed she had any number of broken bones and at least one punctured lung. Items and articles that had spilled from the shelves still clinked and rolled across the floor. The wavering candlelight overhead glinted dully from several metal-shelled eggs. By squinting, she saw two grens, one of them a cylindrical Alsatex concussion flash-bang, and the other an incend.

Visually she backtracked the rolling path of the grens and saw a canvas rucksack on the floor. It was one of two war bags Grant and Kane had brought with them to New Edo. Picking up the grens, she stowed them back in the bag and cast her eyes about for the rest of the equipment. She found a Copperhead, a close-assault chopped-down submachine gun.

Gas operated, with a rate of fire of 700 rounds per minute, the magazine held fifteen 4.85 mm steel-jacketed rounds. It was only two feet in length, and the grip and trigger unit were placed in front of the breech in the "bullpup" design, allowing for one-handed use. An optical image intensifier scope fitted on the top of the frame, as well as a laser autotargeter. Its low recoil allowed the Copperhead to be fired in a long, devastating full-auto burst. All of the Cerberus exiles were required to become reasonably proficient with firearms, and the lightweight "point and shoot" subguns were the easiest for the blaster-impaired to handle.

Brigid dug around in the war bag and found a magazine for the Copperhead. She slapped it into the subgun and glanced toward the fallen cabinet. Yoshika's eyes were closed, and her respiration was fitful. More than likely, Grant's and Kane's Sin Eaters and their body armor were beneath the case, pressing against the girl. She briefly considered trying to wrestle the cabinet off Yoshika, but decided it required effort and time she didn't want to expend.

Slinging the war bag over her shoulder by its strap, and carrying the Copperhead, Brigid left the storage room, looking for the nearest exit to outside. Limping slightly, favoring her left leg, she followed the cacophony of battle into an adjacent chamber and saw a closed *shoji*. She pushed it open and stepped onto an elevated terrace overlooking the broad sward of the lawn.

Standing at the railing, she stared at the swirl of men and the flash of swords, estimated the mob was at its thickest about fifteen yards away. A man mounted on a black stallion commanded her attention. He wielded two swords with deadly skill, and at each stroke, crimson mist and scarlet splashes spattered the air. It took her a moment to recognize Captain Kiyomasa. He spurred his horse among them like a flesh-and-sinew avalanche.

His blades wove lethal nets of flashing steel around him. A quick slash sent a Black Dragon tumbling backward with his entrails oozing from his belly, while a downward chop split a man's skull from crown to chin. Stabbing with one sword, slicing with the other, Kiyomasa wrought crimson havoc. His horse raged like a crazed elephant, and for a moment, he cleared a space of adversaries except for those who lay wounded or dying on the ground.

Then a hail of arrows hissed all around Kiyomasa,

and Brigid saw him jerk in the saddle as a three-foot-long shaft drove through his breastplate. Miraculously, he remained on the horse's back.

Swiftly, she took the flash-bang stun grenade from the bag, pulling the pin and slipping off the spoon all in one smooth motion. She threw it toward a knot of black-kimonoed men advancing on Captain Kiyomasa. Brigid watched as it arced over their heads, then fell out of sight among them. A couple of seconds later, a stunning, painfully loud thunderclap battered at her ears. A blazing nova of dazzling white light accompanied the teeth-jarring concussion of compressed air.

Brigid squinted against the flash, instinctively recoiling. As she stepped back, an arm encircled her neck from behind and yanked her off her feet.

Chapter 3

"Well," Grant announced, knuckling the flash-induced spots from his eyes, "I guess Brigid found our stuff."

The brief shout of triumph voiced by the Black Dragons when they saw Kiyomasa pierced by an arrow clogged in their throats in the aftermath of the gren's detonation. The men closest to the epicenter of the explosion reeled around in agonized shock, hands either clapped over blinded eyes or cradling hemorrhaging ears.

Blinking back the multicolored specks swimming across his vision, Kane saw that Kiyomasa was still in the saddle, but he had dropped the reins and one of his swords. He gripped the animal's mane with one hand as it neighed shrilly and kicked wildly. Its hooves smashed into Black Dragons who were too dazed or dazzled to get out of its panicky path.

Kane waited tensely for more action from Brigid's quarter, even another gren to keep the combatants disoriented. After a few moments when none was forthcoming, he hefted his appropriated *katana* uncertainly. "Something's wrong," he bit out. "I'm going to check it out."

He took several running steps toward the palace, trying to skirt the ebb and flow of Dragons and Tigers. Grant called out to him, but his words were muffled by the noise of battle. Still, he caught the tone and whirled just as a knot of black-kimonoed men broke from the ranks and rushed him, Shizuka and Grant.

A mirror-bright blade lashed at Kane's head. He twisted aside, but its keen edge slid along the top of his right shoulder. He felt the slow, warm spread of blood beneath his shirt.

He slashed swiftly in return, a half cut, half thrust at the Black Dragon's groin, seeking to sever the femoral artery. The blade ripped a straight, clean slash in the kimono, and the man sprang back, crimson streaming from a cut just below his navel.

The Black Dragon's lips drew back from his teeth in a silent snarl, and he lunged, whipping the *katana* in left and right vertical arcs, menacing Kane's head, throat and chest. He had no choice but to leap backward to avoid the razored blade. His heel caught on an irregularity in the lawn, and he stumbled.

The Black Dragon moved in to deliver a killing stroke. Kane glimpsed a flicker, like starlight reflecting off a mirror, and the man came to a halt. His eyes squinted, then widened as they looked at the flat curve of steel protruding from his chest. His mouth opened as if to ask a question, and a flood of vermilion spilled out.

The Black Dragon fell to his knees, then flopped

onto his face. Grant stood behind him, working to free the blade of the *naginata* from the man's back. Two men wearing wicker *tengai* helmets charged, each armed with *kusari-gama,* weapons made of crescent-bladed sickles and lengths of chain. The men spun the weighted ends over their heads, and they whirred like the wings of insects. The Dragons released the chains and the chains shot forth. Kane dodged one, but Grant, still trying to yank the *naginata* from the corpse, was too slow. The chain wrapped twice around his hastily raised right arm.

The Dragon pulled forward, as if he were trying to land to fish. For a moment, Grant dug in his heels and tried to hold his place. The man tugged viciously, tightening the links around Grant's arm. The thick ropes of muscle swelled as he resisted the pressure of the chain. He suddenly lunged forward, kicking himself off the ground.

The Black Dragon stumbled backward when the strain disappeared from the metal links, and he tried to bring the sickle on the end of the chain to bear. As he backpedaled, two long-legged bounds brought Grant within reach. His left arm shot out, and his knotted fist landed solidly in the center of the Dragon's face. The man hurtled over onto his back, his face a smear of blood and broken teeth.

Kane moved in on the other Black Dragon before he could launch his *kusari-gama* a second time. The man didn't try, having seen how quickly his companion was dispatched by the big black gaijin. He assumed a combat stance, his legs planted firmly, his arms held at an angle to his body, his fingers hooked like claws. His slitted eyes glittered, and his lips peeled away from bared teeth. A high-pitched, eerie wail issued from between them.

Kane wasn't intimidated, even though he didn't recognize the posture or the school from which it was derived. Mag martial arts training borrowed shamelessly from every source—from tae kwon do to savate to kung fu. The style focused primarily on the aspects of offense rather than defense. Magistrate doctrine taught never to be defensive when any opportunity presented itself to go on the attack. Most Mags had no idea when or even how to back off.

The Black Dragon launched a roundhouse kick at Kane's midriff in a lightning-swift semicircle. Kane couldn't evade it, so he moved into the arc, striking down with his right elbow an instant before the man's heel made contact. Even over the cacophony of combat, the sharp crack of the shin bone snapping was as loud as a gunshot.

Kane's arm rebounded and straightened, his fist striking the Black Dragon's throat. The man was already overwhelmed by the pain of his broken bone, and so the collapse of his larynx was almost an afterthought.

As he rolled on the ground, spitting up jets of blood and plucking at his lower right leg, which somewhat resembled an inverted L, Kane spun in time to deflect a short sword aimed at his ribs. He back-fisted it aside, hitting the flat of the blade. He spun to his left on one foot while the other swept out and down to scythe behind the Black Dragon's ankle. The man went down, chopping at Kane's legs as he fell in a bid to take him down with him, or at least inflict an incapacitating wound.

Kane jumped straight up, and the *katana* slashed empty air but almost close enough to shave calluses from the soles of his feet. He tried to land on the man's belly with all of his strength, but the Dragon rolled frantically to one side, wrenching himself erect at the same time. The blade of his sword licked out. Kane had no time to dodge.

The man's legs suddenly went out from under him as if he had slipped on an oil slick. As he went down, Kane saw that his features were blurred by a wet red smear. On the fringes of his hearing, he heard the familiar hollow boom of Sin Eater. He spun toward the palace, trying to pinpoint the source of the shot.

Kiyomasa's horse came pounding out of the mob of men, clods of turf flying from beneath its hooves. Kiyomasa slumped in the saddle, clutching at the feathered shaft sprouting from his chest. The animal would have galloped past, but Grant leaped forward and secured a grip on the bridle. The horse screamed, showed its teeth and tried to rear. Kane joined him, grabbing the reins. They exerted all of their upper-body strength and managed to bring the animal to a halt. Kane spoke to it soothingly.

Kiyomasa tried to dismount but with a wheeze he toppled sideways. Shizuka was there to catch him, and to Kane's surprise and admiration she didn't fold beneath his weight. She eased him down as carefully as she could. Kane released the horse, but it didn't run away. It stood trembling, blood trickling from a cut on its flank, its coat shining with lather. Lowering its head, it sniffed at Kiyomasa then pawed the ground nervously.

Cradling Kiyomasa's head in her arms, Shizuka spoke to him briefly. The samurai captain's lips writhed, and he grasped her upper arm convulsively. Kane saw him speak, but he could hear nothing. The man's respiration was labored, and a scarlet froth flecked his lips.

Kiyomasa's mouth creased in a small smile, and he folded his hands over his chest, arranging his legs in a position of grave dignity. He closed his eyes, shuddered almost imperceptibly and died.

Shizuka gently placed his head on the ground and remained crouched over him. Grant reached out and laid a hand on her shoulder. "We can't stay here, Shizuka."

She flung his hand away and sprang to her feet, snatching up Kiyomasa's long *katana* in the process. A mad cry of fury exploded from her throat, and she raced toward the fringes of the battle zone, shrieking words of rage. Grant and Kane went after her.

Shizuka met a Black Dragon who thrust a barbed *yari* spear at her torso. She parried it and swung the flat of the sword in her left hand into the man's stomach. He doubled up from the pain. She didn't follow through with a decapitating stroke. Rather, she screamed, *"Kankou!"*

He spit a word that even to Kane and Grant sounded like an insult, and forced himself to straighten. He whipped the spear in an overhead arc.

Shizuka raised her swords, crossing them to fashion an X, and caught the blow that would otherwise have split open her skull. The force of the blow drove her to one knee. Grimacing, she pushed the spear shaft upward with her two weapons. She strained against the man for a long moment, then flung herself to one side, executing a reverse slash in the same shaved sliver of a second. The edge of her blade surgically removed the Black Dragon's left foot right above the ankle.

He performed a hobbled back jump, his mouth opening as he tried to comprehend why his foot still stayed on the grass when the rest of him had moved away. In that half second of confusion and disbelief, Shizuka's right-hand *katana* sliced through his neck, separating the head from it. A scarlet-foaming fountain spumed from the opened arteries. Blood spattered across her cheek and upper chest in an artless, speckling pattern.

Eyes ablaze, Shizuka whirled toward Kiyomasa's stallion. It still stood over the body of its dead master, nuzzling his face. She pushed between Kane and Grant and ran toward it. The horse didn't shy at her approach, not even when she leaped nimbly into the saddle. It tossed its head, its mane whipping wildly as if impatient to rejoin the battle.

Alarmed, Grant snatched at the bridle. "Wait, goddammit! You can't just charge in there—"

The stallion twisted away, and Shizuka brandished her twin swords. She cried shrilly, "That's exactly what I am going to do! This insanity ends *now!*"

She drove her heels into the horse's ribs, and it bounded toward the field of combat. Grant cast a fearful glance toward Kane and shouted, "Find Brigid and something to give us an edge!"

With *naginata* in hand, he sprinted after Shizuka. Kane started to call him back, but he closed his mouth, not wanting to distract his partner. He watched, expecting at any second to see an arrow fell Shizuka or a sword to pierce her.

He was surprised to see the swords clenched in either fist block and parry thrusts aimed at her. With a savage yell throbbing in Shizuka's throat, woman and stallion thundered among the milling combatants. Without any urging the horse made a leap and launched itself into the press of men and steel.

Then came madness—a din of screams, a forest of blades that waved about Shizuka but parted before her. Both the Black Dragons and the Tigers of Heaven reacted as if the horse and rider had dropped onto them out of the sky. The stallion wallowed a moment across crumpled human bodies, trampling and biting while Shizuka's weapons rose, fell and licked out with terrible effect.

Grant formed a mobile bulwark around Shizuka and her mount, deploying all of the skill and combat acumen he had earned through years of training and bloody experience. Again and again the curved blade of the *naginata* turned a sword from Shizuka's back or beat aside a spear point meant for the horse. The long pole intercepted blows that would have killed the woman. Twice he took superficial cuts on his own body.

Kane clenched his teeth, his jaw muscles knotting as he watched. It wasn't easy to guard another person and keep from being gutted at the same time. He took a few steps toward the mob, then saw a couple of partially armored Tigers of Heaven rallying to Grant's side.

"Ryouko!" Shizuka shouted.

He turned, then, and ran for the palace, toward the overhanging terrace from which he had seen the gren fall. Grasping a low crossbar, he heaved himself up and vaulted over the top rail. He cast a glance over his shoulder to the killing zone.

Shizuka and her stallion formed the leading point of a wedge formation. The Black Dragons couldn't stand up to them, so they parted to both sides, like the sea before the prow of a ship. The Tigers pressed in against one flank, and helped to drive the Dragons relentlessly back until they had to turn to meet another frontal assault.

Back and forth the battle rolled, blades sinking into flesh, piercing chests, hacking into bone, feet churning the ground into crimson-tinged sludge. Shizuka and Grant moved through the whirling, eddying mass of men, shouting and slashing. Again and again a Black Dragon who slashed at her found a blade in his chest before he could strike. Arrows missed her as she moved like a lithe, phantom centaur.

Kane went through the open *shoji* and nearly tripped on a pair of bodies just inside the door. Reflexively, he whipped up his *katana*, squinting to see through the gloom.

In a harsh whisper, Brigid declared, "It's me, Kane—and Lord Takaun."

Stepping closer, Kane saw the daimyo of New Edo lying in a half-prone position, his back against the wall. Takaun was a slender man of medium height. He wore an unadorned red kimono, and his blue sash bore no ornamentation at all. His clean-shaved face was narrow, with heavy eyebrows over hooded eyes. His long black hair, shot through with silvery threads, lay loosely over his shoulders. Even in the poor light, Kane could see how the front of his robe glistened wetly. Brigid kneeled beside him, pressing a rolled-up cloth against the man's midsection.

"He was very nearly assassinated," she said tightly. "By Yoshika."

Kane dredged his memory to place a face with the name. "Yoshika, the geisha? Shizuka's sister?"

"And," Takaun said with a surprising calm, "a Black Dragon. Her masquerade was perfect. She stabbed me with one of her hairpins. I believe it was treated with *fugu* poison."

Kane went to one knee beside him. "What's that?"

"It comes from the sex organs of the globefish. In the old days, my people relished it as both a delicacy and a way to commit suicide."

Brigid said, "The scientific name for it is tetrodotoxin. It's like curare—causes paralysis of the central nervous system. Apparently, Yoshika didn't get in a real good shot."

"What she managed was sufficient," Takaun said mildly. "Already I am suffering from double vision and can barely keep my head up. Soon my lungs will be paralyzed."

"I'll have to give you artificial respiration," Brigid said matter-of-factly. "The fact you're still breathing at all shows the dose she gave you wasn't strong enough to be lethal."

Kane edged closer and on the floor beside Brigid he saw a war bag and an unholstered Sin Eater. Swiftly, he reached across Takaun and snatched the blaster. Although his and Grant's Sin Eaters were virtually identical, he instinctively knew it was his own. He began to holster the big-bored automatic to his right forearm. The Sin Eaters were more than

just weapons; they were almost as much a badge of
office as the Mag duty badges. All Magistrates were
expected to know their assigned side arms more intimately than anything else in the world.

Less than fourteen inches in length at full exten-
sion, the weapon featured a magazine that carried
twenty 9 mm rounds. When not in use, the stock
folded over the top of the weapon, lying perpendic-
ular to the frame, reducing its holstered length to ten
inches. When the Sin Eater was needed, the wrist
tendons were flexed in a certain way, and sensitive,
electrically powered actuators activated a flexible
cable in the holster and snapped the weapon
smoothly into the hand, the stock unfolding in the
same motion. Since the pistol had no trigger guard
or safety, only a firing stud, the Sin Eater fired immediately upon touching the crooked index finger.
Sin Eaters were incredibly lethal weapons and almost impossible for a novice to manage. Recruits
were never allowed live ammunition until a tedious,
six-month-long training period was successfully
completed.

Kane ejected the clip, saw one round was missing
and quirked a questioning eyebrow toward Brigid.
She said, "Lord Takaun had it in his hand when he
came across me."

Weakly, Takaun said, "I had it brought to me so
I could examine it. I'm shamed to admit that its
intricacies eluded me."

"But not you, Baptiste?" Kane inquired with a thin smile.

"I've seen you operate it enough for me to know how to unholster it."

Slamming the clip back into the blaster, he said, "I'm damn glad you're such a quick study. You probably saved me from being filleted."

Her lips creased in a wan smile. "I'd say there was no 'probably' about it."

"How goes the battle?" Takaun rasped.

Once he felt the familiar, comforting weight of the autoblaster, Kane's optimism level rose. "It's been a seesaw. Kiyomasa is dead, and Shizuka has taken command of the Tigers of Heaven."

Picking up the war bag, Kane pawed briefly through its contents, identifying by feel two CS gas grens and another flash-bang. He noted the Copperhead slung over Brigid's shoulder. Taking the concussion gren, he handed the bag to her and turned toward the terrace. "Stay with Takaun."

She stiffened, opening her mouth to voice a protest, but he cut her off with a sharp gesture. "I need you here as my ace. Keep watching me. When you see my signal, lob those gassers."

Her jade eyes narrowed momentarily in worry. "They'll affect both parties."

"Not if my plan works out." He smiled sourly. "And what are the odds of that?"

She smiled at his bit of self-deprecating humor. "Hopefully, they'll be more than one percent."

He grinned fleetingly in appreciation, brought his index finger to his nose and snapped it away smartly in the "one percent" salute. It was a gesture he and Grant had developed during their Mag days, reserved for undertakings that appeared to have vanishingly small chances of success.

Takaun tried to lift an arm and reach out for Kane, but all he accomplished was a spasmodic contraction of his hand and fingers. "Kane-*san*," he croaked, "try to spare the Black Dragons. They are still my people."

"That," replied Kane flatly, "is entirely up to them."

Chapter 4

Kane vaulted over the top rail of the terrace and landed clumsily, going to one knee and nearly dropping the flash-bang. His left ankle twinged. He cursed the weakness in his legs, a consequence of his captivity in the subterranean stud farm beneath Area 51.

Struggling to his feet, Kane jammed the gren into his pocket and loped toward the edge of the battle, trying to find the least fatal area to insert himself. Where the press of combatants was the thickest, he saw Shizuka still astride the black stallion, her two bloodstained swords hewing up and down. Red gashes on her ivory thighs trickled blood, so some weapons had gotten past Grant's guard. Men fought wherever they could, spread out all over the lawn. Taking the palace didn't seem to be the objective any longer.

Both factions had suffered heavy losses, and though Kane felt great respect for the courage of the Tigers and the Dragons, he held little admiration for the tactics they employed. Whoever lost the battle died. The only rule was victory or death, with no middle ground. Kane thought it was monumentally stupid and an incredible waste.

Achieving a goal had become less important than the warriors' own illusory values or honor. Kane had seen egocentric illusions bring death and destruction before. The Magistrates, although not as single-minded about personal honor as the samurai, still put their own arrogance ahead of shrewd strategy. There was certainly nothing shrewd about this butchery.

Still, he couldn't completely condemn either warring faction of samurai. The similarities between the warriors of New Edo and the Magistrates were greater than any minor differences. Both Tiger and Dragon had decided to follow paths laid down by their forebears, eschewing their own identities in favor of those chosen by others.

Grant and Kane had chosen to smother their own identities, as had their fathers and grandfathers before them. All Magistrates followed a patrilineal tradition, assuming the duties and positions of their fathers. They didn't have given names, each taking the surname of the father, as though the first Magistrate to bear the name was the same man as the last.

The originators of the Magistrates had believed that only surnames, family names, engendered a sense of obligation to the duties of their ancestors' office, insuring that subsequent generations never lost touch with their hereditary roles as enforcers.

Last names became badges of social distinction, almost titles.

And like the samurai who had sworn oaths of fealty to a daimyo or an emperor, the black-armored Magistrates ruthlessly enforced the laws of the baronies, believing it was the only way to wring a degree of order out of postnuke chaos. For many years, both Kane and Grant had believed the only way to stem the floodtide of anarchy was to unquestioningly obey the laws of the barons.

As Magistrates, the courses their lives followed had been charted before their births. They had exchanged personal hopes, dreams and desires for a life of service. They were destined to live, fight and die, usually violently, as they fulfilled their oaths to impose a degree of order upon the chaos of postnukecaust America. Kane's life had taken another course, but he learned later he was following the secret path laid down by his father.

Reaching the swirling eddy of battle, Kane paused uncertainly. Figures were locked in a mass of combat, falling to the ground beneath the impacts of blades and spears. Black Dragon and Tiger of Heaven ran this way and that, in disorganized clusters of terror and fury.

A Tiger fell at Kane's feet with a wheeze, clutching his hands to his upper body where a feathered shaft sprouted. A spattering of arrows fell. The thrum of loosed bowstrings vibrated through the air, and more warriors fell gasping and crying out.

Taking a deep breath of resolve, Kane lowered his head and lunged into the melee, using the heavy metal frame of his Sin Eater as a bludgeon to clear a path. He whacked skulls, knocking black-kimonoed men out of his way. He didn't want to shoot any of the Black Dragons, even though he was fairly certain neither they nor the Tigers carried firearms. Shizuka had told them New Edo possessed a very limited supply of blasters, and an even more limited supply of ammunition, claiming they didn't have the natural resources to manufacture much of it themselves.

Over his head came a faint whoosh, a glint of some dark metal, and a stinging force ripped the *katana* from his hand. Kane flung himself backward, trying to shake some feeling back into his numbed hand. A large black-robed man sprang from the press of battle, whirling a metal flail or whip in his right hand. Connected to a wooden pole about four feet long, the *chigiriki* was a series of iron rods linked together by metal rings. A heavy iron weight with beveled edges dangled from the end.

Kane hastily leveled his Sin Eater, but the flail snapped out again and smashed hard into the frame of the blaster. His pistol snapped back into the holster, and he realized with a mixture of disgust and fear the spring-release-cable mechanism had been knocked askew. He knew from past experience it couldn't be repaired quickly.

Kane backed away, keeping his eyes on the man's

feet. The whirling lengths of metal hummed through
the air in a blurry circle. He knew better than to
stare at them, because the spinning motion induced
a mild hypnotic effect.

Feinting to the left, Kane leaped to the right, pivoted and swung his left leg up and around in a perfect crescent kick. The Black Dragon surged forward
in the opposite direction. Kane's foot grazed his
head, but the weighted end of the *chigiriki* slapped
into Kane's ribs, smashing all the wind out of him
and knocking him backward.

Trying to ignore the needles of intense pain lanc-
ing up his rib cage, fighting for breath, Kane recovered his balance. His eyes searched the ground for
his *katana*.

The Black Dragon snapped the jointed lengths of
iron at him like a bullwhip. Kane ducked, and the
weighted end went over his head and slammed into
the ground, knocking a fist-sized divot out of it.

While the Dragon reeled in the *chigiriki,* Kane
launched himself forward. Doubling the metal rods,
the samurai met Kane's attack by whacking him
across the midsection. Dazed and nauseated, Kane
managed to shift the weight of his body, and he
caromed against the Black Dragon, grabbing a double fistful of kimono as he went down. Both men
fell heavily, and Kane struggled and heaved and
achieved a kneeling position atop the samurai.

He pinioned the man's right wrist under his knee.
With his free hand, the Dragon clawed savagely at

Kane's eyes. Batting aside the hand, Kane dashed a straight right into the snarling face under him, and started a flow of blood from the lips.

With a nimble twist and sidewise wrench of his whole body, the Black Dragon managed to shove Kane to one side and club at him with the doubled *chigiriki*. The blow glanced off Kane's raised forearm. He rolled and came swiftly to his feet, and planted a foot on the side of the man's neck as he tried to rise.

The Black Dragon went over on his back, but he unleashed the full length of the *chigiriki* in a snakelike strike directly at Kane's head. Kane leaned backward, and the weighted end only brushed the collar of his shirt. Arcing past him, it crashed between the shoulder blades of a Black Dragon, knocking him face first to the ground, probably with a fractured spine.

Thrown off balance, the Dragon tried to lift the heavy rods for a backhand blow, but Kane took a quick step forward and stab-kicked hard at his hand. There was a sharp snap as a wrist bone broke.

The Black Dragon yelled with pain, and his fingers slackened around the leather-bound handle. Kane kicked the *chigiriki* out of his grasp.

The Dragon hugged his broken wrist, and his left hand groped for something on his right hip. Raising his voice, he yelled, *"Zensen!"*

Kane slashed down with a stiffened hand. Weighted by the Sin Eater, his right arm fell like a pile driver. The heel of his hand chopped into the base of the Black Dragon's neck. With a liquid gurgle, the man sagged to the ground and lay still.

Kane wasn't sure if he was breathing or not, and at the moment he didn't give much of a damn. Metacarpal bones in hands still aching, he pulled the flash-bang from his pocket, thumbed away the spoon and hurled the gren toward a clot of Black Dragons closing in around Shizuka and Grant.

The gren bounced unnoticed over the ground and detonated at the men's feet. Kane turned his head just as a star seemed to go nova. An intolerable white glare blazed, bleaching all of the shadows out of the area. Amid the flash of light, pebbles, dirt and pieces of turf were flung in all directions.

The very air shuddered with the concussion, and even over the shivering echoes of the explosion, Kane heard men crying out in pain. He saw at least three men writhing on the ground, faces bloody from wounds inflicted by fragments of the gren's casing.

With alarmed shouts, the Black Dragons started to run toward the palace, but Brigid's Copperhead stuttered from the terrace, the bullets kicking up dirt divots in front of them, stinging them with rock particles. The Black Dragons began a stumbling, stubborn retreat toward the gate.

When the horde reached a certain point, Kane lifted both arms over his head in two fast, frantic waves. While the Dragons tried to rally and bring their weapons to bear, Kane saw Brigid at the terrace rail, hurling a cylinder with a looping overarm toss. It passed over the heads of the Black Dragons, trailing a little stream of acrid vapor. It landed among them and burst with a loud pop. Billowing plumes of white smoke erupted from it.

Yells and shouted commands became incomprehensible coughs as the CS gas seared eyes, lungs and nostrils. Gagging and choking, the Black Dragons made a blind, blundering rush for the gate and fresh air. They stumbled into the waiting blades of the Tigers of Heaven, but even they were coughing and weeping.

Kane's lungs, throat and eyes began to burn. As he tried to clear his vision, a rush of bodies bowled him off his feet, knocking him sprawling. Sandaled feet trampled him, kicked him, stumbled over him. Tigers and Dragons alike fought above him.

As he knuckled tears from his eyes, an adrenaline-fueled panic forced him to his knees. He started to rise, but the movement attracted the attention of a nearby Dragon. He yelled and started to lunge with a *yari* spear meant to impale him. He suddenly dropped to his hands and knees and vomited copiously.

Getting to his feet, Kane tried to move with the flow of the fight, but he realized it had swiftly become a rout. The Black Dragons fled toward the gate, groping their way through the shifting clouds of chemical vapor.

Shizuka, still astride Kiyomasa's black stallion,

blocked the way. She was bleeding from a score of wounds on her legs and arms, but her dark eyes glittered with a strange, intense light. She swept her twin blades back and forth, driving the half-blind Black Dragons back, shouting at them at the same time, *"Kankou! Koufuku!"*

The Dragons milled away uncertainly, their faces stained with tears and mucus. They were instantly surrounded by sword and spear points, most of them caked with blood. The Tigers of Heaven didn't lower their weapons, but they didn't carry through with an attack, either. Shizuka continued to shout, and then a man wearing one of the wicker *tengai* helmets pushed from the crowd and with a sword gestured imperiously to her. A torrent of harsh syllables came through the crosshatched square in the helmet.

Shizuka instantly sprang from the saddle and with a shout and a slap sent the horse galloping through the archway. She advanced on the helmeted man, sweeping her swords in elaborate patterns, warning friend and foe alike this was a single combat. At once the two figures were alone in a little cleared space.

Kane didn't understand what either person had said, but he guessed Shizuka had issued a challenge to the titular leader of the Black Dragons. He came forward to settle the civil war on New Edo once and for all.

Shizuka and the Black Dragon faced each other

only two yards apart. They bowed to each other. Then the swords of both combatants swung in whistling curves and shocked together with little star-bursts of sparks at the point of impact. There was a ringing clash of steel, and Shizuka's left sword fell to the ground. Kane could tell her hand, if not her entire arm, was numbed by the force of the sword stroke. She stumbled back half a pace, pain glinting for an instant in her eyes.

The Black Dragon leaped into the air, his *katana* high over his head, his arms coming down in a powerful stroke that would split Shizuka from shoulder to hip. Then Shizuka shifted her body, dropping down, knees bending her low to the ground but her upper body erect as if she were still standing. With a whipping, corkscrewing motion, she drove her sword upward. From all sides came murmurs and gasps of fear.

Shizuka's *katana* entered the Black Dragon leader's body at his left hip. It cut deep, the curved tip extending nearly six inches from the man's back. It slid with ease through the kimono, flesh, muscle and bone, moving up at angle until the blade slashed free of the Dragon's body at the junction of his left shoulder. Scarlet sprayed from cleanly severed arteries.

The Black Dragon dropped on his side to the earth, his intestines slithering out of his body cavity. Shizuka's *katana* rose and fell one final time, and the *tengai* helmet fell away from the man's shoulders. His head rolled from it, like a melon from a basket of fruit.

Shizuka bent and caught up the head, holding it aloft by its samurai topknot. Kane couldn't tell much of the dead man's face, only that it was contorted in a grimace of astonishment. Facing the Tigers and Dragons, Shizuka made a short, grim speech, shaking the head for emphasis. Blood sprinkled from the severed neck, spattering those who stood nearest to her.

Shizuka stopped speaking and stood motionless, her breasts heaving with passion. She glared into the stricken faces around her. Finally, the Tigers of Heaven found their tongue. "Shizuka! Shizuka! Shizuka!"

They shook their red-stained weapons over their heads as they shouted. The crashing chant, repeated over and over, took possession of the Black Dragons, and within moments they were screaming her name with just as much fevered reverence.

Kane wasn't particularly surprised by the change of heart. The rebellious Dragons saw only two options—to continue to press their coup and die to a man, or to swear loyalty to the samurai who had slain their leader. From here on, they would obey her every command, appease her every whim with a kind of devotion different yet more powerful than that they would have given to a man.

Kane recalled she was named in honor of Shizuka Gozen, a heroine of feudal Japan. She was a member of a great samurai family during the eleventh-century reign of Yoritomo, the first shogun. She fell in love with Yoritomo's brother and rival for the throne, Yoshitsure. When he became a fugitive, Shizuka was forced into Yoritomo's harem. One evening, when she was ordered to entertain him, she defiantly sang a song in praise of his brother. The shogun was so enraged that when Shizuka gave birth to a male child, he had the baby murdered before her eyes. She became a martyr to women's rights in male-dominated Japan.

But now Shizuka was no longer a woman or even a Tiger of Heaven—she was a goddess.

Grant's voice rumbled into his ear, "I guess this little war is finally settled."

Kane turned to see him standing just behind him, his face blood streaked and battered, his eyes squinting in pain. "Yeah," he replied, nodding toward the pinnacle of the cliff from which the bell still tolled. "Just in time for us to fight a new one."

Chapter 5

Ramirez stood aft by the rail of the CG-47 cruiser, looking at the mile-distant jagged peaks looming up from the sea. They were highlighted by the rays of the setting sun, which washed them with variegated smears of pastel color. The glittering stars above the cliffs, the first of the evening, were like powdered diamonds, sprinkled onto a vast dark blue velvet tapestry.

He pulled his gaze away from the sky, slightly ashamed of his own frivolity of thought. The ability to conceptualize lyrical similes wasn't part of his Magistrate training. A thing was what it was, black and white, A or B, dead or alive, with no neutral ground in between. The destination of the CG-47 cruiser certainly wasn't neutral ground.

The island of New Edo was the largest of a smaller string consisting of four islets. The main landmass reared out of the sea like a massive cube of black volcanic rock. He could barely discern the touch of green vegetation on the summit of a small peak. Atop it, he saw the silhouette of a watch or bell tower. Castellated escarpments loomed at least a hundred feet above the surface of the Cific. Thundering waves crashed and broke on the bare rock, spraying foam in all directions. He couldn't see the passage at the base of cliffs, though Intel claimed it was there.

Still, the sight of the dark cliffs beneath star-speckled indigo was beautiful, strange and ominous. There was something ominous about all of the Western Isles. The term was a catchall to describe a region in the Cific ocean of old and new landmasses. The tectonic shifts triggered by the nukecaust dropped most of California south of the San Andreas Fault into the sea. During the intervening two centuries, undersea quakes raised new volcanic islands. Because the soil was scraped up from the seabed, most of the islands became fertile very quickly, except for the Blight Belt—islands that were originally part of California but were still irradiated.

Despite being born in the coastal barony of Snakefish, Ramirez had only rarely ventured into the sea. At twenty-four, he had spent most of his life either patrolling the Tartarus Pits or the ville's outlying territories. His smooth, boyish face was clean shaved and bore no scars. His short, crisp black hair was of regulation length, and was neatly parted on the right. His brown eyes didn't possess the flint-hard gleam of a man who had seen and participated in so much violence he'd become inured to it. Until a few days ago, he had never even chilled another human, much less commanded a Magistrate strike force.

Ramirez repressed a shiver as a breeze gusted across the Cific and lightly caressed his face. The waves seemed to flutter and send black shadows writhing beneath them. He didn't know why he shivered, since the breeze was warm and held a hint of jasmine.

A vibration ran through the contoured hull of the cruiser, and its forward progress slowed. He gripped the handrails as her sharp prow of dark riveted metal cut through the sea with hissing ripples. Purple twilight deepened toward the ship.

The CG-47 was the only long-distance vessel in the small fleet of Snakefish. There were a handful of patrol boats, even sailboats, but most of them were better suited for hugging coastlines than braving the open ocean, but the CG-47 was something special. Ships of her class had been so even before the nukecaust. He had been told by Carpenter, her pilot, she was a "smart ship," but what made an inanimate vessel smart hadn't as yet been explained, nor was Ramirez told where she and all the ordnance aboard her had originated. Ramirez hadn't asked, either. It was sufficient that they still functioned.

The CG-47 was a sleek, high-prowed craft, painted a flat dark military gray. Its streamlined hull stretched 567 feet from bow to stern. Rising from enclosed housings amidships was the weapons cluster—two missile launchers, two five-inch cannons and four machine-gun mounts, one pair .54 caliber, and the other .50 caliber. There were also four torpedo tubes.

The CG-47 was powered by twin LM-2500 gas turbine engines possessing eighty thousand shaft horsepower. When Ramirez was informed of that, he tried to appear suitably impressed, although he had trouble visualizing even eighty horses, much less eighty thousand of them. All he knew was that the engines could sustain a maximum speed of thirty knots on smooth seas.

Ramirez had been told the ship was a true treasure, regardless of how Baron Snakefish ended up with it. He was familiar with enough postnukecaust history to know that Stockpiles, caches of material and technology, had been laid down by the predark government, just in case of a national emergency. He also knew that many of the original barons had built their power bases with the Stockpiles, but all of that was a long time ago, nearly a century before the Program of Unification and its initial rallying cry, "Unity through Action."

The doctrine of Unity through Action stated that humans were too intrinsically destructive to be allowed free will and free rein. Since the ruined planet was mute testimony to that philosophy, very few people argued with it. As it was, the old predark system of smoldering desperation and unchecked societal chaos, which burned out in a final megacull, was inferior in every way to the ville societies conceived during the Program of Unification.

It was more than a theory, nearly a century after the fact. It had been proved at least to Ramirez's satisfaction, regardless of a few contradictions in its implementation. One of the contradictions was the stated belief that none of the predark advances in science were of lasting value, that all of the technological achievements meant absolutely nothing. Yet those same predark achievements had been the building blocks of the Program of Unification. Without access to that technology, ville society couldn't have been built.

Ramirez knew very little about the century preceding the skydark, but he knew the technologies developed by the people of that time was still in use. The CG-47 was one such example, but he wasn't particularly thrilled by any machine. Instead, he was anxious to put his feet on dry ground again, even if the ground was hostile. The voyage had seemed endless despite the fact it had taken them a little less than eight hours to sail from Port Morninglight.

As it was, Ramirez felt as if he were just beginning to understand the sequence of events that had led him to be standing on the deck of the CG-47. It seemed almost impossible that only three weeks ago, he had been performing standard support duties to the Intel section when he was summoned into the division administrator's office on Level C of Snakefish's Administrative Monolith.

The barony of Snakefish, like eight others, had been consolidated by the Program of Unification into a network of city-states, walled fortresses that were almost sovereign nations. They were named after the barons who ruled them, and they all conformed to standardized specs and layouts—fifty-foot-high walls with Vulcan-Phalanx gun towers mounted on each intersecting corner. There was a single legal way into and out of the villes, and that path was deadly to anyone who didn't have business walking it.

Inside the walls, the ville elite lived in the residential Enclaves, four multileveled towers connected by pedestrian walkways. A certain amount of predark technology was available to the elite, the so-called high towers. Only four thousand people were allowed to live in the Enclaves. Another thousand lived below, in the Tartarus Pits. Since ville society was strictly class and caste based, the higher a citizen's standing, the higher he or she might live in one of the residential towers.

At the bottom level of the villes was the servant class, who lived in abject squalor in the Pits. The population was ruthlessly controlled, so as not to exceed a thousand. The Pits were consciously designed as ghettos.

The residential towers were connected by major promenades to the Administrative Monolith, a massive cylinder of white stone jutting three hundred feet into the air, the tallest building in every ville.

Every level of the Administrative Monolith fulfilled a specific ville function. The base level, Epsilon, was the manufacturing facility. Delta Level was devoted to the growth, preservation and distribution of food stuffs. Cappa Level held the Magistrate Division and Beta Level housed the Historical Division.

The work of the administrators was conducted on the highest level, Alpha, and in the spire above that reigned the barons, unapproachable and invisible.

Like most other ville citizens, Ramirez had no clear idea what went on in A Level. The secrecy surrounding Baron Snakefish and the administrators' activities was deliberate, and jealously guarded. Almost everybody in all the other divisions were kept in ignorance about the actual number and identities of the administrators. Fraternization between division personnel was strongly discouraged, presumably so no one would know anything that the administrators didn't want them to know.

The administrator of the Snakefish's Magistrate Division was a man named Hauk. Ramirez had exchanged maybe five words with him, years before, so he was a little bewildered when the personal summons reached him.

Like all administrative offices, Hauk's was shaped like a small oval with one end chopped off. Hauk sat behind a desk in front of a broad window framing the towers of the residential Enclaves. Three large squares of stiff paper were the only items on the desktop.

He nodded toward the single chair when Ramirez

entered. Hauk wasn't tall. He was a little over medium-size with the thick, square body of a man who intimately knew the ways of close and bloody combat. The eyes above the high-collared, pearl-gray bodysuit brought a cold feeling deep inside Ramirez's bowels.

Hauk's face was that of a man in the prime of his life—a hard life. If it hadn't been for the deep cicatrix scar creasing his left cheek from the corner of his gray eye to his chin, he wouldn't have drawn any attention in a crowded room.

His blond hair was pulled back and knotted at his nape. Absently, Ramirez noted it wasn't quite regulation length, but he supposed ville division administrators were allowed a certain leeway as long as they performed their jobs to the baron's satisfaction. It occurred to him Hauk looked a shade too young to be a division administrator, but then he had no clear idea of the criteria by which such transfers were granted.

Magistrates were legally allowed to marry and produce legitimate offspring only when they held an administrative post, and being appointed as an administrator in any of the ville divisions wasn't a promotion exactly, nor was it completely based on age. The quality of service was the most important consideration.

Hauk didn't waste time on a preamble. In a flat, uninflected tone of voice, he launched into a narrative. "War is breaking out among the nine barons.

I don't know the reasons, so don't ask me. We've already had an incursion from Cobaltville.''

Ramirez managed to keep his face a blank, but he mentally replayed the rumors about a covert invasion that had filtered out of the Intel section.

"A seaside settlement called Port Morninglight was attacked," Hauk continued. "The outlanders living there were abducted. One of our patrols came across the place and tracked the perps to a predark ville near the Sierra Nevadas.''

Ramirez knew that when the nukes flew and the mushroom clouds boiled their way into the heavens, the San Andreas Fault had given one tortured final heave, and thousands of square miles of California coastline dropped into the sea. For the past two centuries, the Cific had lapped less than thirty miles from the foothills of the Sierras.

"They found a force of twenty Magistrates," Hauk went on mildly, "slaughtered to a man.''

Ramirez tried not to allow the surge of shock he felt to register on his face. Hoarsely, he asked, "How do you know they were from Cobaltville?''

"Because some of them carried that ville's scrip on them. As for who slaughtered them, that's a little more complicated. Our patrol recovered the prisoners and persuaded a couple of them to talk.''

Ramirez didn't need to ask about the forms of persuasion. Stone-faced, he watched as Hauk flipped over the three squares of paper on his desk. He slid them toward him. ''Judging by the descriptions they provided, these three were implicated,'' he said.

Ramirez looked at the three grainy photographs, all head-and-shoulders shots and obviously reproduced from ID pix. He knew instantly who they were, though he had never met them. Every Mag in every ville knew who they were. His dismay grew into outright fear.

He looked at a high-planed, clean-shaved face beneath short, crisp, neatly combed dark hair. A pair of cold eyes shone above a pair of regal cheekbones. It was a hard face, but not brutish. ''Kane,'' he said.

The next pix was of a black man, heavy through the chest and wide about the shoulders. His face was square jawed and weather-beaten, brow-shadowed eyes shrewd and watchful. ''Grant.''

The third photo depicted a young woman with big, feline-slanted eyes and thick mounds of hair tumbling around her shoulders. He could barely see the dusting of freckles over the bridge of her nose. Despite the feminine softness in her features, there was a hint of iron resolve in them, too. ''Brigid Baptiste.''

No copy complemented the photographs, and Ramirez wasn't surprised. The pix had been circulated in the Outlands, and most outlanders were illiterate, but nobody needed to read to have heard all about the two renegade Cobaltville Magistrates and the insurrectionist archivist. For the past year, all of the nine villes in the continent-spanning network had engaged in a cooperative search for them. The search concentrated mainly in the old military redoubts, scattered across the face of America.

Ramirez knew only that the subterranean installations were constructed two centuries before to house the most advanced scientific miracles of the day, but they had been sealed for generations, since the Program of Unification.

Over the past few months, the redoubts located in ville territories were methodically visited and inspected by the respective baron's Magistrates. More than one had shown signs of recent occupation, as if the quarry knew they were being sought and moved from redoubt to redoubt to escape capture and confuse the trail. If anyone knew how they managed to move so swiftly from place to place, the information wasn't shared with Ramirez.

But other events had occurred during the search for the seditionists. A squad of Sharpeville Magistrates was obliterated in Redoubt Papa, and Baron Sharpe himself was seriously wounded—by a man in the black Magistrate armor.

A few weeks after that, a report was filed from Baron Samarium's territory in Louisiana, stating that several swamp dwellers had encountered Kane. Shortly thereafter, Baron Ragnar in Minnesota was assassinated in his own private chamber by a woman, though the reports of the incident were garbled. The true identity of the woman had yet to be determined, but the names of Kane and Grant figured prominently in reports filed by a pair of Mags who had secured a redoubt in Ragnarville's territory.

The attempted homicide of one baron, coupled with the successful assassination of another, was more than distressingly unprecedented—the two events were blasphemous on a scale not witnessed since the institution of the unification program, ninety years before. Tales of the renegades' exploits were already circulating through the Outlands, giving rise not only to rebellious thoughts, but also to outright acts of resistance. To chill a baron was tantamount to chilling a god.

Ramirez started to speak, but his vocal cords seemed paralyzed. He coughed, cleared his throat and asked, "How could the three of them chill a twenty-man squad of hard-contact Mags?"

Hauk's thin eyebrows knitted at the bridge of his nose as if the question irritated him. "Obviously, they had help."

"From whom?" Ramirez demanded.

Hauk pursed his lips as if tasting the next word he was about to utter. He looked as if it tasted very repulsive. "The Tigers of Heaven."

"The who of what?" Ramirez's voice was ragged, his tone incredulous.

"The Tigers of Heaven. Apparently, they're based on one of the Western Isles and maintained a trading relationship with Port Morninglight."

Ramirez narrowed his eyes. "We're not talking about an invasion, are we?"

One of the official reasons for fortifying the villes was century-old paranoia of an invasion from foreign nuke-scarred nations. There wasn't any evidence that such an attempt was ever made, primarily because the larger countries, particularly those allied with the United States, were first-strike targets. Certainly the nations allied with the Soviet Union were in no shape, a century after the nukecaust, to mount an army large enough to establish anything other than a remote beachhead in the hinterlands.

Of course, the threat of mutie clans unifying and sweeping across the country was a longtime fear. A hundred years or so before, charismatic mutie leaders had waged a few sporadic wars against the norms, but the fighting had never spread beyond isolated pockets of the Deathlands. Still, the memory of the menace was burned deep in the collective minds of the baronial hierarchies. It had burned so brightly that a major aspect of the Program of Unification had been a campaign of genocide against mutie settlements in ville territories.

The primary threat over the past three decades had derived from within, rather than without. Ramirez knew about the Preservationists, an underground seditious movement scattered throughout the nine villes. The Preservationists represented an underground resistance movement following an idealistic principle of someday freeing humanity from the heel of the barons by revealing the "truth."

Ramirez had never wondered what comprised the

Preservationists' concept of the truth. He knew only if it weren't for the laws of the barons, established over ninety years during the Program of Unification, the descendants of nukecaust survivors would still be barbarians, trying to reconstruct all the horrors of the predark world that led to skydark.

He was very familiar with the dogma, the doctrine, the articles of faith that justified the barons and their sometimes ruthless laws. People couldn't be trusted to govern themselves, and they were responsible for the war that had nearly transformed the world into a smoldering, lifeless cinder spinning darkly in space.

All people were responsible for irresponsibility. Russian people, American people, Asian people. Irresponsible people had put irresponsible people into positions of responsibility, so ergo, the responsibility for the nukecaust was the responsibility of humanity as a whole.

Ramirez believed that, of course. Certainly, he had never seen any reason to question it. Humankind had been judged guilty, and the sentence carried out forthwith.

Hauk's voice brought him back to the present. "Not an invasion in the strict definition. More like a trespass," he said.

Reaching beneath his desk, the division administrator brought out two items and handed them to Ramirez to inspect. He turned the longbow over in his hands, admiring the beautifully crafted, smooth, red-lacquered wood. There was an elegance, an artistry to it, and he knew no wandering tribe of ragged Roamers possessed the skill to make it.

The other object was shaped like a paddle, but Ramirez quickly identified it as an oversize hand fan. It was imprinted with a sunburst symbol enclosing three geometric shapes.

Hauk nodded toward the fan. "Intel tells me the marking on that is called an ideograph. It's Japanese. According to the Historical Division, it's a warning."

Ramirez inspected it closely. "What kind of warning?"

Hauk shrugged. "They weren't specific. Probably the way it's waved tells the story, like a semaphore code."

"So you want me to track down these so-called Tigers of Heaven?"

"Not right away. We've got other, more pressing concerns on our table right now."

Ramirez felt his eyebrows crawling toward his hairline in astonishment. "What the hell could be more important than identifying and neutralizing a foreign threat to the barony?"

"Following the baron's orders for one thing." A steel edge slipped into Hauk's voice. "And not just Baron Snakefish, either."

That announcement so stunned Ramirez he asked no further questions. When Hauk rose and beckoned him forward, he moved without a word. He followed

his superior into the corridor, following him past
office suites, then past the armory. Ramirez always
experienced a quiver of unease when he came near
the huge storage facility that occupied nearly a quarter of C Level.

A pair of gray-uniformed men, their eyes masked
by dark, Mag-issue glasses, stood before the re-
cessed, massive vanadium-alloy sec door. They held
full-auto Commando Arms carbines across their
chests, and they didn't acknowledge either Hauk or
Ramirez with a murmur of greeting or so much as
a nod. Although Hauk was their superior officer, and
Ramirez was on good terms with both men, the duty
protocol of armory sentries was very simple—chill
anyone who tried to gain entrance, regardless of
rank or social standing. Only a direct voice author-
ization from Baron Snakefish allowed them to admit
anyone.

Ramirez completely understood the reasons for
the strict regulations—the huge chamber contained
rack after rack of assorted weaponry, everything
from rifles and shotguns, to pistols, mortars and
rocket launchers. Crates of ammunition were
stacked up to the ceiling. Armored assault vehicles
were also parked there, the Hussar Hotspurs and the
Hummers, not to mention disassembled Deathbirds.

Almost all of it was original issue, dating from
right before skydark. The planners of the old Continuity of Government—COG—programs, had pru-
dently recognized that technology and particularly

weapons—unlike food, medicine and clothing—could, if kept sheltered, endure the test of time and last generation after generation. Arms and equipment of every sort had been placed in deep-storage locations all over the United States, within vaults filled with nitrogen gas to maintain below-freezing temperatures.

Unfortunately, the COG planners hadn't foreseen that the nukecaust would be such a colossal overkill, that the very people the Stockpiles had been intended for would perish like all the other useless eaters. Some survivors of the nukecaust and their descendants carved out lucrative careers looting and trading the contents of the Stockpiles. Hordes of exceptionally well-armed people once rampaged across the length and breadth of the Deathlands.

When the Program of Unification was instituted during the Council of Front Royal, one of the fundamental agreements was that the people had to be disarmed and the remaining Stockpiles secured. Of course, to institute this action, the barons and their security forces not only had to be better armed than the Deathlands hordes, but they also had to know the locations of the Stockpiles. The barons were provided with both, and far more.

At a lift disk, Hauk and Ramirez showed the sentry on duty their badges. The sentry keyed in the numbers on a miniature three-digit tabulator, and the door panel rolled aside. The elevator was one of six shafts on C Level that dropped directly to the Tartarus Pits. The largest of the shafts was positioned in the armory and could accommodate an armored wag filled with a Magistrate squad, just in case a Pit outbreak had to be quelled.

After they stepped into the car, the sentry, with studied casualness, pressed a control toggle and set the lift for a fast descent. The disk platform bumped to a stop, and the door panel slid aside. The base of the Administrative Monolith was completely enclosed by a walled compound made of six feet of rockcrete. The twenty-foot-high walls were rigged with proximity alarms. The sun, at its zenith, glinted from the sharp points of the coils of razor wire stretched out over the tops of the walls. The massive sec door was made of vanadium alloy and powered by a buried hydraulic system.

The impregnable perimeter hadn't been built simply to protect the tower from invasion by outraged Pit dwellers. Far below, in a sublevel, rested the primary output station that supplied the ville's power. Ramirez didn't know for sure, but he thought electricity was provided by nuke generators.

The breeze wafting in from the Tartarus Pits was redolent with the mixed odors of cook fires, rotting meat, unwashed bodies, urine, human and animal droppings. Hauk led Ramirez along a narrow rail-enclosed footpath. Like a channel, it wended its way around the outer limits of the Tartarus Pits. The pathway was strictly forbidden to anyone but Magistrates. Vid spy-eyes affixed to posts made sure no Pit denizen planted a muddy foot on it.

The path entered an adjacent walled compound. It was also topped by coils of razor wire. Parked beneath an overhang were a number of vehicles, Land Rovers, personnel carriers and armored Sandcats.

They walked past an attendant whose leather belt was weighed down by so many hand tools Ramirez was surprised he could even move. Despite the grease and grime smearing his face, his complexion was paper pale, as if he were struggling to recover from a terrible emotional shock. Hauk paid him no attention and strode into the garage itself. Ramirez followed him, his impatience now at an intolerable level.

The interior of the garage was filthy. Rust-scabbed pipes crisscrossed at all angles along the walls and the ceiling. There was a cracked and grease-filmed porcelain toilet affixed to a wall; judging by the effluvium it exuded, it hadn't been flushed in a couple of years. The floor tiles were layered with ancient grease and grime in the shape of boot soles. A long row of dented, dilapidated metal lockers lined one wall.

Hauk entered a workshop, illuminated poorly by overhead naked light bulbs. It was filled with heavy trestle tables, tools, chain vises, band saws and drill presses. Ramirez took a deep breath, preparing himself to snap out a profane demand to know why

Hauk had led him down here, regardless of what reprimands might come his way.

When he glimpsed the two figures in the shadowed room, his resolve vanished like an ice cube on a hot sidewalk, and the demands clogged in his throat. His knees suddenly felt as if they were filled with water, and his heart thudded wildly inside his chest like a bird battering at a cage.

Hauk inclined his head toward the figures and said reverently, "My lord baron, this is Ramirez. I've chosen him."

The figure stepped forward and said in a lilting, fluting voice, "I am Baron Sharpe. You may have heard of me."

Baron Sharpe was small and slender, despite the bulky camouflage jacket and pants he wore. A bright blue scarf was wrapped around his short, slim throat. Ramirez doubted he was more than five and half feet tall and might weigh out at 130 pounds.

The baron's hair was close-cropped, blond and possessing an odd, feathery duck-down texture. His milky blue eyes, the cold color of mountain meltwater, were very large, shadowed by sweeping supraorbital ridges. His cranium was very high and smooth, the ears small and set very low on the head.

Ramirez couldn't speak. The few cogent thoughts in his head scattered like burglars reacting to a sudden alarm. He had never dreamed he would stand in the presence of his own baron, much less one from another ville. He understood that audiences with barons were exceedingly rare and conducted with great ceremony and secrecy.

He had heard stories of the barons, of course. Anyone serving in any division in any ville had heard them. Part of his mind knew that maintaining a baron's mystique was contrived, an intimidation strategy, an old psychological gambit. But still, the baronial oligarchy ruling the nine villes was more than the governing body of postnukecaust America. The barons were god-kings, serving as a bridge between predark and postdark man, the avatars of a new order. To find Baron Sharpe—any of the barons, for that matter—in a filthy workshop on the outskirts of the Tartarus Pits wasn't only bizarre but strangely heretical.

"And this," said Baron Sharpe in that same musical voice, "is my high councilor. You may call him Crawler. I forget his birth name, if ever he had one."

Ramirez flicked his gaze downward and choked back a cry of mingled surprise and revulsion. His stomach turned a cold flip-flop. The creature scrabbled forward on heavily muscled arms. Thick calluses covered his elbows, and his pale legs trailed behind him like a pair of boneless tentacles. He wore a leather harness and velvet loincloth. The harness displayed his exceptionally well developed upper body. His torso looked to be all muscle from the neck down to his hips.

Whereas the harness showed off his bulging biceps and dinner-plate-size pectorals, the loincloth did nothing to disguise his shriveled, atrophied legs. They stretched out behind him like flaccid, flesh-colored stockings half-filled with mud. Even in the dim light, Ramirez could make out the red scars bisecting the back of his knees. His nausea grew when he realized the man had been crippled deliberately.

Crawler lifted his shaved head and gazed at Ramirez speculatively with dark eyes. Ramirez couldn't tell if they were black or a deep brown, but he experienced a shuddery sensation of ghostly fingers riffling through his memories.

With a jolt of terror, Ramirez realized Crawler was a doomseer, a mutant gifted—or cursed—with the psychic ability to sniff out forthcoming death.

Ramirez had been taught that doomies didn't exist anymore. Most of the mutie strains spawned after the nukecaust were extinct, either dying because of their twisted biologics, or hunted and exterminated during the early years of the unification program. Stickies, screamers, scabbies, swampies and almost every other breed exhibiting warped genetics had all but vanished. Or so he had been taught.

Crawler smiled and in a surprising well-modulated, even educated voice stated, "He is far from being honored in our presence, Lord Baron. He is petrified. Still, he has courage and cunning."

Baron Sharpe's neatly compressed lips creased in a small smile. He stepped toward Ramirez with the grace of a dancer. It required all of Ramirez's self-control not to recoil. With an index finger nearly as long as the Magistrate's entire hand, the baron stroked his cheek. Ramirez felt his bowels loosen and he clenched his jaw muscles to keep his teeth from chattering.

"Do not fear me," Baron Sharpe said in a low, soothing voice. "We're going to be great friends. We're all going to embark on a fantastic adventure. Aren't we, Crawler?"

The crippled man only smirked in response, a smirk Ramirez felt was disrespectful. The baron took Ramirez by the arm and led him toward a chair. "Look how the poor boy's legs are shaking. We'd best sit you down before you collapse and get your nice clean uniform all soiled."

Dazedly, Ramirez allowed Baron Sharpe to seat him in the chair as if he were an enfeebled old man gone faint. The baron patted him on the shoulder solicitously. "Let me explain all of this."

The baron did so in his trilling, contralto voice. First Baron Sharpe provided him with biographical information, which though interesting, didn't seem particularly relevant—at first.

Baron Sharpe told him he had been dead for a long time, but he had gotten better. Not waiting for Ramirez to question him on his quiet claim, he explained how he had one day, nearly ten years before, succumbed to an infection. He wasn't sure what it was, but he suspected it was some airborne filth that had floated up from either Sharpeville's Tartarus Pits or wafted in from the rad-rich Outlands.

Since Sharpeville was located near ground zero, Washington Hole, the baron's territories were still the most active and deadly hellzones in the country. Baron Sharpe coughed up blood-tinted phlegm for two days before lapsing into a coma. Members of his personal staff had whisked him, via mat-trans gateway, to a medical facility in Dulce, New Mexico. There, physicians who were intimately familiar with all the limitations of the unique baronial immune systems worked on him for a week. Ramirez was perplexed by this comment, but he continued to sit silently.

When, at the end of those seven days, Baron Sharpe opened his big blue eyes and sat up, the doctors told him he was cured, that his metabolism had been adjusted, his tainted blood replaced and detoxified, his damaged organs replaced. They told him he was cured, but the baron knew better. He was dead, regardless of the fact that he walked, talked, ate and breathed.

At first, his condition disturbed him since no one else seemed to notice it. After a few months, he grew accustomed to being dead and found it oddly liberating, even exhilarating. Very infrequently, the notion that he might not be dead but simply deluded intruded on Baron Sharpe's peace of mind. He was the most powerful and gifted member of the baronial oligarchy, and therefore he had powerful responsibilities that he couldn't shirk, alive or dead, comatose or awake.

Slowly, Ramirez began to understand that Baron Sharpe believed he couldn't die; therefore he wasn't afraid to mix with his subjects and embark on what he termed "adventures." At the same time, Ramirez also realized Baron Sharpe was quite mad.

Somewhere during Sharpe's droning monologue, Ramirez became acutely aware that Hauk had silently drifted away, leaving him alone with the baron. Ramirez was alone, utterly alone in the dark and dirty workshop with Baron Sharpe.

All the moisture dried in his mouth, and he fought against the crazed impulse to leap from his chair and flee the room like a terrified deer.

Only a fractionally tiny percentage of people had private audiences with barons, and those few were members of his personal staff. As far as Ramirez knew, not even Hauk had ever met Baron Snakefish.

Completely oblivious to Ramirez's new surge of fear, Baron Sharpe went on speaking. "You have been selected for a singular honor. You have been chosen to act as the commander of an elite combined unit consisting of men from my ville and those from yours."

After a moment of straining effort, Ramirez managed to dredge up the tone, if not the appearance of a veteran hard-contact Mag. "Our mission objective, my lord?"

"Nevada. A place called Area 51."

Ramirez had never heard of the place, which didn't surprise him much.

"We will displace the forces already there," Sharpe continued, "and occupy it ourselves."

Ramirez's mind raced with speculation and fearful conjecture. He tilted his head back, forcing himself to meet Baron Sharpe's gaze. To his relief, he saw the baron wasn't even looking at him. Instead, with a frown on his finely drawn features, he was inspecting his fingernails.

"My lord baron," Ramirez inquired, "who are the forces occupying it? Where are they from?"

With a studied nonchalance, Sharpe answered, "Cobaltville. Baron Cobalt claimed the place, and Baron Snakefish and I propose to take it away from him."

He gestured negligently with the hand he had been studying. "I'm sure there will be violence, so pick men who know their way around a blaster." Suddenly, a grin split his face. "I'm hoping it will be a lot of fun."

THE DECK OF THE CG-47 suddenly lurched, and Ramirez was hurled against the handrail and back into the present. He saw water foaming at the sides as the ship rose and fell. He remembered how the ocean's name, the Pacific, was something of a mockery. According to nautical lore, the Pacific Ocean was anything but peaceful.

Boots rang on a grille-floored gangway over his

head, and he looked up to see Sprague, one of his men, leaning down toward him. He called out, "The pilot says there's rough water ahead. Maybe a submerged reef or shoal. He recommends we weigh anchor until sunrise so we can see what we're up against."

Ramirez nodded. "Good idea. I wouldn't want to run aground after coming all this way." With a sour smile, he added, "Even if it would meet Baron Sharpe's standards of 'fun.'"

Sprague didn't respond. Ramirez hadn't really expected him to.

Chapter 6

Grant, Brigid, Kane and half a dozen samurai struggled up the rough trail leading to the brow of the escarpment and the watch post. In the fast-fading light, it looked as if only mountain goats could possibly manage the trails, but a number of hand- and footholds had been chipped into the rock.

Pitons had also been hammered into the stone at regular intervals to serve as braces. It was still an arduous climb, partly because of the heavy war bags slung around Kane's and Grant's shoulders, as well as the Sin Eaters holstered to their forearms.

After only a few hundred yards, all three outlanders understood why New Edo's watchmen pulled forty-eight-hour-long shifts. The prospect of making the climb twice inside of a day would probably drive them to commit seppuku.

The bell no longer tolled its brazen warning. Using one of New Edo's small hand comms, Brigid had contacted the watchman and told him those down below were aware of the situation. The range of the comms was limited to about three miles, so they had to reach the halfway point in the long ascent before she was able to apprise the man in the tower. Still, it was remarkably powerful for such a small device. Its range was greater than their own, larger trans-comms.

The last few minutes of sunset were strikingly beautiful. Sunsets always were spectacular in the Outlands, due to the pollutants and lingering radiation in the upper atmosphere.

Full night fell swiftly, like the lowering of a curtain, and the crags above them were swathed in deep shadow. Kane and Brigid took out their Nighthawk microlights. Though they emitted a five-thousand-minicandlepower beam, the illumination they cast didn't pierce the shadows more than ten feet over their heads.

The group halted after forty minutes of toiling in order to catch their breath. Panting, Kane looked below him. The view of New Edo's harbor was very peaceful, hauntingly so with the starlight dancing on the dark waters. Beyond it swept a crescent moon of a white sandy beach, bracketed by stunted palm trees and tropical ferns. The beach circled the bay like a band of pearls.

Several quays and docks were built around a spit of volcanic rock that jutted into the blue waters of a lagoon. A cluster of vessels was tied up there, mainly barges and skiffs, but there were also three large vessels that Shizuka claimed were built to be warships.

Kane found her claim dubious. They were all similar in size and contour, riding high above the waterline, consisting of sharp angles, three high masts, with arches and flaring buttresses surrounding the deck. The sails reminded him of window blinds, but he knew they were made of coarse cotton and braced flat by bamboo strips and battens.

He noticed that the prows of the ships were broad and flat, rather than pointed. The bottoms of the boats were flat with very small keels. The wooden rudders were very long. All three vessels were about sixty feet in length.

Looking up the trail stretching above them, Kane grimaced, then smiled ruefully. If Domi was with them, she would have scampered over the summit by now. He recalled Grant had often compared her climbing ability to that of a scalded monkey.

Kane squeezed his eyes shut momentarily against the wave of images crowding into his mind. He shook his head, trying to clear it of his last sight of Domi.

During the last few minutes of the battle for control of Area 51, Domi had darted from an elevator cupola, scooped up a fallen implode gren in one hand and cocked her arm to throw it at a Sandcat. Grant rushed toward her, bellowing at the top of his lungs, ''Domi, no! Get back in the—''

Again Kane saw the blindingly white incandescent glare swallowing her small form. A tremendous roar, half explosion, half gale-force wind, slammed against his eardrums. The shock wave of the concussion felt like a riptide, gripping his body and yanking him forward in a head-over-heels tumble, dragging them all into clumsy somersaults.

A cascade of air, dust, rock particles and powdery sand swirled around him as it was irresistibly sucked toward the wedge of vacuum that followed the detonation of the implode gren. When the maelstrom effect created by the implosive device collapsed in on itself, Kane was too stunned to do anything other than lie on the ground as fragments of debris pattered down all around him.

He recalled drunkenly shambling to his feet and staggering to the detonation point of the gren. He saw no crater, only a charred star-shaped pattern on the concrete. Wisps of smoke curled from its center. Several black-armored bodies were sprawled nearby, their arms and legs elongated to unnatural lengths. Flat crimson ribbons stretched from their heads toward the epicenter of the implosion.

He knew that beneath the polycarbonate, the Mags' bodies were mangled lumps of flesh, their eardrums shattered by the brutal decompression, their eyeballs pulled from their sockets, internal organs burst, blood from ruptured vessels flowing from every orifice, their lungs collapsed to wafers of tissue. Several more men at the edge of the effect radius were unconscious due to the sudden lack of oxygen.

Kane saw absolutely nothing that might have been the girl's body. Although he wasn't an expert on explosives, he was fairly certain implode grens didn't vaporize organic matter without leaving some trace—a spattering of blood, a scrap of bone, a hank of hair.

For the past few days, he had tried very hard to think of anything but Domi, but the unreliable human mind always zeroed in on the most painful image. His mind kept replaying his last sight of Domi, her small figure vanishing in the blinding flare of light. Every time he closed his eyes, he saw her standing there, her arm poised to hurl the gren, like a poorly edited vid tape on continuous loop. The image lingered in his heart and head like a wound that refused to heal.

He had no trouble admitting to himself that not only had he yet to come to terms with her death, but also he couldn't even grasp the concept except in the most abstract way. The very notion ghosted through his mind like a wisp of smoke.

It wasn't as if Kane didn't recognize the inevitability of death. He was accustomed to a lot of inevitables—loneliness, pain, fear, the emptiness of dreams. He had accepted all of them with equanimity, yet he couldn't accept the fact Domi was truly dead. Something inside of him, an almost visceral reaction, didn't allow his mind to acknowledge it. He knew his denial was due in part to his ingrained opposition to blindly embracing the superficial.

A suspicion lurked at the very back of his mind that what he had seen, what all of them had seen, wasn't Domi disintegrating in the explosion. A subliminal afterimage of an object or movement at the very instant of detonation bobbed at the fringes of his memory, but his conscious mind couldn't analyze it. On a deeper, more instinctual level, Domi's death simply felt wrong, as if it weren't supposed to have happened. It was an error, a miscalculation.

Kane glanced toward Grant, who stared back down the trail, his face as immobile as if it were carved from teak. He knew he hadn't the time to come to terms with Domi's death, either, but then even if he had, the big man's expression wouldn't show it. His face didn't register the pain his wounds had to have been causing him, so it wouldn't display an inner pain, either.

As if sensing Kane's thoughts, Grant announced gruffly, "Let's see what we're dealing with here. Sooner we take a look, sooner we can make a plan."

Brigid hefted the palm-sized comm unit. "According to Mohri, the lookout, it's a ship. A damn big ship."

Grant only shrugged. He turned and breached the unspoken protocol observed between him and Kane by taking point. In their dozen or so years serving as Magistrates together, Kane almost always assumed the position of point man. When stealth was required, Kane could be a silent, almost graceful wraith. In a dangerous setting, his senses became uncannily acute, sharply tuned to every nuance of any environment. It was a prerequisite for survival he had learned in a hard school.

Kane didn't say anything as Grant literally began clawing his way up the cliff face. He exchanged a quizzical look with Brigid, then simply fell in behind him. The cliff grew ever steeper, but they scrambled on, pulling themselves forward by handfuls of undergrowth. Pebbles and dirt spilled down the slope from under their feet.

The cliff bulged outward near the escarpment's summit, and the strain on muscle and tendon became nearly intolerable. Kane didn't envy the six Tigers in their party, but he did resent their placid stoicism in the face of such a labor.

The Tigers of Heaven were attired in full suits of segmented armor made from wafers of metal held together by small, delicate chain. Overlaid with a dark brown lacquer, the interlocked and overlapping plates were trimmed in scarlet and gold. Between flaring shoulder epaulets, war helmets fanned out with sweeping curves of metal. Some resembled wings, others horns. The face guards, wrought of a semitransparent material, presented the inhuman visage of a snarling tiger.

Quivers of arrows dangled from their shoulders, and longbows made of lacquered wood were strapped to their backs. Each samurai carried two longswords in black scabbards, swinging back from each hip. None of them carried firearms, but their skill with the swords and the bows was such they didn't really need them even if they had access to them.

Their progress slowed as they reached the bulge, and more than once miniature avalanches started beneath their feet. They crawled on hands and knees when the angle of the slant became too sharp. Finally, after what felt like a rope of intertwined eternities, the crag's pinnacle blotted out the stars a scant twenty feet above them.

Within a narrow, rock-ribbed cleft dangled a ladder made of rope and bamboo. Grasping the rungs, Grant hauled himself up, hand over hand. His eight companions clambered up one at a time onto a sort of hilly plateau. They could barely see the watchtower, which looked like a little hut built on twenty-foot stilts. It was mounted on a promontory on the far edge of the plateau about a half mile away. A labyrinthine tumble of rocks, ridges and slopes lay in their way.

Without pausing to rest, the party headed toward the tower. Despite its great height, no breeze stirred the foliage or tropical vegetation atop the plateau. Kane felt sweat collect at the roots of his hair and slowly trickle down his forehead. He wished he had followed his first impulse after the battle with the Black Dragons, and left New Edo by the same way they had arrived.

But Shizuka had asked them to visit the watchtower to try to identify the nature of the threat. Her presence was required in the palace to restore at least an imitation of order on the madness that had reigned unchecked briefly but violently.

The chief of the Black Dragons had turned out to be a man named Ugo, a rank-and-file member of the Tigers of Heaven. Apparently, when his ambition won out over his loyalty to the daimyo, he had concocted a coup. The appearance of the outlanders on the shores of New Edo had been the spark that lit the fuse of rebellion.

In a little over an hour, much had transpired. Fortunately, it appeared Lord Takaun would recover from the fugu poison, though Kane guessed Shizuka would never get over her sister's betrayal. Takaun at least didn't seem to hold Yoshika's assassination attempt against her. The court physician prescribed a long period of bed rest for the daimyo until the toxin ran its course, and Takaun handed over the reins of power to Shizuka.

Just as fortunately, when the defeated Black Dragons were told about a possible invasion, they set aside their political differences and hatred of the gaijin and eagerly rejoined the ranks of the Tigers of Heaven. Of course, Kane reflected bleakly, having their death sentences commuted had something to do with their enthusiasm.

Of the six samurai who accompanied them, he had no idea how many might bear the small tattoo of the Black Dragon somewhere on their bodies. Nor did he care to check. He, Grant and Brigid needed all the goodwill they could wring out of the New Edoans. The moon had risen, but the pale light it shed wasn't adequate. At one time or another, all of them stumbled as they put feet in holes, climbed pillars of sharp volcanic stone, trod through the ferns, long grasses, over rocks and up slopes so sheer that one samurai tumbled headlong down the other side.

There was much resentful and bitter muttering among the Tigers, and never mind Shizuka's orders; they wouldn't fight for the daimyo but for New Edo—and against gaijin invaders, even though it was gaijin who may have led the invaders to their island home.

Finally, weary eyed and footsore, they reached the promontory on which the watchtower stood. Grant, Kane and Brigid climbed up the rickety, cobbled-together stairs that led to the top and swarmed up the ladder to the roofed platform.

The frightened Mohri still stood there. He was a small, middle-aged man, and he spoke wildly, gesturing first to the brass, tripod-mounted telescope, and then to the open sea beyond the leading lip of the escarpment. Although most New Edoans could speak a smattering of English, Mohri had apparently forgotten every word of it in his fear and excitement.

Pushing the man aside, Grant bent and squinted into the telescope's eyepiece, while Brigid took a pair of compact binoculars from a war bag and raised them to her face. Kane searched the Cific with his naked gaze and glimpsed a long, dark shape floating on the darker surface of the sea. He guessed it was about a half mile away.

Grant grunted and adjusted the focus. "It's a cruiser, and it looks like it's packing heavy artillery. It sure as hell isn't a pirate schooner from Autarkic or one of the islands."

Brigid peered through the binoculars, the ruby-coated lenses diminishing the shadow and seeming to make the distant ship's running lights glow brighter. Although she was slightly astigmatic, her far vision was excellent, especially aided by the 8x12 magnifying power of the binoculars.

"Does it match up with anything either of you are familiar with?" Kane asked, a little irritated that he could only strain his eyes trying to see the vessel through the moonlit murk.

Although Grant was something of a military-history buff, his interest lay primarily with firearms, and could barely qualify as a hobby. Brigid, however, was a trained historian, spending nearly half of her twenty-eight years as an archivist in the Cobaltville Historical Division, but there was more to her storehouse of knowledge than simple training.

Almost everyone who worked in the ville divisions kept secrets, whether they were infractions of the law, unrealized ambitions or deviant sexual predilections. Brigid Baptiste's secret was more arcane than petty crimes or manipulating the system for personal aggrandizement.

Her secret was the ability to produce eidetic images. Centuries earlier, it had been called a photographic memory. She could, after viewing an object or scanning a document, retain exceptionally vivid and detailed visual memories. When she was growing up, she feared she was a psi-mutie, but she later learned that the ability was relatively common among children, and usually disappeared by adolescence. It was supposedly very rare among adults. Brigid was one of the exceptions.

Since her forced exile, she had taken full advantage of the Cerberus redoubt's vast database, and as an intellectual omnivore she grazed in all fields. Coupled with her eidetic memory, her profound knowledge of an extensive and eclectic range of topics made her something of an ambulatory encyclopedia. This trait often irritated Kane, but just as often it had tipped the scales between life and death.

Examining the dark gray ship with its raised superstructure and armored gun emplacements, she said, "I'd judge it to be of the CG class...one of the old Ticonderoga cruisers. If it is, it's state-of-the-art...or it was in the late twentieth century."

"Like the Imperium Brittania's stealth boat, the *Cromwell?*" Kane asked.

She lowered the binoculars and handed them to him. "Not exactly, though some of the same technologies were utilized. If I recall the specs correctly—"

"And there's no reason you wouldn't," Kane murmured, peering into the eyepieces.

Brigid affected not to have heard the comment. "This class of vessel was called 'smart ships.'"

"Why?" Kane asked, studying the barrels of the artillery pieces.

In a curt, uninflected and scholarly tone, Brigid said, "Two centuries ago, the CGs were part of the U.S. Navy, cruisers armed with guided missiles that performed primarily in a battle-force role. Due to their extensive combat capability, ships of the CG class had been designated as battle-force capable units. They were built as support of aircraft-carrier battle groups, amphibious assault groups, as well as interdiction and escort missions. Like all of its class, the ship was built in sections, called modules, which were then fitted together to form the hull of the ship, and the deckhouse sections were then lifted aboard."

"I'm not interested in the damn thing's construction history," Kane said. "What kind of weapons is that thing carrying?"

"I don't know about now," she replied, "but their primary armament was the vertical launching system, which employed both the long-range surface-to-surface Tomahawk missiles, and the standard surface-to-air missiles. The multifunction ships were capable of sustained combat operations in any combination of antiair, antisubmarine, antisurface and strike-warfare environments. The CG-47 class vessels were the first surface combatant ships equipped with the Aegis weapons system, the most sophisticated air-defense system in the predark world."

"What was so sophisticated about it?" Grant wanted to know.

"The heart of the Aegis system was the SPY-1A radar, which automatically detected and tracked air contacts to beyond two hundred miles. The Aegis weapons system was designed to defeat attacking missiles and provide quick reaction, high firepower and jamming resistance to deal with the antiair warfare threats."

"They won't have to worry about that," Kane commented dryly. "What can they throw against us?"

"As you can see," Brigid answered, "there are two five-inch gun mounts that can bombard shore targets. In addition, the ships carried a strong anti-submarine weapons suite and an advanced under-water-surveillance system."

"What made it so smart?" Grant asked.

Brigid smiled slightly. "For one thing, integrated automated piloting systems, which controlled the ship's course and track, as well as automated damage-control management. Ideally, you could program it to target and fire its weapons while the bridge crew sat around and had coffee. The smart-ship innovations allowed the bridge team to go from thirteen personnel on watch at a time down to three. It also allowed the entire central crew complement to be reduced from fifty people down to a dozen or so."

Kane lowered the binoculars and remarked,

"Sounds impressive. But how much of that smart tech still works?"

Brigid shrugged. "Who can say? Even if only a little of the automation is functional, that ship poses a serious threat, especially if they get through the strait. They can sit in the harbor and pound New Edo to dust."

The ship made a slow, sweeping turn to starboard, presenting its port side to the watchtower.

In reaction to Brigid's words, Grant snorted with derision. "Even if all those bells and whistles are still functional after two centuries, they'd need somebody who knows what they're doing to operate them. What are the odds of that? Pretty damn slim I'd say—" He broke off, his shoulders stiffening. He growled, "Son of a bitch."

"Who?" Kane wanted to know.

Grant stared fixedly into the eyepiece, centering the telescope on a man standing at the aft port-side rail. Although he was dressed very differently from the last time he'd seen him, Grant recognized the crisp, neatly combed dark hair and the arrogant tilt of the young man's head. His brown eyes didn't possess the gimlet hard glint of a man who had seen and participated in so much violence he couldn't conceive of solving a problem without a blaster or bludgeon. But, as Grant had reason to know, he wasn't a stranger to violence, either.

"No doubt about who sent the ship now," he declared flatly, straightening and stepping away from the telescope.

Kane trained the binoculars on the ship again. "Why do you say that?"

"I see Ramirez on board."

Brigid swiveled her head toward him, then stooped over the telescope. "Ramirez? Are you sure?"

Kane said, "I didn't see the bastard without his helmet. You sure it's him?"

"It's him," Brigid stated coldly, backing away from the telescope. "Baron Snakefish sent the ship."

"The bastard must have trailed us from Nevada to Port Morninglight," said Grant. "It wouldn't have been hard with the tracks the war wag left. He was probably a day behind us all the time. When he reached the village, he made a call to the ville and the ship was sent to pick up him and his squad."

He paused and added darkly, "Just like I was afraid of."

Kane cast a glance at the samurai assembled at the base of the promontory. "Just like the Black Dragons were afraid of, too." He handed the binoculars back to Brigid. "Do you think that ship is narrow enough to squeeze through the strait into the harbor?"

Raising them to her eyes, she nibbled her underlip as she mentally compared the width of the passage between the two ramparts of rock, and the breadth of the cruiser. Hesitantly, she said, "It's hard to say for sure. It may be a replay of the *Argo* and the Clashing Rocks."

"Spare us the classical comparisons, Baptiste. Do you think he'll take the risk?" Kane spoke more harshly than he intended.

Lowering the binoculars, she threw him a slit-eyed glare. "It depends less on the width of the ship than Ramirez's orders. You were a Mag. If a baron commanded you to eliminate a threat, would you risk it?"

Kane nodded gravely. "If I wanted to stay a Mag and alive, yes, I would."

Grant, still squinting into the telescope, said, "They're weighing anchor. If they're going to take the risk, they'll wait until dawn so they can see the passage."

Kane exhaled a long, weary breath. "We have until sunrise to decide what to do about the ship out there, or we'll have another uprising to contend with. And one in a twenty-four hour period is my limit."

Brigid angled an eyebrow toward him. "You have a plan?"

Kane turned toward the ladder. "By the time Ramirez makes up his mind what to do, I will."

Grant shook his head in disgust and gave the telescope an angry slap, sending it spinning on its gimbal. "Like I've said before—why does this shit always happen to us?"

Chapter 7

Grant's question was pretty much rhetorical so neither Brigid nor Kane bothered answering it. He had asked the same question on several occasions over the past year or so. This time, if either of his two friends had cared to respond to it, the answer was complicated and stretched back nearly five months to a night in the New Mexican desert.

He, Kane, Brigid Baptiste and Domi had inadvertently destroyed the medical facility beneath the Archuleta Mesa in New Mexico. The barons depended on the facility to bolster their immune systems. Once a year, the oligarchy traveled to the installation for medical treatments. They received fresh transfusions of blood and a regimen of biochemical genetic therapy designed to strengthen their autoimmune systems, thus granting them another year of life and power. Grant knew the six-leveled facility in New Mexico had originally been constructed to house two main divisions of the Totality Concept, Overproject Whisper and Overproject Excalibur. One dealt with finding new pathways across space and time, and the other was exclusively involved in creating new forms of life. According to

Lakesh, after the institution of the unification program, only Excalibur's biological section was revived to maintain the lives of the barons and to grow new hybrids.

Although all the hybrids were extremely long-lived, cellular and metabolic deterioration was part and parcel of what they were—hybrids of human and Archon DNA. The treatments involved infusions of human genetic material, and the barons relied upon an aircraft to locate sources of raw material in the Outlands, kill the donors, harvest their organs and tissues, and return with the merchandise, as they referred to it, to the mesa to be processed.

Before the nukecaust, the aircraft had been the pinnacle of avionic achievement. Code-named Aurora, it enjoyed the status of the most closely guarded of military secrets. Supremely maneuverable, the aircraft was capable of astonishingly swift ascent and descent, could take off vertically and hover absolutely motionless. Powered by pulsating integrated gravity wave engines and magnetohydrodynamic air spikes, the Aurora was a true marauder of the skies.

Grant and his companions had traveled to the New Mexico desert to eliminate the barons' method of harvesting the fresh material. Grant shot down the Aurora with a rocket launcher while it hovered above its underground hangar. When it crashed into the hangar, the impact breached the magnetic-field container of a fusion generator—or at least that was Brigid Baptiste's theory.

Whatever happened, none of them could argue with the cataclysmic aftermath. The result had been akin to unleashing the energy of the sun inside a cellar. Although much of the kinetic force and heat was channeled upward and out through the hangar doors, a scorching wave of destruction smashed through the installation. As he learned later, if not for the series of vanadium blast-shield bulkheads, the entire mesa could have come tumbling down.

Despite the fact their actions in the desert that night had been the single most devastating blow struck against baronial tyranny, it set into a motion a sequence of consequences that none of them could have foreseen. It began with an innocuous-seeming transmission picked up on the Cerberus redoubt's Comsat relay.

Although most satellites were little more than free-floating scrap metal now, Cerberus possessed the proper electronic ears and eyes to receive the transmissions from at least two of them. One was of the Vela reconnaissance class, which carried narrow-band multispectral scanners. It could detect the electromagnetic radiation reflected by every object on Earth, including subsurface geomagnetic waves. The scanner was tied into an extremely high resolution photographic relay system.

The other satellite to which the redoubt was up-linked was a Comsat, which for many months was used primarily to keep track of Cerberus personnel when they were out in the field. Everyone in the installation had been injected with a subcutaneous transponder, which transmitted heart rate, respiration, blood count and brain-wave patterns. Based on organic nanotechnology, the transponder was a nonharmful radioactive chemical that bound itself to an individual's glucose and the middle layers of the epidermis. The signal was relayed to the redoubt by the Comsat, and the Cerberus computer systems recorded every byte of data. Sophisticated scanning filters combed through the telemetry using special human biological encoding. The digital data stream was then routed through a locational program to precisely isolate an individual's position in space and time.

Over the past few months, Bry, the resident tech head of Cerberus, had established a communications linkup with the Comsat satellite to both personnel out in the field and the Cobaltville computer systems. Since all the villes had a form of wireless communication, the primary obstacle was finding an undetected method of patching into the channels, and Bry had come up with a solution that involved using the redoubt's satellite uplinks. The overall objective was to find weak areas in Cobaltville defenses and baron-sanctioned operations in the Outlands that could be exploited. The technique was far from perfect; the electronic eavesdropping could be adversely affected by weather fronts or sun spots.

The last thing any of them expected to overhear was a plan to covertly dispatch Mags from Cobaltville into the territory of Baron Snakefish. Such an act was not only unprecedented, but it was also strictly forbidden by the terms established in the Program of Unification.

Grant, Kane, Domi and Brigid used the Cerberus gateway to make the mat-trans jump to the nearest redoubt in the Sierra Nevada range. The gateways were major aspects of the predark scientific undertaking known as the Totality Concept. Most of the units were buried in subterranean military complexes, known as redoubts, in the United States. Only a handful of people knew they even existed, and only half a handful knew all their locations. The knowledge had been lost after the nukecaust, rediscovered a century later, and then jealously, ruthlessly guarded. There were, however, units in other countries—Japan, England, South America and Mongolia.

From Sierra Nevada, they traveled overland but were too late to stop the massacre at Port Morninglight, so they set out to free the captives and find out why Baron Cobalt had undertaken such a risky endeavor as invading the territory of a brother baron.

During the course of trailing the Cobaltville Mags, they met Shizuka and the Tigers of Heaven for the first time, and together they wiped out the Mags and set free the prisoners.

However, that was only the beginning. Back at

the Cerberus redoubt in the Bitterroot Range of
Montana, investigation showed that the legendary
Area 51 somehow figured in Baron Cobalt's plans.
Brigid found a gateway destination-lock code, and
Kane and Domi volunteered to perform a recce
wherever the code might take them.

When Kane and Domi stepped into the Cerberus
gateway unit to jump to Area 51, they might as well
have jumped to another planet or dimension. The
telemetric signals transmitted by their biolink transponders vanished from the tracking screen like can-
dle flames snuffed out by a sudden breeze. Nor did
their successful transit register on the huge Mercator
relief map that displayed all the known working
mat-trans units in the Cerberus network.

At the time, no one in the redoubt panicked. Any
number of reasons presented themselves for the ces-
sation of the transponder's transmissions, from sun
spots interfering with the Comsat's uplink to the signals being blocked by either vanadium shielding or
iron ore. Either one was a possibility, inasmuch as
intel on Area 51 was fragmented. The redoubt's database had yielded very little of use.

Lakesh told them Area 51 was, in the latter years
of the twentieth century, a place as fabulous to
Americans as Avalon had been to Britons a thousand years earlier. This particular Avalon, however,
was very real and financed by the government. Also
known as Dreamland and Groom Lake, Area 51 was
a secret military facility about ninety miles north of

Las Vegas. The number referred to a six-by-ten-mile block of land, at the center of which was located a large air base the predark government only reluctantly admitted even existed.

Lakesh claimed the site was selected in the mid-1950s for testing of the U-2 spy plane, and later, due to its remoteness, Groom Lake became America's traditional testing ground for experimental "black budget" aircraft. The sprawling facility and surrounding areas were also associated with UFO and conspiracy stories in which alien technology was reverse-engineered and retrofitted. According to Lakesh, Area 51 was a popular symbol for the alleged U.S. government cover-up of UFO activity.

Grant had no reason to doubt Lakesh's history, since one of the experimental aircraft that rolled from the hidden hangars of the Area 51 complex was the Aurora. Kane, Brigid and Lakesh had seen to the destruction of a far larger and more deadly Aurora aircraft kept in deep storage beneath Mount Rushmore.

At any rate, since the Dreamland complex was alleged to be mainly underground, Lakesh opined Kane and Domi materialized in a subterranean section where the biolink signals were blocked. As for the mat-trans materialization not registering on the Cerberus sensor web, Lakesh had an explanation for that, too. The unit in Area 51 wasn't among the indexed gateways.

Since both Grant and Brigid knew that the Cerberus redoubt had served as a manufacturing facility where the gateway units were mass-produced in modular form, they accepted his hypotheses with only a little bit of dread.

After a full twenty-four hours passed without so much as a squirt of a signal from the transponders, Grant and Brigid decided to go after them. When the gateway's autosequencer couldn't achieve a coordinate lock with the target unit, their dread turned to fear. An active transit lock couldn't be established, so there was no way to tell if the jump line had been cut from the other end, or if Kane and Domi were speeding madly through the entire Cerberus network in the form of disembodied digital information.

The decision about the next course of action was reached very quickly. They would travel overland, from Montana to Nevada, and either rescue Domi and Kane or discover their fates. Grant told him how he planned to enlist the aid of Sky Dog and the war wag. The question of whether the Amerindians would help them never entered anyone's minds. The tribes people owed them several debts, not the smallest of which was the virtual annihilation of a band of Roamers who had attacked their village and carried off a number of women and children.

Grant and Brigid chose the Hussar Hotspur Land Rover, one of the redoubt's two mil-spec vehicles, and crammed it full with a dozen ten-gallon jerricans of fuel, self-heat MRE ration packs, armament, maps, first-aid and survival supplies and Grant's Magistrate body armor.

The Amerindians were the Cerberus installation's nearest neighbors—its only neighbors, for that matter. Only a few months before, direct contact had been established between the redoubt's personnel and the tribespeople. Kane had managed to turn a potentially tragic misunderstanding into a budding alliance with Sky Dog.

Not so much a chief as a shaman, a warrior priest, Sky Dog was Cobaltville-bred as they were. Unlike them, he had been exiled from the ville while still a youth due to his Lakota ancestry. He joined a band of Cheyenne and Sioux living in the foothills of the Bitterroot Range, and eventually earned a position of high authority and respect among them. Part of that position was to serve as the keeper of his people's great secret—the war wag.

According to tribal lore, nearly a century before, a group of adventurers had ridden inside its iron belly up the single treacherous road wending its way around deep ravines to the mountain plateau. When the vehicle made its return journey, it ran out of fuel and the Amerindians had set upon the people inside of it. After killing them all, they had hidden the huge machine and removed all of its weapons except the fixed emplacements.

When a set of circumstances brought Grant, Brigid and Kane into first conflict, then alliance with the Indians, Sky Dog proposed the people living on the mountain plateau make the vehicle operational again. They had agreed, since a fully restored and armed war wag would make a solid first line of defense against a possible incursion from Cobaltville. The task to bring a machine back to life that had lain dormant for at least a hundred years entailed far more effort and time than any of them, particularly Kane, had foreseen.

Periodically over the past couple of months, Grant and Kane visited the Indian settlement to complete the refitting of the war wag. The front-mounted 20 mm cannons had been repaired, the side and rear rocket pods made fully functional and a drum-fed RPK light machine gun reinstalled in the roof turret. Once the huge vehicle was completely operational with all of its weaponry in perfect working order, it became a true dreadnought, a mobile skirmish line, far superior to the ville Sandcats. Although the war wag was not as maneuverable or as fast as the smaller Cats, it was essentially unstoppable, as all of them had reason to know. It had completely routed a Magistrate assault force a short time before, disabling the two Sandcats that had ferried the force from Cobaltville.

All of the ordnance that rearmed the war wag came from the Cerberus armory, an arsenal literally stacked from floor to ceiling with predark weaponry. It in turn had been supplied from caches of matériel stored in hermetically sealed Continuity of Government installations. Protected from the ravages of time and the nuke-ravaged environment, all the ordnance and munitions were as pristine as the day they rolled off the assembly line.

Lakesh himself put the arsenal together over several decades, envisioning it as the major supply depot for a rebel army. The army never materialized—at least, not in the fashion Lakesh hoped it would. Therefore, Cerberus was blessed with a surplus of death-dealing equipment that would turn the most militaristic baron green with envy or give the most pacifistic of them heart failure—if they indeed possessed hearts. Cerberus could afford to be generous not only in the refurbishing of the war wag, but outfitting Sky Dog's warriors, as well.

As Grant and Brigid assumed, Sky Dog hadn't hesitated about offering the MCP or volunteering himself and his best warriors to join the mission.

Eventually, they caught up to their companions and enjoyed a brief alliance of convenience with Ramirez and his assault force of Mags dispatched from both Snakefish and Sharpeville. Domi had apparently been killed in the battle, and Kane had yet to tell either Brigid or Grant what had happened to him during his two weeks of captivity.

Grant swallowed a sigh and tried to focus on the present. After a brief discussion that included the six Tigers of Heaven, Kane removed four high-ex grens from his war bag and gave them to Grant. They split up. Kane, Brigid and half the contingent of Tigers made the long descent back to the fortress, while

Grant and the other three samurai elected to remain
on the escarpment.

The samurai led Grant across the rock-littered plateau and through the heavy undergrowth to the cliff
edge that overhung the strait. Upon reaching a crev-
ice in the escarpment floor, they came to a halt. Even
in the uncertain light provided by the stars and the
rising moon, Grant could see how the opening had
been widened and the edges smoothed with digging
tools. A rope ladder was anchored to a pair of stakes
driven into the ground, and it dangled down into the
dark, rocky slant.

Without hesitation the Tigers of Heaven climbed
down into the shadowy throat. Grant waited uneasily
until he heard a questioning whisper from below.
"Grant-*san?*"

Swallowing a sigh, Grant swung his big body into
the hole, his broad shoulders scraping against stone.
The climb was short, less than three yards, and he
set foot in a combination cave and redoubt. When
he arrived at New Edo early that morning he had
noticed how both bastion walls of the strait were
defended.

Squat, boxlike structures were built over deep
clefts in the cliff face, one opposite the other. They
were little more than crude but effective walls of
shored-up rocks, fortifying an outthrusting shelf.
Windlasses and ballista arms extended outward for
the dropping and drawing of nets across the narrow
passage. The interior was very small and cramped,

holding only a pair of floor futons, rope and jugs of water. He couldn't stand to his full height within the little fortification.

Two helmeted men were present, standing by the cable-wrapped drum winch. Even in the wavering lantern light, their eyes showed trepidation of the giant black man. Grant nodded shortly to them, then stepped to the wall, peering over it. Nearly two hundred feet below he could barely see the black waters of the inlet. A huge net was stretched drum tight across the strait.

Leaning out as far as he could, Grant tilted his head back to study the cliff face above the little box fortification. Then he examined the stone wall, kicking experimentally at the supporting props. They were wedged firmly and wouldn't budge.

When he turned, he saw the New Edoans gazing at him expectantly as if he were a sage and about to utter words of eternal wisdom. Gesturing to the winch, Grant declared, "The net won't stop a ship of the cruiser's size. If it makes it into the strait, the best we can hope for is to slow it down for a couple of minutes...and we'll take full advantage of them."

Addressing the redoubt's guardsmen, he asked, "Do you have comms?"

When he received blank, uncomprehending looks as replies, Grant put his hand near his mouth and pretended to speak into it. "Comms. Radios."

One of the guardsmen nodded in understanding. *"Hai."* He fished around in a pocket and brought out a small transceiver. He extended it to Grant, who waved it away. He pointed to the outpost on the opposite side of the passage. "Call the men over there and tell them to start taking out the timbers from the wall. You do the same here."

All the men regarded him dubiously, then the one with the comm shrugged and made the call. Grant picked up the coil of heavy rope from the floor, hefted it and climbed back up the ladder, bidding the three Tigers to follow him.

Out on the escarpment, Grant walked cautiously and carefully to its very lip and craned his neck to look over. He removed the holstered Sin Eater from his right forearm and knotted the rope under his arms. Tersely, he explained to the Tigers what he had in mind. Although they cast him skeptical glances, they took the length of rope, wound it once around the base of a boulder and all three of them secured grips on it, anchoring it firmly.

Dropping to all fours, Grant slowly crawled backward to the cliff edge. He opened the Velcro tabs on the war bag and eased off the rock lip, a few inches at a time. When his legs dangled over the water far below, he pushed himself off. The loop of rope bit cruelly into his thick lattissimus dorsi muscles as the Tigers fed him slack and lowered him a few feet.

Trying to minimize his body's tendency to sway back and forth, he clutched at knobs of rock, his feet seeking toeholds on small ledges. The cliff face was interlaced with cracks and fissures, just as he had seen from below. He looked down, trying to estimate the position of the fortification.

Digging his fingers into cracks, he pulled himself to the right, twisting his upper torso. The rope suddenly jerked and for an instant it went slack. For a heart-stopping second, Grant thought the rope had broken but it snapped taut again, bringing a grunt of pain to his lips. His newly bandaged wounds burned with agony, and he felt the slow seep of blood from a shallow gash along his rib cage.

Breathing heavily, he managed to jam the steel-reinforced toes of his boots into a wide crack and so take some of the strain off the rope and the men who held it. Awkwardly, Grant took out a high-ex gren from his bag and worked it into a fissure running horizontally to the lip of the cliff. He didn't push it too far, but he made sure it wasn't going anywhere. He planted another gren in a vertical crack a couple feet above it and a third beside it.

When he was done, he eyed them critically. The high-exs had percussion-charge detonators, and a hard jolt was all that was required to set them off. He figured the grens were close enough to each other that if one detonated, the explosion would be sufficient to set off the others. He called out, and the Tigers of Heaven dutifully began hauling him back up to the top of the escarpment. He gritted his teeth as his cuts pulled and stretched, silently enduring the pain.

The Tigers looked a little winded from the strain, but one of them, a man named Suki, asked, "Now what, Grant-*san?*"

Grant looked around for a place not covered with rocks and sat down. "Now we make ourselves comfortable. We've got a long wait."

Chapter 8

By the time Brigid and Kane completed the arduous return journey from the plateau, all of New Edo was in a high state of war excitement. Citizens rushed back and forth, dragging the materials to build a palisade across the road that led to the palace. Shizuka herself oversaw the erection of breastworks on all sides of the bay.

She stood atop a stack of crates, shouting orders and calling out encouragement. She was in full armor except for her helmet, and despite her small size she seemed to tower against the sky. Kane easily understood Grant's almost instant attraction to her. He couldn't help but smile sourly at the irony—instead of overthrowing the gaijin-loving daimyo and putting one of their own number in his place, the Black Dragons had succeeded in investing with power a woman whose attitude toward outsiders was even more liberal than Takaun's.

An old man broke out of the crowd and approached Kane and Brigid. He had a mop of white hair and a drooping leonine mustache, and his skin was the color and consistency of cured leather. It was Dubois, the sole remaining occupant of Port

Morninglight, who had brought them to New Edo in his sailboat.

Brigid greeted him and said, "You may want to get in your boat and get out of here before dawn. Things are liable to be a little rough."

Dubois lifted a knobby shoulder in a shrug. "I would if I could. But I can't."

"Why not?" Kane asked.

Dubois saluted the sky. "Storm front's movin' in. I figure it'll bust loose right around daybreak."

Kane and Brigid exchanged quick glances. "How do you know that?" Kane inquired.

Dubois regarded him scornfully, touching his nose. "I was borned to the sea. I can smell everything from a squall to a hurricane."

Kane nodded, repressing a smile. "I hope your smeller is as reliable as your seamanship."

Shizuka caught sight of them and gestured for Kane and Brigid to join her. Brigid had already radioed in a description of the cruiser, its crew and its likely armament. Strategy was the focus now, and was a question of concentrating only on defense or mounting an offense.

As she stepped down from the crate, Kane told her grimly, "We can assume the ship will try to make it through the pass. Grant will do what he can to make it as difficult as possible for them."

Shizuka tilted her head at a quizzical angle. "How?"

"I don't know. But he'll find a way."

"He has talent for making things difficult for enemies," Brigid interposed.

Shizuka threw her a fleeting smile and said, "What vexes us now is how to deal with the invaders once they make it through the strait. We are severely outgunned."

Kane glanced at the bustle of activity swirling around them and said, "The ordnance we brought with us is yours to use. We might be able to stretch it out a little with some improvising."

Shizuka nodded. "You're the expert on these Magistrates. What may we expect them to do?"

"More than likely, once they're in the harbor, they'll launch landing boats under the cover of artillery fire." Kane gestured to the junks moored at the quay. "My suggestion is to engage them on the water as soon as they make it through the pass. It won't be anything like an even contest, but at the very least we can confuse them a little, maybe make them think they're dealing with an entire flotilla of warships."

Shizuka's eyes narrowed, then widened with a sudden thought. "Perhaps I may have a way to tip the scales just a little bit in our favor. Come with me."

Brigid and Kane followed Shizuka along the shoreline. She was stopped a few times by agitated civilians who peppered her with panicky questions. She responded to them in a cool, calm tone that lessened the fear in the people's demeanors appreciably.

Shizuka led the way across a pebble-strewed beach into a small cove, made almost invisible by foliage and the leafy boughs of trees drooping on either side. The three of them waded through the shallows until they saw a long shape humping up from the water.

Brigid and Kane turned on their Nighthawk microlights and cast the amber beams on the big, oblong shape resting in the water. "A submarine!" Kane blurted.

"Not exactly. It's a *kobukson*," Brigid said.

"Exactly," Shizuka agreed.

"What the hell is a *kobukson?*" Kane demanded, stumbling a bit over the pronunciation.

"A turtle ship," Brigid translated.

As he drew closer to it, Kane realized the vessel was aptly named. Although the vessel's streamlined contours bore some resemblance to the submarine he had seen on Ambika's Isle of the Lioness, what he had mistaken for a conning tower was actually more of a figurehead. Rising from near the bow, it was a stylized representation of a horned dragon's head, baleful and demonic of expression. Its fanged jaws hung open in a ferocious snarl.

Kane ran his hands over the ship's hull. The planking felt like tough pine, almost as hard as iron. The entire top deck was enclosed by a hexagonal framework that gradually rose amidships to give it the appearance of a turtle's shell. Within the three-foot-wide frames gleamed tightly linked steel mesh. All the ship's lines were gently rounded, and even the figurehead blended into its overall gracefulness. He guessed its overall length at around thirty feet.

"It was built at the direction of Lord Takaun," Shizuka declared.

"Why?" Kane demanded.

"It's the next best thing to an ironclad," Brigid said. "Actually, a turtle ship like this was probably the first ironclad."

Interested in spite of himself, Kane asked, "What do you mean?"

"In the sixteenth century," Shizuka replied, "Japan was torn by civil strife. A shogun named Oda Nobunga managed to temporarily call a truce among the warring clans and houses. He was assassinated and Toyotomi Hideyoshi rose to power in 1590. Hideyoshi's problem was to find a way to weaken the powerful feudal lords of the western part of Japan. In this explosive domestic situation, he looked abroad and decided that an invasion of China would provide the outlet needed for a peaceful solution at home. He sought Korea's aid in this undertaking."

"I see," Kane said, though he really didn't.

"When Korea rejected Hideyoshi's request for aid in attacking China," Shizuka continued, "he ordered his generals to invade Korea in 1592. The Japanese army, armed with matchlock guns with which Korean soldiers were not familiar, reached Seoul within two weeks. They had attempted to invade the granary province of Cholla-do, only to meet the strong resistance of the people led by General Kim Shi-min at Chinju. They then turned back toward Seoul.''

Shizuka looked expectantly toward Brigid. ''You seem passingly familiar with my country's history. Do you know what happened next?''

Brigid smiled wryly. ''Korea's King Sonjo and the royal princes fled to the northern provinces and appealed to the Ming emperor for aid against the invaders. The Japanese generals squabbled among themselves, while Korean Admiral Yi Sun-shin conducted a brilliant series of operations in the Korean Straits, destroying many Japanese ships. The ironclad *kobukson*, which Admiral Yi improved with plated armor resembling a turtle shell, protected the sailors and marines, and was more than a match for anything else afloat.''

Kane glanced over his shoulder at Shizuka. ''And the Japanese then borrowed the design?''

She nodded. ''And this one is almost an exact duplicate of the one that defeated the Japanese navy. Lord Takaun personally selected all the wood. The ribs are of oak, and the pine planks were made pliant by steaming them over boiling seawater.'' She shrugged. ''It was something of a hobby of his, but the ship is also functional. He named it the *Gameramaru*.''

Sounding a little perplexed, Brigid asked, "Does that name have any historical significance?"

"Mythological, perhaps," Shizuka answered. "Before skydark, there was a body of legends about a giant fire-breathing turtle that acted as the guardian of Nippon."

Kane walked the length of the turtle ship, stepping over the mooring lines, noting with a degree of dismay the rust pitting the metal mesh within the framework. At its bow, he nearly tripped over a long ramming sprit just below the surface. It was about twelve feet in length, made of sturdy oak and wrapped with hammered-out strips of metal wound around it for reinforcement. The shaft terminated in a broad-bladed iron triangle, like a plowshare.

Turning to Shizuka, he asked, "How does this thing move? I don't see any sails or oarlocks. What does it use—hamsters on a treadmill?"

If Shizuka understood his comment, she didn't react to it. "It's powered by a diesel engine," she replied.

Kane whirled toward her. "Diesel engine? Does it work? Do you have fuel?"

She gestured toward the vessel. "See for yourself, Kane-*san*."

He circled the turtle ship, splashed through the water and found where prop blades protruded astern. Following Shizuka's instructions, he opened a hatch on the starboard side aft, and heaved himself into the interior. The moonlight coming through the chain-link mesh had a honeycomb pattern, but he saw the vessel was smaller than he expected from the outside. He figured the beam was narrower because the *Gamera-maru*'s speed and maneuverability were more important than a smooth ride.

Three rows of wooden benches were bolted to the deck, and in the bow he saw a large copper caldron sitting on stone blocks. A wide-mouthed pipe with tin skirting hung over the pot and angled upward. The contents of the caldron exuded a strong, astringent odor, which he could even taste. "What's in this pot?" he called out.

"You should be able to smell that for yourself," Shizuka called back. "A mixture of sulfur and saltpeter. When it's ignited, it produces a smoke screen."

Examining the pipe, Kane saw how it funneled up through the hollow throat of the dragon figurehead. The smoke would pour from its mouth, which he thought was appropriate, since the vessel was named after a fire-breathing turtle. He saw how the bulkheads were perforated with ob and weapons ports. A mast was stowed away in a crutch below the deck, but was easily pulled out and stepped into its socket, with the aid of massive oaken wedges. The sail, unlike those on the junks, was a square of coarse white linen. Takaun had taken into consideration the possibility of running out of fuel while at sea.

At the rear of the ship he found an ancient engine block, and unscrewed the lid to the fuel tank. The dipstick showed it was about three-quarters full. He checked the oil sump and found it full. "I'm going to give it a try," he half shouted.

"Go ahead," Shizuka replied.

He thumbed the priming button several times. Bracing his feet, he jerked the starting cord, but nothing happened. He yanked again and again. After the third failure, he checked the plugs, the coil wires and the choke. He pumped the prime again, then grasped the cord tightly by its handle, held his breath and pulled violently.

With a staccato pop-popping the engine roared to life, the props churning the water to a froth. Noxious fumes floated from the exhaust, as the turtle ship slid forward, then came to a stop when it reached the end of the mooring lines. Kane managed to figure out how to steer the ungainly craft with a rudder handle and a crude wheel. He experimented with the motor, increasing the rpm, the thudding growl of the pistons rising in volume. The ship probably could achieve twenty knots on calm seas.

To turn off the engine, he worked a jury-rigged throttle made of wire and springs and closed off the fuel pump. The motor made a wheezing gasp and died. Kane climbed out of the hatch and rejoined Brigid and Shizuka on the shoreline.

"What's the average crew complement of the *Gamera-maru*?" he asked.

Shizuka shook her head. "I know she can comfortably fit a dozen people. We sailed on her to Port Morninglight.''

"Where'd you get the sulfur and saltpeter?''

"Here. It's in abundance. This is a volcanic island after all.''

A half smile lifted one corner of Brigid's mouth. "Then you're not quite as outgunned as you may think.''

"How so?'' Shizuka asked.

Kane took her by the elbow, guiding her back toward the quayside. "Show us what else New Edo has in abundance and we'll let you know.''

Chapter 9

The horizon was as thin as a pencil line and seemed to curve slightly downward. Despite the rising sun, the sea was gray and the sky was gray. Ramirez felt as if the CG-47 were pressed between the two. He saw nothing but inestimable miles of uninterrupted, heaving gray.

Thunder rumbled, the wind picked up and the ocean swells grew. Still, the cruiser cut a foaming path through the boiling sea on a direct heading toward the strait.

Like the rest of the men on deck, Ramirez wore his full suit of battle armor. As a wave crashed over the prow and the spray wet him, he ran his fingers over the joints of the armor, making certain all the seals were secure. The armor was close-fitting, molded to conform to the biceps, triceps, pectorals and abdomen. Even with its Kevlar undersheathing, the armor was lightweight and provided no loose folds to snag against projections. The only spot of color anywhere on it was the small, disk-shaped badge of office emblazoned on the left pectoral. It depicted, in crimson, a stylized, balanced scales of justice, superimposed over a nine-spoked wheel.

The badge symbolized the Magistrate's oath to

keep the wheels of justice turning in the nine baronies, and the wheels turned ruthlessly and inexora-
bly, grinding anyone who stood in their way.

He felt the touch of the chill wind against his
exposed chin, and he palmed away the droplets of
moisture on his helmet's visor. Like the armor en-
casing his body, the helmet was made of black polycarbonate, and fit over the upper half and back of
his head, leaving only a portion of the mouth and
chin exposed. The slightly concave, red-tinted visor
served several functions—it protected the eyes from
foreign particles, and the electrochemical polymer
was connected to a passive night sight that intensi-
fied ambient light to permit one-color night vision.

The tiny image-enhancer sensor mounted on the
forehead of the helmet didn't emit detectable rays,
though its range was only twenty-five feet, even on
a fairly clear night with strong moonlight.

At the moment, the image enhancer was of no
use. Ramirez lifted the visor and placed a pair of
binoculars to his eyes. They showed surf breaking
over a coral line that was exposed by an outgoing
tide. He could barely make out a vertical slit between the two tall bastions of cliffs.

The closer the cruiser drew to it, the more the
wind gusted, sweeping in at random from what
seemed like five different directions at once. Waves
seethed over the sides, completely drenching anyone
who so much as put a foot on the deck. Ramirez
hooked the binoculars onto his web belt so he could
grasp the rail with both hands. Despite his body ar-

mor's relative light weight, he knew if he fell overboard he would still sink like a stone, burdened as he was with his Sin Eater and heavy combat knife.

It started to rain, a slow, almost laconic drizzle, like a gentle spring shower. A loud boom of thunder exploded, and the air shivered with its vibration like the striking of a gong. Lightning crowded the sky, the brilliant flash turning the dim gray dawn to a blazing high noon. A moment later, a howling squall hit the cruiser broadside. It tossed the ship about as if she were a twig caught in rapids.

The CG-47 bucked and slammed up and down. A swell peaked like a wet mountain beneath the keel, and the cruiser slid down it. The ship tobogganed to the next gray-green mountain that loomed up out of the sea. Ramirez gripped the railing with all the strength in his hands, afraid to glance over his shoulder at the wheelhouse. If Carpenter the pilot failed to keep the ship's bow up, the CG-47 would wallow, take on water and go swiftly to the bottom.

The pumps worked steadily, yet all the while more of the sea sluiced over the deck and into the bilge. Ramirez saw one of his men clinging to a stanchion like a barnacle on a rock. The Mag quickly became violently seasick. His complexion turned as greenish gray as the sea. His shoulders heaved, and he vomited until there was nothing left in his stomach but burning acids. The waves rinsed the deck clean.

A voice filtered into his ear through the helmet's comm-link, but it was so hashy with static he couldn't understand a word. Carefully, he turned to look at the elevated bridge housing, and he saw Carpenter at the wheel, gesturing to him.

Clenching his teeth, Ramirez pushed himself away from the rail just as another huge wave buffeted the CG-47. Ramirez stumbled, and he saw the sick Magistrate lose his grip and roll across the foredeck, tumbling like a log. Ramirez reached for him, but a wave surged over the deck, engulfed him, and he was gone.

Ramirez opened his mouth to roar out an obscenity, but a bucketful of seawater struck him directly in the face. He coughed and sputtered and spit, and left the rail, heading toward the bridge. Despite the thick treads of his boots, he staggered and slid on the deck plates, gracelessly falling on his rear end more than once. He crawled to the ladder leading to the wheelhouse, and pulled himself up the rungs, his wet gloves slipping on the railing.

Once inside the cabin, he breathed deeply with relief. A handful of his Mags were present, and they all appeared both frightened and motion sick. There were twenty Magistrates aboard, and even those from Snakefish in the cabins belowdecks possessed little hard seamanship experience. Ramirez could only hope that by the time they squeezed through the strait, they wouldn't be too busy throwing up to achieve their mission objective.

Carpenter, a man with a weather-beaten face and ash-blond hair, said flatly, "The seas are so rough we may pile up inside the passage. We could wait until the storm passes.''

"How long will that be?" Ramirez asked, stumbling as the cruiser pitched to starboard.

Carpenter shrugged. "I couldn't say."

"You're the official pilot of this boat—"

"Ship," Carpenter corrected automatically.

Ramirez acted as if he hadn't heard. "—so you know better than anybody what it can take and what it can't."

Carpenter's leathery lips compressed. "I've never been in these seas before. But I do know this—the baron loves this ship. If she's scuttled, if she's sunk, if she's wrecked, all of us better go down with her. Baron Snakefish won't listen to any excuses about how she was lost."

Ramirez's belly turned a cold flip-flop but not from seasickness. He knew full well that Carpenter spoke the truth. Regardless of the mission the baron had assigned him, Ramirez was expected to return the cruiser to the ville more or less in the same shape in which it had left.

He was positive the New Edoans were aware of their presence by now. And if Kane, Grant and the renegade historian Baptiste were there, they would have told them what they could expect in the way of opposition. Still, he knew from the onset, based on the intel Carpenter had provided, that it would be impossible to approach the island unseen. They wouldn't be able to sneak in through the strait unchallenged and unopposed.

Another huge wave crashed over the prow of the CG-47, and Carpenter wrestled with the wheel. He decreased the rpm of the two turbine engines, and the boat shook with a stem-to-stern vibration. The wipers flicked steadily back and forth, but they were unable to keep the windshield clear for more than a microsecond at a time. One of the Mags suddenly bent forward and vomited. No one paid him any attention, and Ramirez didn't rebuke him. He was glad to be in the stuffy bridge rather than down below or on deck.

Then, as the CG-47 rode the crest of a swell, Ramirez saw dead ahead the vague outline of the strait. He guessed it was only a hundred yards away, and wouldn't have been visible through the mist and flying spray, except for dim lights on the far side of it.

"Make up your mind," Carpenter said grimly. "Are we going to thread the needle or not?"

Ramirez swallowed hard. He understood that regardless of Baron Snakefish's affection for the boat—ship—he wouldn't countenance the Mag force turning back after reaching the very doorstep of their goal.

"We go," he said tersely.

Carpenter turned the wheel and grunted, "Aye, aye, sir."

The ship's bow turned toward the opening and the craft picked up speed, although the engines were still coasting on low revs. Responding to Ramirez's questioning look, Carpenter said calmly, "We're caught in the current, the undertow. I expected as much. It's apt to get rougher.''

Plucking a microphone from the instrument panel, Ramirez opened the channel to all of the ship's sections and announced, "We're going through the strait. Everyone stow your equipment and hang on."

The gap between the bastions of rock seemed to widen. With appalling suddenness, it became a gushing channel swirling around broken rocks, spray rising like mist.

Carpenter spun the wheel to port, then to starboard. The ship quivered, then flew like an unguided missile into the heart of the foaming, churning passage. Ramirez braced himself tightly on the edges of the plot board as the CG-47 arrowed into the wild current. Mist and foam completely covered the windshield.

The cruiser plunged madly along the strait between the towering, kelp-draped walls of the cliffs. It pitched and yawed as it picked up speed, shooting forward, threading its way between upthrusts of pitted rock. The deck was saturated by the crashing waves and flying foam.

The current seemed to draw the CG-47 forward like a toy at the end of a string. The cruiser's prow cleaved through the narrow channel like a knife blade. Ramirez prayed the high speed in shallow water wouldn't have the very possible effect of putting the ship's stern down to touch bottom and smother the spinning props in the sand.

Expertly handled by Carpenter, the CG-47 rushed

down the strip of water between the two high ramparts of dark stone. Ramirez heard the scream of metal as the hull scraped the walls. The vessel shuddered under the glancing impact but kept on going. Seconds later she bucked heavily to starboard as her bow smashed sideways into rock.

The pilot spun the wheel, veering away, and sent her back on course with no slackening of her speed. She raced on through, heading clear and free toward the open water beyond the strait.

The frothing sea calmed the farther the ship moved down the throat of the passage. The end of it was in sight. Within seconds, it seemed to Ramirez the cruiser barely moved.

"The worst of it is behind us," Carpenter declared gruffly.

Ramirez didn't even try to suppress his sigh of relief. He spoke into the microphone. "We're through. All hands on deck. Standard deployment of arms and personnel. Prepare the landing boats."

On the heels of his last order came the sharp crack of an explosion. For an instant, he thought it was a thunderclap. Then a torrent of stone rained from above, completely obliterating any view of what lay beyond the strait.

Chapter 10

Grant had certainly spent worse nights out in the open than the one he suffered atop the plateau, but his discomfort wasn't simply physical. He lay under a sheltering fern atop one of the futons provided by the outpost guards, so he wasn't too uncomfortable.

Through the foliage, he gazed up at the starlit sky, absently noting how the scudding clouds thickened across the face of the moon. The breeze carried the faint whiff of ozone, and he guessed a storm front was moving in.

He knew he should have been exhausted, both from the battle and the climb—not to mention his lovemaking with Shizuka—but he couldn't force himself to sleep. He had trained himself to catch sleep whenever he could, so as to build up a backlog in case he had to go for long periods without it, but this night he could barely nap much less drift off into deep slumber.

His mind raced like an out-of-control engine, thoughts, memories and images careening wildly within the walls of his skull. One image predominated—an outlander girl, barely five feet tall, slender yet curvaceous of build. She looked to be in her teens, but by her own admission she didn't know her true age. She could be anywhere from sixteen to twenty-six.

Her skin was the hue of a pearl, her bone-white hair ragged and cropped very short, her eyes a burning red. Her hips were flaring, her legs long and slim, and her breasts were small but perky.

He had no trouble mentally conjuring up his first glimpse of her on a muddy street in Cobaltville's Tartarus Pits. Her hair was held away from her piquant, hollow-cheeked face by a length of satiny cloth. She wore a T-shirt and a pair of red, high-cut shorts that showed off her pale slim legs.

Grant easily recalled how a minute after his first sight of her, she had led him, Kane and another Magistrate into an ambush. Domi had been acting under duress, put in fear of her life by the Pit boss, Guana Teague. At her first opportunity, she rectified her treachery by cutting Teague's throat.

Teague was crushing the life out of Grant beneath his three-hundred-plus pounds of flab when Domi expertly slit his throat for him. After that, Domi attached herself to Grant, viewing him as a gallant black knight who rescued her from the shackles of Guana Teague's slavery, even though in reality quite the reverse was true. As something of a memento, she always carried the hunting knife with the nine-inch serrated blade that had done the deed.

For more than a year, she made it fiercely clear that Grant was hers and hers alone, and she had been

jealous of DeFore, the Cerberus medic, suspecting
the woman of having designs on Grant. He fought
hard to make sure there was nothing but friendship
between him and Domi, but he feared it was a fight
he would eventually lose. He had no idea of Domi's
true age; he was pushing forty and felt twice as old.
Still, he could never deny he was attracted to her
youthfulness, her high spirits and her uninhibited
sexuality.

But more than that, Domi had proved herself to
be a tough and resourceful if not altogether stable
partner. At one point she had saved his, Brigid's,
and Kane's lives when the Cerberus mat-trans unit
was sabotaged. Even being in her debt didn't make
him more understanding of her, or appreciate her
uniqueness. He realized he had never really known
her. It hadn't occurred to him they had forged a
relationship deeper than he knew or cared to admit.

Always before, he had tried to make the gap in
their ages the reason he didn't want to get involved
with her, sexually or otherwise. Domi had been pa-
tient and understanding for a year until she grew
tired of waiting. In truth, Grant had deliberately
maintained a distance between himself and Domi,
so if either she or he died—or simply went away—
the vacuum wouldn't be so difficult to endure. He
recalled with crystal clarity what she had said to him
a month or so ago, when she confronted him: "If
you can't do it, if you're impotent, then let me know
right now so I can make plans."

When he angrily denied a physical disability was the reason, she snarled, "Then it is me, you lying sack of shit." Then, with contempt dripping from every syllable, she said, "Big man, big chest, big shoulders, legs like trees. Guess they don't tell the story, huh?"

That was the last private conversation they had. Her angry outburst cut him like the knife she had turned on Guana Teague. When he remembered the recrimination in her voice, he knew he couldn't make up for anything he had done to hurt her. And he knew he had hurt Domi dreadfully when she spied him and Shizuka locked in a passionate embrace. He didn't speak to her about it. Part of his reluctance was due to shame, another part due to pride, but more than anything else, fear made him hold his tongue.

It was Grant's habit to keep some emotional distance between himself and everyone he knew, even Kane. The reason was simple—if one were lost, the other could go on. He realized bleakly the distance was nothing but a manifestation of inner fear, a terror of not being able to accept the inevitability of personal loss or his lack of control of the fates of others.

He remembered his helplessness and rage when Olivia had been torn from him by the caste standards of the villes. He could only watch stoically as she drifted away from him and his life. The hole her absence left was never filled, but the pain left in its place strengthened him—he had silently vowed never to let anyone take control from him again. Now, because of that vow, Domi would never know how much she meant to him. She had died feeling used and discarded. Guilt and self-loathing filled him.

Grant's eyes stung and his throat constricted. He breathed harshly but regularly until the tension in his throat relaxed. He wiped his eyes and thought about Shizuka. Although she was closer to his own age, and much more mature than Domi, he realized bleakly her heart and soul were inextricably bound to New Edo. Those ties were even stronger now after the death of Kiyomasa and the incapacitation of Lord Takaun. She would never leave as long as she perceived New Edo needed her.

The notion of remaining on the little island monarchy definitely appealed to him, but Shizuka hadn't mentioned it to him, and Grant didn't feel it was his place to raise the issue with her.

And if by chance she ever did make the proposition to him, and he accepted, he was fairly certain Kane would accuse him of desertion, despite the fact he had taken no vows or sworn oaths of service to battle the barons. Kane was his partner, true enough, and it was a matter of Mag policy never to desert a partner regardless of the circumstances, but they weren't Mags any longer. Kane had more of a personal vested interest in seeing the barons overthrown than he did, anyway. It was Kane's vendetta, his vengeance trail, not Grant's. His primary contribution was to cover Kane's back.

Besides, judging by what Baron Sharpe had revealed to him and Brigid during their meeting in Las Vegas, the involvement of Cerberus in overthrowing the barons might not be necessary at all. The baronies were poised on the brink of civil war, sparked by one of their own. If so, the strife had its roots thousands of years in the past.

Grant had believed the barons were under the sway of the Archon Directorate, a nonhuman race who influenced human affairs for thousands of years. In fact, Lakesh claimed the entirety of human history was intertwined with the activities of the entities called Archons, although they were referred to by many names over many centuries—angels, demons, visitors, ETs, saucer people, grays. Beginning at the dawn of human history, the Archons subtly— and sometimes not so subtly—influenced human affairs. The concept of humanity as a slave race, owned by some mysterious power, was expressed thousands of years ago in humankind's earliest recorded religious and historical texts.

Allegedly, the sinister thread linking all of humankind's darkest hours led back to a nonhuman presence that conspired to control humanity through political chaos, staged wars, famines, plagues and natural disasters. The nuclear apocalypse of 2001 was all part of the Archon Directorate's strategy. With the destruction of social structures and severe depopulation, the Archons established the nine barons and distributed predark technology among them to consolidate their power over Earth and its disenfranchised, spiritually beaten human inhabitants. Lakesh believed the conspiracy continued to the present, aided and abetted first by willing human allies and then the hybrid barons, their plenipotentiaries on Earth. The gene pool of the barons was a collection of superior traits derived from both human and Archon DNA.

The supposed goal of the Directorate and the barons was the unification of the world under their complete control, with all nonessential and nonproductive humans eliminated. Nearly two hundred years after the nukecaust, that objective had almost been achieved. The small population was easier to manipulate. But unification wasn't as easy to sustain as it was to gain.

But over the past few months, all of them had learned that the elaborate explanation was a ruse, bits of truth mixed in with outrageous fiction. The Archon Directorate didn't exist except as a vast cover story, created in the twentieth century and embellished with each succeeding generation. The only so-called Archon on Earth was Balam, the last of an extinct race that had once shared the planet with humankind.

After three years of imprisonment in the Cerberus redoubt, Balam finally revealed the truth behind the Directorate and the hybridization program initiated centuries before. Balam claimed that the Archon Directorate existed only as an appellation and a myth created by the predark government agencies as a control mechanism. Lakesh referred to it as the Oz Effect, wherein a single vulnerable entity created the illusion of being the representative of an all-powerful body.

Balam himself may have even coined the term Archon to describe his people. In ancient Gnostic texts, *Archon* was applied to a parahuman world-governing force that imprisoned the divine spark in human souls. Kane had often wondered over the past few months if Balam had indeed created that appellation as a cryptic code to warn future generations.

Even more shocking was Balam's assertion that he and his ancient folk were of human stock, not alien but alienated. They still didn't know how much to believe. But if nothing else, none of the Cerberus personnel any longer subscribed to the fatalistic belief that the human race had had its day and only extinction lay ahead. Balam had indicated that wasn't true, only another control mechanism.

Regardless of scraping away the myth and exposing the truth, the barons, the half-human hybrids spawned from Balam's DNA, still ruled. Although all of the fortress-cities with their individual, allegedly immortal god-kings were supposed to be interdependent, the baronies still operated on insular principles. Cooperation among the barons was grudging despite their shared goal of a unified world. They perceived humanity in general as either servants or as living storage vessels for transplanted organs and fresh genetic material.

The barons weren't immortal, but they were as close as flesh-and-blood creatures could come to it. Due to their hybrid metabolisms, their longevities far exceeded those of humans. Barring accidents, illnesses—or assassinations—the barons' life spans could conceivably be measured in centuries. Grant figured that even the youngest of them was close to one hundred years old.

But the price paid by the barons for their extended life spans wasn't cheap. They were physically fragile, prone to lethargy and their metabolisms were easy prey for infections, which was one reason they tended to sequester themselves from the ville-bred humans they ruled. In severe cases, even damaged organs were replaced from the storage banks of stockpiled organic material. The full scope of the medical procedures and treatments was unknown.

What was not an unknown was how the vast genetic engineering facility beneath the Archuleta Mesa in Dulce had served as a combination of gestation, birthing ward and medical treatment center. The hybrids, the self-proclaimed new humans, were born there, the half-human spawn created to inherit the nuke-scoured Earth.

None of the hybrids reproduced in conventional fashion. They reproduced by a form of cloning and gene splicing, but it hadn't seemed reasonable they would rely completely on the subterranean facilities beneath the Archuleta Mesa. And if that were so, if they didn't have access to a secondary installation, then extinction for the barons was less than a generation away. Or so Grant and all the Cerberus exiles fervently hoped, with the Dulce installation now destroyed.

That hope vanished quickly when Lakesh informed them of the Area 51 complex and the body of legends that claimed alien involvement with the top-secret facility. The so-called aliens weren't referred to by name, but they fit the general physical description of Balam's people. If that was indeed the case, Lakesh theorized that the medical facilities that might exist in Area 51 would be of great use to the barons, since they would already be designed for their metabolisms. Baron Cobalt could reactivate the processing and treatment center without having to rebuild from scratch. He could have transferred the medical personnel from the Dulce facility.

Grant repressed a shudder when he recollected his conversation with Baron Sharpe, who essentially confirmed Lakesh's hypothesis. Sharpe declared that Baron Cobalt's forces had occupied the Dreamland complex, and proposed doling out the means of baronial survival as he saw fit. Sharpe had said, "He vexed the barons with an ultimatum, you see—to place him in the position of final authority as the imperator, or to die."

Imperator. Grant rolled the title around in his

drowsy mind. During Kane's captivity in Area 51, he'd been told about a mysterious figure called the imperator who intended to set himself up as overlord of the villes, with the barons subservient to him. That bit of news was surprising enough, but it quickly turned shocking when Kane said his informant claimed none other than Balam, whom they had thought was gone forever, supported this so-called imperator.

Grant closed his eyes and beckoned sleep. To his distant surprise, he felt himself drifting off. He was awakened almost immediately, it seemed, by a spatter of cold rain, followed by the rumble of thunder.

He opened his eyes and groggily raised his wrist chron to his face. According to the LED, the time was close to 5:00 a.m. He had slept for more than seven hours, but he didn't feel particularly rested and certainly not refreshed.

As he pushed himself up on his elbows, thunder boomed again, this time sounding much closer. Lightning flickered briefly in the cloud-clogged sky. The boom bled off into the sudden tolling of the alarm bell.

Galvanized by the clanging, and with his heart pounding, he struggled to his feet, wincing as his cuts twinged. He surveyed the sky, seeing a mountainous thunderhead skimming out of the east, almost blotting out the rising sun. The floating, billowing mass thickened rapidly, casting deep shadow over the entire plateau, bringing a sudden and op-

pressive gloom. The atmosphere seemed to gain
weight, pressing against his eardrums, making respiration labored. The stormy blackness slowly
spread like a blanket. Another thunderclap made the
rocks underfoot tremble.

Antoku rushed up to him from the vicinity of the
watchtower, barking into the small comm unit in his
hand. Even over the brassy ringing of the bell, Grant
heard Mohri's agitated voice speaking frantically
over the transceiver.

Breathlessly, Antoku said, "Mohri reports the
ship is under way, on a direct heading with the strait.
The seas are very rough this morning, so it's moving
slowly. We have a little time."

Grant only nodded and climbed down into the
cleft leading to the cramped cavern. By the lantern
light, he noted with approval the guardsmen had removed all the support stakes and braces from the
stone wall. He nudged it with a foot and the rocks
shifted. Peering down into the strait, he saw nothing
but darkness. Although the sun was higher, the
heavy cloud cover prevented its light from penetrating the channel. The morning sky was the dismal
color of old lead.

The wind increased, and within moments it
howled along the cliff face, whistling eerily through
crevices and cracks. Craning his neck, Grant looked
toward the overhang where he had planted the grens.
They were invisible in the gloom. He withdrew back
into the cave, fervently hoping that by the time the

ship entered the strait, the light would be stronger. If not, he figured he could hose bullets from his Sin Eater in the general vicinity of the grens and hope for a lucky shot.

The guardsmen and the Tigers of Heaven whispered urgently among themselves, fidgeting with their *katanas,* which were about as useful at the moment as a stickie with a manicure.

"No need to get so wired up," Grant calmly told them. "They'll get here when they get here—if at all."

For a few minutes, Mohri kept them updated on the cruiser's progress over the comm, but as the wind strengthened and drizzle became a raging downpour, the transmissions became garbled and finally ceased altogether.

They waited out the storm in the little cave, wincing at the near deafening claps of thunder, and flinching from lightning strokes so frighteningly close Grant fancied he felt his hair standing on end due to the static electricity.

As the storm lashed at the plateau, even Grant grew nervous and impatient. There wasn't enough space in the hollowed-out room to pace, so he contented himself with first cracking his knuckles, then drumming his fingers on the rock wall.

At length, the front moved off, the wind lessened in its fury and the rain tapered to a drizzle. The dark mass of clouds slowly broke up, allowing weak sunlight to filter through. Grant leaned against the wall,

hazarding a peek down. It took his eyes a moment
to adjust to the gloom of the strait, and he could
barely make out the storm-tossed whitecaps in the
dark water far below. He wouldn't have seen the
ship at all except for the lights feebly glowing
through the window of the wheelhouse.

The comm in Antoku's hand suddenly blared with
Mohri's frantic voice. "He can't see the ship," Antoku translated.

"I can." Grant pointed downward. "And here
she comes."

The Tigers and the guardsmen crowded around
him, elbowing one another. They pushed Grant
against the wall, and he felt it shift beneath his
weight, dislodging a few of the smaller stones. With
a curse, he pushed them back. "Spread out. One at
a time or you'll be on the ship's deck."

The men took turns gazing down at the cruiser as
it eased past the mouth of the channel. They uttered
hissing whispers of fear and anger, and stepped
back, instinctively clutching at their swords. A couple of them glared at him in silent accusation.

Grant ignored them and leaned over the fortification, squinting as the last of the wind-whipped
rain dampened his face. From below arose the strong
odor of brine. Silently, he watched as the churning
waters of the strait pummeled and buffeted the
cruiser, lifting it, dropping it and smashing it sideways against one wall.

More than once he expected to see the vessel pile

up against the rocks, but each time a head-on collision was avoided. As it was, he heard the tortured screech of metal against stone echoing like the cry of a damned soul. He felt a moment's grudging admiration for the skill of the ship's pilot.

The sea calmed as the cruiser progressed into the channel. Grant tensed as it approached the net spanning the width of the passage. The prow struck it dead center, and as he had anticipated and predicted, the ship's weight and momentum ripped the net loose from its moorings. Cables snapped with loud semimusical twangs, and wood splintered from the armatures with prolonged cracks.

Without turning his head, Grant said curtly, "Everybody out. Move a fair distance away. It's time to test my brilliant plan. Signal the others to get ready."

Swiftly, the guardsmen and the Tigers of Heaven climbed up the rope ladder and out of the cave. Grant leaned farther out over the wall, looking up. He gusted out a sigh of relief when his eyes picked out the grens jammed in the fissures.

He flexed his wrist tendons and the Sin Eater slapped solidly into his waiting palm. Carefully, he brought one gray-shelled egg into target acquisition, took and held a breath, then squeezed the trigger.

The 9 mm round penetrated the thin metal shell, and the overhang dissolved in a blinding flash, a clap of thunder and a blooming burst of hell-hued

light. The other two grens detonated almost simultaneously.

Grant ducked back into the cave and rushed for
the cleft and the rope ladder as the air shivered with
the echoes of the explosions. Ugly black fissures
spread out in a spiderweb pattern around the cleft.
Dust and rock sifted down from above. He looked
back once to see the entire cliff face in roaring motion. Rocks struck the wall and sheared it away,
breaking it apart in hundreds of smaller pieces.

As Grant struggled up the ladder, the entire section of the cliff that held the cave collapsed with an
earsplitting roar. Tons of rock plunged downward
and very nearly carried him with it. Grant secured a
tight double-fisted grip on the bamboo rungs, but his
legs flailed for a foothold. He spit out grit, and his
eyes watered from dust. The avalanche roared and
rumbled into a continuous thunder.

Pelted by stones, stung by pebbles, he dangled at
the end of the ladder over the strait. Slowly, he
heaved his body up, chinning himself on a rung.
There was a crack of splitting rock, and Grant felt
one side of the ladder slipping downward. He fought
to dig the toes of his boots into the hard volcanic
rock.

Then a hand closed over his right wrist. Grant
tilted his head back, blinking, and saw Antoku lying
belly down with the rock rim in his armpits. "Grab
me with your other hand," the samurai directed
through clenched teeth.

Grant seized his wrist, and Antoku said a few sharp words over his shoulder. The other men held Antoku by the ankles, and they began to back away from the cliff. Grant didn't try to pull. With his greater weight, he probably could have pulled Antoku and the others right down into the strait.

By the time Grant was lifted to the point where he could rest his weight on the ladder, Antoku's limbs quivered violently with the strain.

Grant heaved himself up, threw an arm over the edge, then pulled his body over. For a long minute, all anyone could do was pant and gasp. When he recovered sufficient wind to do so, he husked out, "Thanks."

The New Edoans nodded casually as if what they had accomplished were nothing to expend words of gratitude about. Grant didn't stand. He sat and tried to catch his breath, looking across the channel to the fortification on the opposite rampart. The guardsmen there had kicked and shoved their stone wall down into the chasm.

So now his part of the plan was complete. If the next step—whatever Kane might have concocted— worked as well, the invasion would be decisively met and repulsed. The battle would be over.

He earnestly hoped so. He was very tired.

Chapter 11

From Ramirez's vantage point, the catastrophe arrived between one heartbeat and another. He felt numb, completely disassociated from his body and surroundings. It was as if his mind hovered high above the CG-47 and observed the disaster with a kind of aloof bemusement.

A roaring, seething avalanche of roaring rock slabs and dirt cascaded down the steep face of the cliff, augmenting its bellowing fury with tons of stone torn loose by its rush. Great crags and shards rained on the deck of the cruiser, smashing, pulverizing and crushing anything beneath it, including the few men who had ventured out on deck after the storm.

Tons of granite and shale thundered down on the CG-47, boulders rolling and bouncing. Dimly, above the grinding rumble, Ramirez heard the terrified screams of the Magistrates in the wheelhouse as they backed up against the far bulkhead.

He watched in openmouthed astonishment as a boulder the size of a landing boat tumbled end over end toward the wheelhouse. Carpenter bleated in shock, right before the window shattered inward in a glittering, razor-edged spray of glass. Fragments rattled violently against the walls, and Ramirez felt several sharp blows against his upraised, armored arms.

A flying splinter of glass nicked his chin and suddenly, as if he had been booted in the rear, he was back in the bridge room again, not floating above it. Ramirez flung himself backward, wedging himself in a corner between the door frame and the wall, paralyzed by terror and shock.

Carpenter began to bellow, to curse and wrestle with the wheel, but it did no good. The CG-47 shuddered brutally under the barrage of falling stone. The lights in the wheelhouse flickered. The ship rocked to and fro, and Ramirez had to grab one of his men to keep him from staggering into the pilot. They fought each other to open the door.

Under other circumstances, Ramirez would have shouted orders to bring his men under control. Instead, he made only gagging noises, his eyes blinded by hot tears. He felt a stream of urine scorching its way down his leg.

The wheelhouse shook with such violence his teeth clattered. Fissures spread out on the ceiling. The bulkheads buckled and the ceiling cracked, split in the middle and folded inward in a shower of debris.

Ramirez kicked himself away from the corner as a seething cascade of metal braces, lath work and insulation rained to the deck. He caught only a fleeting glimpse of the pile of wreckage covering Carpenter and the other Magistrates. His shoulder slammed the door open, and Ramirez toppled unceremoniously past the ladder, landing on his right side with a clatter of polycarbonate. His helmeted head smacked sharply against the deck plates.

Air exploded from between his lips, and multicolored spirals spun before his eyes. A rock the size of a pumpkin hurtled over his head and smashed into pieces against the superstructure.

Ramirez elbowed himself to his knees, then used the rungs of the ladder to achieve a crouching posture. He dragged air into his laboring lungs, swung his head up and saw that the wave of shattered stone sweeping down the cliff face was bleeding itself out.

He sheltered himself as best he could from flying fragments, although a couple of fist-sized chunks of granite rebounded painfully from his shoulders. He crouched there as the ship heaved and trembled around him.

The shuddering crash of tumbling, rolling rock slowly faded. Settling stone continued to click and grate. Cautiously standing, he peered through the thick pall of rising dust at the high heap of shale and boulders completely blanketing the deck.

Ramirez looked beyond the CG-47's bows and saw an open expanse of fairly calm water. The ship was through the strait and in a natural bay. Rather than sighing with relief, he froze in fear. A flotilla of strange-looking ships hove out of the dust and the

early-morning murk. They encircled the CG-47.
Two of them rode high in the water, their sails filled
with the wind. They had a peculiar, lacquered appearance. One was a bit longer and broader in the
beam than the other, but both ships were essentially
identical.

He caught only a glimpse of the third ship, and
unlike the others, it was low-slung with no superstructure to speak of. He was irresistibly reminded
of a giant turtle, but then its shape was lost by
wreaths of yellow mist floating up and around its
hull.

Within seconds, the vapor thickened to the consistency of a fog bank billowing and rolling across
the surface of the bay. Faintly, he heard the steady
throb of an engine. He could see only a blurry outline of the ship through the vapor shrouding the hull.
He caught the acrid stench of sulfur.

By now, Magistrates ran in crazed confusion all
around the stone-littered deck, stumbling over rocks,
colliding with one another, screaming a babble of
orders and counterorders. A couple of them opened
up with their Sin Eaters, shooting toward the ships,
though the range was far too great for handblasters.

Climbing halfway up the ladder, Ramirez opened
the all-channel comm-link frequency and shouted at
the top of his lungs, "Man the cannons! Man the
fucking cannons, you assholes!"

A couple of Mags scrambled to obey, scaling the
ladders and dashing along the gangways to the

shielded gun housings. From starboard of the lacquered ship bearing down on them erupted what appeared to be a shower of flaming meteors. They
arced up over the water and down again. Ramirez
blinked first in astonishment, then in derision. Fire
arrows! Even with as much damage as the CG-47
had incurred, a shower of flaming arrows would
have about as much effect on the armored ship as a
handful of matchsticks.

The flight of three-foot-long arrows landed on the
amidships deckwork, some falling short and dropping with little hisses into the bay. Others splintered
against stone and metal.

Ramirez ignored even the couple that thudded
near him. He continued to bellow orders. "Get to
the machine guns! Fire at will! Prep the landing
boats!"

The last word of his order was drowned out by a
brutal detonation. From somewhere behind him a
hell-flower bloomed, petals of flame curving and
spreading outward. Spewing from the end of every
petal was a rain of shrapnel, ripping into bodies and
bulkheads. A few fragments rattled violently against
his armored back, knocking him from the ladder and
onto all fours. The rolling echoes of the explosion
faded, punctuated by screams of men in agony.

The acrid chemical odor of high explosive filled
his nostrils, and his belly lurched sideways. At least
one of the flight of arrows had been tipped with a

frag gren, and he knew it probably wouldn't be the
only one flying their way.

DESPITE THE VISOR of her helmet, Brigid could see
the cruiser bearing down on the *Gamera-maru*. The
ship was still very fast, even with the damage she
had taken not just from the rock fall but from the
frag gren. The turtle boat moved sluggishly, the hull
seeming to drag. Clouds of sulfurous smoke spewed
from the figurehead, so strong in odor she wondered
how Kane and the handful of men aboard the ship
could possibly stand it.

Still the smoke screen was effective; a stream of
fire from the cruiser's MG emplacements did little
more than punch holes in the vapor. It also provided
cover for Dubois and his little sailboat, with its little
packet of high explosive. At least she hoped the reason she couldn't see him was due to the smoke. If
Dubois had reneged on his contribution to the little
war, Kane would be more than disappointed; he
would be enraged. He had spent hours creating a
shaped charge from most of their grens.

Brigid stood on the prow deck of the junk next
to Shizuka, wearing Tigers of Heaven body armor
with a Copperhead slung over her shoulder. All of
the men aboard the ship wore some form of armor,
even those who weren't samurai but volunteers from
the New Edoan citizenry. The volunteers wore hard
leather cuirasses and were equipped with bows and
full quivers.

From the deck of the ship, it was a frightening spectacle. The awkward junks wallowed slowly toward the dark, streamlined cruiser. The New Edoan vessels in the bay were trying to act as a barricade force, but they were having a hard time maneuvering. The winds weren't with them.

However, the CG-47 didn't have much of an advantage, either. With the wheelhouse crushed by several boulders, the ship drifted. The currents and tides were forcing the ship in close to the rocks at the base of the cliffs where it was in danger of breaking up on submerged reefs or being beached. Shading her eyes, Brigid thought she spied Ramirez on deck. She resisted the impulse to look behind her to the quays.

Shizuka shouted out orders, and her words were repeated until they reached the dozen archers lining the rail. In unison, they nocked their long arrows, bowstrings hummed simultaneously and they loosed another flight of flaming arrows at the cruiser. They landed on its battered, stone-strewed deck, and within seconds came the crump of an explosion and a hot orange flash. The sound was different than the fragger, and Brigid knew that the gren this time was one that Kane had improvised out of a small ceramic jar filled with sulfur, saltpeter and a sampling of chemicals borrowed from a gren in their war bags.

Shizuka snapped out another order, and the man at the wheel obeyed instantly, but not quite fast enough. The junk began a starboard turn just as the twin cannons aboard the cruiser fired with ear-knocking reports. The double volley began with the forward cannon, and stepped raggedly back toward the stern. With a sound as of a gigantic piece of stiff cloth being ripped, the shell screamed across the surface of the bay and struck the junk's bow low, almost at the waterline. Brigid and Shizuka staggered backward, drenched by the geyser of water fountaining up over the side. Men went sprawling. Some stayed on their feet by clutching the deck rail.

The second shell went into the quarterdeck, smashing wood, flinging deadly man-size splinters. The jagged shards of broken timber slashed at the samurai in the vicinity. One man went down, folded around a long sharp stake, his intestines oozing out along the point of bloody wood.

As Brigid regained her balance, she saw the cruiser's tripod-mounted machine guns spit flickering spear points of flame. Steel-jacketed bullets sped across the rolling waves and sang through the rigging and sails. The blastermen didn't have the range yet, and miniature water spouts sprayed up just behind the junk's stern.

The CG-47's cannon fired again, but the shell missed entirely, miraculously passing through the narrow clear space between sail and mast and striking the water on the other side. The current slowly pushed the cruiser in a counterclockwise circle, moving the bore of the cannons away from their ship. The next thunderous volley soared up and over the bay, and impacted on the shoreline. The shells reduced a large section of the newly erected palisade blockade to splinters.

None of the Magistrates aboard the cruiser seemed to notice the second, smaller junk cutting an oblique course toward their vessel. They weren't aware of its proximity until a flight of fire arrows hummed almost straight up and over the side of the CG-47.

A series of small explosions lit up the cruiser's deck with little balls of orange-red flame. The machine gunners turned their aim toward the wooden ship, and a stream of bullets chewed through sails, rope and flesh. Fist-size holes appeared in the cloth, giving it the likeness of Swiss cheese.

The archers on Shizuka's ship poured another hail of arrows onto the deck of the CG-47. Three explosions lit up the postdawn gloom like flares, and dark smoke boiled up from the detonation points. The machine gun stopped chattering. The second junk drew alongside the cruiser, and coils of rope licked out, the grappling hooks catching fast on the port side forward.

Heart pounding, her breath coming hard and fast, Brigid looked toward the turtle ship and saw it was completely concealed now by a pall of smoke that spread like streamers of filthy lace over the roiling surface of the bay. She couldn't even make out the haziest outline of Dubois's sailboat.

The junk slid closer to the cruiser, and the two

ships smashed together with a nerve-stinging crunch. The vessels were locked together and though the cruiser's greater bulk overwhelmed the New Edoan ship, the junk rode slightly higher and so the samurai didn't have to climb up to the deck. Unsheathed *katanas* in hand, voicing shrill fierce cries, the Tigers of Heaven leaped down onto the cruiser.

Nothing was calm and organized about boarding the cruiser. Brigid hadn't believed the samurai were in for an easy fight, and she was right. They were met in the smoke on the cruiser's deck by armored men every bit as fierce and deadly as the samurai. First there were the cracks of blasters and the stutter of subguns. The first wave of boarders folded over, some falling between the ships to the bay. Then swords flashed and the slaughter commenced in earnest.

Shizuka cried out commands, and laboriously the junk began to come about, moving toward the cruiser's starboard side. The ship foundered, wallowing and listing like a drunken dolphin.

She stood immobile at the rail, one hand on the hilt of her *katana,* and the other resting on the pommel of her *tanto.* Her face was completely expressionless except for the glitter in her dark eyes. A wild bullet fired from the cruiser thumped the air between them, and although Brigid instinctively ducked, Shizuka paid it no more attention than the buzzing of a gnat.

Brigid contemplated warning Shizuka that just because the Magistrates were occupied with her samurai, it didn't necessarily mean they wouldn't direct fire toward them. She realized Shizuka wasn't deliberately inviting injury. With her helmet's visor raised, she was showing herself to her followers, presenting the image of implacable determination, the very embodiment of Bushido, the way of the warrior and *otoko ni michi*, the ancient and honorable code of the samurai. She didn't even appear to notice how the junk was taking on water.

Brigid inhaled a deep calming breath and stood beside her, figuring she could present the same example—at least outwardly.

Chapter 12

The deck was awash with looping liquid ribbons of scarlet, adding to its already slick quality. Several Magistrates sprawled across it, their black polycarbonate exoskeletons sliced open, fluids leaking from the splits and gashes.

On his knees behind a tumble of stone, Ramirez watched in incredulous horror as one of the armored boarders hacked off a Mag's right arm at the elbow with a lightning-fast sword stroke. The man opened his mouth to scream, but the sword blade lifted, fell and cleaved his helmet and the skull beneath it nearly in two. He realized now why they were called Tigers, but they seemed to spring from Hell not from Heaven.

Other Magistrates screamed in soul-deep terror as blades far sharper than razors licked out, inflicting deep wounds in their bodies. Ramirez saw one of the swordsmen make a whirling movement, and his sword cut wheels through the streamers of smoke. The edge of his blade sank into the junction of a man's jaw and the Magistrate's throat opened in a jetting of crimson.

The same Tiger caught sight of Ramirez and scuttled close, sword held at a right angle to his body, positioning himself for a decapitation. He laughed, an animal, guttural sound like a throaty gargle. The cruiser lurched on a swell, staggering the Tiger sideways for an instant.

Ramirez drew up his knees in a protective gesture, fumbled with a Copperhead he had picked up from the deck and put the targeting pipper on the figure. The red kill dot bloomed on the breastplate like a tiny pinhead of blood. The Tiger made a derisive snort and brushed at it contemptuously as if it were a piece of lint. Rage replaced Ramirez's fear, at least for a moment. With a howl of fury, he depressed the subgun's trigger and a triburst stitched holes in the Tiger's upper chest, knocking him backward and down.

Realizing the armored killers were mortal, Ramirez rose to his feet, his training finally kicking in. He shifted the Copperhead's barrel, retargeted and fired again, the pipper flicking across a brass-colored back. The burst twisted the Tiger's legs beneath his body in midstride, sending him flying headlong over the side.

"To me! Regroup! Regroup!" he shouted.

Turning at the sound of his voice, a masked and armored figure bounded toward him, sword held aloft. The pipper from Ramirez's autotargeter touched the molded visor of the helmet. He stroked the Copperhead's trigger, and the burst of 4.85 mm steel-jacketed rounds pounded into the visor. The man struck a bulkhead wall, bounced off and fell heavily to the deck, almost atop Ramirez.

As Ramirez lifted himself above the corpse, he risked a swift glance over the heaped rocks. He saw a confusing turmoil of running shapes and smears of orange flame from weapons. From out of the shifting planes of dust and smoke plunged a howling mob of crazed Magistrates, shrieking bloodthirsty cries. They fired their blasters as they came.

The samurai swarmed to meet them like slinking shadows, moving with blurring speed in great leaps and bounds.

The two forces crashed headlong into each other. Wherever a long blade touched a Mag, it began to hack him apart. The Magistrates shot, battered and clubbed at the samurai in maniacal fury, but where one Tiger of Heaven fell, three of their own number went down.

The Magistrates finally set up a concentrated pattern of fire and began moving toward Ramirez. The racket of the fusillade was almost deafening with half a dozen Sin Eaters blasting all at once. The Tigers took cover behind the wreckage littering the deck of the cruiser.

"Into the boats!" he shouted. "Assault force into the boats!"

Then Ramirez glimpsed a flaming arrow arcing overhead, dropping between him and his men. He opened his mouth to scream a warning, but a thunderclap blast slammed his words back into his throat.

Without hesitation, Ramirez dived forward. He hit the deck, going into a shoulder roll. He was still rolling when the area lit up in a red flash. Flying tongues of flame billowed outward. The detonation of the incendiary gren hurled fire-wreathed bodies into the air, the concussion shattering bones and rupturing internal organs.

The shock of the concussion slammed into Ramirez, bowling him over. As he somersaulted, he felt the brief wave of searing heat against his back. He elbowed himself over onto his back, his stunned eardrums registering little but a surflike throb. A fine rain of pulverized pebbles and droplets of blood drizzled to the deck.

Ramirez peered through the ragged scraps of smoke and settling dust. Two Magistrates thrashed around in blind agony, screaming as they tried to beat out the flames on their clothes and hair.

Using his elbows and the sides of his feet, Ramirez began crawling backward in the general direction of the landing-boat berths. A shadow shifted in the planes of dust and smoke. Propping the Copperhead's barrel on a rock, he fired a long burst. The multiple impacts smashed the Mag sideways, and even as Ramirez recognized the black armor, the firing pin of his subgun clicked dry on an empty magazine.

Rising to his feet, Ramirez ran broken-field style,

blinking back the runnels of sweat sliding into his eyes. His breath burned hot and heavy in his throat. He heard the twang of bowstrings and the crack of shafts splintering on rock. The skin between his polycarbonate-sheathed shoulder blades crawled in anticipation of one of the long arrows planting its barbed head there.

The rational segment of his mind knew an arrow couldn't possibly penetrate the armor, but rationally the Magistrates shouldn't be facing defeat from a numerically inferior and underarmed enemy, either.

He sprinted half the distance to the landing-boat berths before his ears registered a bone-jarring concussion. The CG-47 rocked violently, as if it had been struck from below by a monstrous wrecking ball. The white-red flash of an explosion belled up from the starboard bow. The shock wave picked him up and threw him down like a rag doll. The world seemed to be hammered apart under a series of blows in an explosion so violent and close he thought for a crazed instant the cruiser would fly apart.

Lifting his head, he saw an umbrella of black smoke rising in the sky, and his nostrils caught a sweetish whiff of high explosive. The metal deck plates under his body shivered with a prolonged vibration, and the entire ship tilted several degrees to port, sending him rolling. Clattering creaks and groans of overstressed metal surrounded him. He heard hull plates tearing with prolonged screeches and the gurgling of water rushing to fill a vacuum.

Choking back bleats of terror and humiliation, Ramirez dragged himself forward by his elbows, then regained his feet and began a shambling, staggering run. He knew what had happened—somehow, some way, an explosive device, a bomb or a mine had been attached to the cruiser's hull. With his crew's attention diverted, it had been ridiculously easy for a slagger to float or swim close enough to plant the device.

When Ramirez finally made it to the berths, he saw he wasn't the only Mag with the same idea. A group of his men had already activated the hydraulic hoist and winch system to lower the pair of launches. Cables and grapnels were connected to the gunwales of the craft. Each of the boats was twelve feet long with high, metal-reinforced sides. Outboard motors were clamped to the squared-off sterns.

The men scrambled aboard both of the boats, taking orders from a man named Quint. Ramirez clambered aboard one carrying eight men, and they regarded him with sour, contemptuous looks. Pretending not notice, he announced autocratically, "We've got to get back through the strait and head for one of the other islands."

No one responded to his declaration. With a creaking of the pulley mechanisms, the boats were smoothly lowered into the bay. Ramirez started the outboard with a single yank of the pull cord while another Mag snapped open and cast off the grapnel. He gunned the engine, the prow riding on a rush of foam.

He paid no attention to the junk wallowing a few hundred yards away. He knew it was sinking. He cast an over-the-shoulder glance to the CG-47. A gaping cavity showed in her hull and water cascaded into it. With a gurgling rumble, the cruiser settled low in the water. Ramirez swallowed hard.

At a snarling cry from Quint in the other boat, he turned. "There's the son of a bitch who did it!"

A small sailboat angled its way back toward the shoreline. An elderly, white-haired man held the tiller. When he saw he was the focus of their attention, he threw back his head and voiced a howl of malicious triumph. He thrust one arm up into the air, the middle finger extended in an ancient and unmistakable gesture.

Lips peeled back over his teeth in a snarl of fury, Quint turned the bow of his craft toward the sailboat. Alarmed, Ramirez shouted, "What are you doing? Leave him! We've got to get out of here!"

Quint ignored his words, gunning the engine.

"That's an order!" Ramirez bellowed.

Quint turned his head toward him long enough to yell, "Fuck you and your orders!"

TIGHT-LIPPED, KANE TOOK the helm from the man at the turtle boat's rudder and held it in a straight line, not bothering about current. Despite the scraps of smoke, his eyes had already spotted the Mags abandoning the cruiser. Their craft would reach Dubois's sailboat about the same time as the *Gamera-maru.*

The craft was making fifteen knots now, but it wasn't fast enough for Kane. They were bearing down on the sailboat, and Dubois's back was to them. So absorbed was the man in shouting obscenities at the Mag craft, he didn't see the approach of the turtle boat. His back was to them.

The launch's engines bellowed throatily, and the craft's props chopped the water to froth. The boat lunged toward the sailboat, its prow like the snout of a gray killer whale arrowing in on helpless prey. The wake it kicked up was the lashing tail fin of a voracious sea beast. The sound of the launch's engine rose in pitch, and the craft churned forward.

Kane swung his helm to starboard, cutting a course that would head him directly for the landing craft instead of the sailboat. He shouted over the drone of the diesel engine to the four-man crew, "Brace yourselves! I'm going to ram!"

A low mutter of dismay arose from the men, but they clutched davits and cleats and the edges of the benches. Even though they didn't care for the idea, they knew there was no other option. Their own weapons were at a grave disadvantage against the heavily armed Magistrates.

Shizuka's floundering junk managed to cut close

behind Dubois's little craft, and Kane steered a course that would carry them past it, on a collision course with the Mag boat. Dubois was still unaware of their approach.

Kane saw Dubois rise, level a revolver at the boat and stand there, awaiting the death from the Magistrates when they opened up with their weapons. Kane could spare the old man only a quick sideways glance, and his eyes flickered with admiration for the man's guts.

Then he had no time for anything but the matter at hand. The crew of the landing boat suddenly noticed the *Gamera-maru* plunging out of the pall of smoke, and directed a hail of machine-gun fire at it. They had expected the junk to come close to the sailboat and take off its occupant. It never occurred to them that the crazy-looking boat would ram them.

Cries of terror burst from the men aboard the Mag boat. A man with a Copperhead abruptly sprang up and dived over the far side when he realized what Kane intended to do. The man at the wheel screamed at him to veer off. The crew added their own panic-shrill voices to his screams. They knew if their boat sank, their armor, as light weight as it was, would still be an impediment in the water.

The rest of the man's shout was overwhelmed by the shattering crash of the impact of the turtle boat's ramming sprit against the landing boat. The prow of the boat splintered, planks wrenching, groaning and tearing in splinters twice as long as a man.

Kane reversed the engines, and the propeller of the *Gamera-maru* churned up great geysers of water as it dragged the vessel astern. There was another great rending crash, and the turtle boat dragged itself clear of the Mag launch, its prow-mounted ram sliding out and leaving a huge raw wound in the craft's side.

The bay rushed into the space the prow opened up, and boat listed to port. A couple of the black-armored crew toppled over into the bay, but the others clung to the sides. With appalling quickness, the enemy boat seemed to be swallowed down into the dark water as if dragged by a thousand undersea hands.

The turtle boat kept churning astern, and Kane ordered a line thrown over the side. One of his men lifted a wooden hull frame and tossed a coil of rope to the sailboat. Dubois caught it, winding the hawser twice around a cleat.

Taking the sailboat in tow, the *Gamera-maru* headed toward the crippled junk. Somehow its crew had kept the ship from sinking though she listed low in the water. Kane saw Brigid and Shizuka standing at the highest point in the bow, but they weren't looking at him.

Kane turned to follow their gaze. The second junk of the flotilla moved away from the CG-47, having cut its grappling lines. The cruiser, with a hissing gurgle, sank beneath the surface of the bay, leaving a great round saucer of suction that dragged debris and bodies with it. At the sight, the crews of all three ships cheered wildly.

Dubois took Shizuka and Brigid aboard his boat. The crew of the ship remained aboard, pumping and bailing until their sister junk arrived and hooked up tow lines. They laboriously rowed back to the quays.

The New Edoans greeted them with cheers of unrestrained jubilation and improvised dance steps of joy. Kane, Brigid, Dubois and Shizuka walked a gauntlet of bowing, hand-shaking people, their faces wet with tears of joy and relief.

The artillery fire from the CG-47 had taken only a modest toll. Three New Edoans were dead, and two seriously wounded. Nine others suffered injuries from minor to incapacitating, but none of these were life-threatening, only burns and shrapnel cuts.

They drank victory cups of stinging sake, and within twenty minutes, Grant appeared, out of breath, dirty and glowering as if angry or disappointed. Usually the deeper his scowl the more satisfied he was with a situation, and his scowl was very deep.

Before anyone could greet or congratulate him, he said peevishly, "A boatload of the bastards got away."

"We know," Kane retorted, imitating his testy tone. "They probably won't make it through the strait."

"They made it," Grant stated. "And Ramirez was with them."

Shizuka's lips compressed. "We'll hunt them down, Grant-*san*. Do not fear they shall escape us."

"I don't doubt you'll hunt them down. I just wish you wouldn't," Grant said quietly.

Shizuka shot him a glare of incredulous outrage. "We can't let them return to the baron and report what they saw."

"No, we can't," Grant replied mildly. "I wasn't proposing that we do. I'm requesting that you and your Tigers stand down and let us deal with them."

He gestured to himself, Brigid and Kane. Shizuka's dark eyes widened in surprise, then she nodded in sudden understanding. When the Tigers of Heaven had tracked down the Magistrates responsible for the Port Morninglight massacre, many of them were tortured to death. She remembered Kane's and Grant's objection to the samurai version of justice.

"Very well," she said. "You should not have any great difficulty locating them on the open sea, even in *Gamera-maru*."

Brigid removed her helmet and shook her mane of hair free. "I don't think they'll strike out for the mainland in broad daylight. They'll find a place to hole up, to tend to their wounds and wait for dark."

"Hole up where?" Grant asked. "They're out of the strait so—" He broke off, comprehension gleaming in his eyes.

Grimly, Shizuka said, "There is only one place. Ikazuchi Kojima—Thunder Isle."

Chapter 13

Lakesh gazed in awed fascination at the transparent sphere. Six feet in diameter, it occupied the center of the room from floor to ceiling—at least, Lakesh assumed the room had a floor and ceiling even if he couldn't see them. The walls, ceiling and floor of the room were so totally black that they seemed to absorb all light, like a vast ebony sponge. It was a blackness usually associated with the gulfs of deep space.

But within the suspended globe glittered thousands of pinpoints of light, scattered seemingly at random, but all connected by glowing lines similar to the Mercator relief map in the redoubt that delineated all the functioning gateway units of the Cerberus network. But the map had never gripped his imagination like the sphere.

He couldn't tear his eyes away from the flashing splendor, recalling how Plato had looked up at the stars and dreamed that each one made its own heavenly music. It was as though he stood before the whole blazing, wheeling galaxy in miniature. He felt as if he were a disembodied spirit flying through space, rather than standing in a room looking at a three-dimensional representation of the electromagnetic power grid of the planet.

Erica van Sloan sidled up from the blackness, her satiny blouse rustling softly. In a voice no less soft and rustling, she said, "Impressive, isn't it? I thought at first it was a work of art."

Lakesh nodded distractedly. "In a way it is. It's not just a geomantic map of Earth, but my entire field of study condensed and captured."

He gestured to the flickering points of light. "The power points of the planet, places that naturally generate specific types of energy. Some have positive and projective frequencies, while others are negative and receptive. There are funnel-type vortexes, cylindrical and even beacon types."

Pointing to one glowing speck, brighter than the rest, he said, "Chomolungma in the Himalayas—Mount Everest. According to ancient lore, that vortex is the single most powerful point on the planet. The energy it radiates sustains life and spreads *prana* all over the globe."

She cocked her raven-tressed head quizzically. *"Prana?"*

"An old Sanskrit term, meaning in a general way, the world soul."

"Was that what you were you trying to spread with your quantum interphase mat-trans inducers?"

Lakesh chuckled self-consciously. "I was just trying to make quota. At the time, I didn't know I was going over ground already broken the millennia before.''

Lakesh had achieved his breakthrough in the Project Cerberus quantum interphase researches only by coming to the conclusion that matter transmission was absolutely impossible through the employment of Einsteinian physics. Only quantum physics, coupled with quantum mechanics, had made it work.

But he was by no means the first to make this discovery. The forebears of Balam's people possessed the knowledge of hyperdimensional physics. The so-called Archons shared this knowledge in piecemeal fashion with the scientists of the Totality Concept. But they hadn't shared their knowledge that the gateways could accomplish far more than linear travel from point to point along a quantum channel.

The Totality Concept itself was the umbrella designation for a long-range experimental program to explore arcane and esoteric scientific areas, from time travel to genetics. The research dated back to World War II, when German scientists were laboring to build what turned out to be purely theoretical secret weapons for the Third Reich. The Allied powers adopted the researches, as well as many of the scientists, and constructed underground bases, primarily in the western U.S., to further the experiments.

The Totality Concept was classified above top secret. It was known only to a few very high ranking military officers and politicians. Few of the presidents who held office during its existence were even aware of the full ramifications.

Overproject Whisper was the division under which Project Cerberus and its sister subdivision, Operation Chronos, fell. They were aspects of the same phenomenon; only the applications of the principle differed. It had occurred to Lakesh that perhaps the entire undertaking had been code-named the Totality Concept because it encompassed the totality of everything, the entire workings of the universe. Project Cerberus was considered to be an appropriate code name for an undertaking devoted to ripping open the gates between heaven and hell.

Under the aegis of the Totality Concept, utilizing bits of preexisting technology, the aim of Project Cerberus was essentially the conversion of matter to energy and back again to matter. The entire principle behind matter transmission was that everything organic and inorganic could be reduced to encoded information. The primary stumbling block to actually moving from the theoretical to the practical was the sheer quantity of information that had to be transmitted, received and reconstituted without making any errors in the decoding.

The string of information required to program a computer with every bit and byte of data pertaining to the transmitted subject, particularly the reconstruction of a complex biochemical organism out of a digitized carrier wave, ran to the trillions of binary digits. Scientists labored over a way to make this possible for nearly fifty years, financed by funds funneled away from other government projects.

Lakesh glanced toward Sloan, then looked away as he felt a rush of shyness and even a little inferiority. Erica van Sloan was tall and beautiful with a flawless complexion the hue of fine honey. Her long, straight hair, swept back from a high forehead and pronounced widow's peak, tumbled artlessly about her shoulders. It was so black as to be blue when the light caught it.

The large, feline-slanted eyes above high, regal cheekbones looked almost the same color, but glints of violet swam in them. The mark of an aristocrat showed in her delicate features, with the delicate arch of brows, and her thin-bridged nose.

A graceful, swanlike neck led to a slender body encased in a strange uniform—high black boots, jodhpurs of a shiny black fabric, with an ebony satin tunic tailored to conform to the thrust of her full breasts. Emblazoned on the left sleeve was a familiar symbol. A thick-walled pyramid was worked in red thread, enclosing and partially bisected by three elongated but reversed triangles. Small disks topped each one, lending them a resemblance to round-hilted daggers. Once it had served as the unifying insignia of the Archon Directorate, and then was adopted by Overproject Excalibur, the Totality Concept's division devoted to genetic engineering.

Wearing a white bodysuit that bagged on his

scarecrow frame, Lakesh felt distinctly underdressed in her company. As a man who was chronologically a shade under 250 years old, he felt he looked better than he should have, even though he was a long-nosed, wizened cadaver of a man. He wore thick-lensed glasses with a hearing aid attached to the right earpiece. He had rheumy blue eyes, and his hair was the color and texture of ash.

But, he told himself, he still looked better than Erica the last time he had seen her, twelve years ago during a council of the nine barons at Front Royal. She was wheelchair bound, almost completely paralyzed, a stereotypical crone. Before that meeting, he had occasionally crossed paths with the woman in the Anthill. Then she had been beautiful, vibrant and haughty. But that was before the nukecaust, almost two centuries ago.

The Anthill, so named because of its similarity in layout to an ant colony, had been the most ambitious COG facility. Because of its size, the Anthill was constructed inside Mount Rushmore using the most advanced tunneling and digging machines of the day.

As the overseer of Project Cerberus, Lakesh and the majority of Totality Concept scientists had been taken there days before the nuclear war. Project Cerberus, like all the other Totality Concept researches, was classified above top secret. A device that could transmit matter, particularly soldiers and weapons, was a more important offensive weapon than America's entire nuclear Stockpile.

The matter-transfer units had other, less destructive applications, as well. Given wide use, the technology could eliminate inefficient transportation systems and be used for space exploration and colonizing planets in the solar system without the time- and money-consuming efforts necessary to build spaceships.

Mohandas Lakesh Singh, the project's overseer, engineered the breakthrough that led to the production of gateway units. To streamline the mass production of the quantum interphase mat-trans inducers, the project was moved from Dulce, New Mexico, and headquartered in a redoubt on an exceptionally remote mountain plateau in Montana's Bitterroot Range.

Lakesh had been stationed in the Cerberus redoubt for only a year before he was relocated to the Anthill, along with the key staff members of other Totality Concept divisions. He and many of others had spent the following century or so in cryogenic stasis to spare the installation's strained resources.

He barely remembered Erica van Sloan from the Anthill, but that wasn't unusual. There were many people there, and all of them seemed to have their own concerns. He recalled she had been attached not just to Operation Chronos, but to the project overseer, Dr. Torrence Silas Burr. He built on Lakesh's

mat-trans breakthroughs to spin off his own innovations and achieve his own successes.

Operation Chronos dealt in the mechanics of time
travel, forcing temporal breaches in the chronon
structure. The purpose of Chronos was to find a way
to enter "probability gaps" between one interval of
time and another. Inasmuch as Cerberus utilized
quantum events to reduce organic and inorganic material to digital information and transmit it through
hyperdimensional space, Chronos relied on that
same principle to peep into other time lines and even
"trawl" living matter from the past and the future.

Since the nature of time couldn't be measured or
accurately perceived in the quantum stream, the
brief temporal dilation was the primary reason Operation Chronos had used reconfigured gateway
units in their time-traveling experiments.

Lakesh never knew what happened to Burr. He
simply vanished from the Anthill one day, leaving
Erica van Sloan behind. And, like Lakesh, she had
been revived when the Program of Unification had
reached a certain stage. She was only one of several
preholocaust humans, known as freezies in current
vernacular, resurrected to serve the baronies. He
tried but failed to reconcile the memory of the with-
ered old hag hunched in a wheelchair with the tall,
superbly built beauty regarding him from the base
of the jump platform.

Erica van Sloan had contacted Lakesh through a
circuitous and unusual path—a telepathic commu-

nication from Balam using Banks, one of the Cerberus redoubt's personnel, as the conduit. Because of his long association with Balam as his keeper, and due to his latent psionic abilities, Banks had empathetically melded with the entity to facilitate a verbal dialogue between warder and prisoner. It was possible, even probable, the link hadn't been as temporary or as one-way as both Lakesh and Banks initially believed.

Erica said, "I was attached to Operation Chronos, remember? It was your first successes with the mattrans inducers that allowed us to pierce the chronon stream."

Of course, the human scientists and military officials involved in the endeavor were too fixated on reaching short-term goals, making quota and earning bonuses, to devote much thought to the workings of the universe, or even where the basic components to build the first mat-trans unit had come from. Lakesh included himself in this number, although he hadn't been so much fixated as blinded to the vast sea of disastrous consequences that could result from the Totality Concept's myriad divisions.

"I know," Lakesh replied. "But every bit of Totality Concept technology was only a synthetic imitation of the power Balam's folk tapped into and wielded." He smiled bitterly. "We were all frauds, you know."

Lakesh still remembered his dismay and outright shock when, in his position of Project Cerberus

overseer, he had learned that the scientific principles
by which the gateways operated were less a form of
new physics than a rediscovery of ancient knowledge.

Before and after the nukecaust, he had studied the
body of scientific theory that megalithic structures,
such as the dolmens of Newgrange in Ireland and
Stonehenge in England, were expressions of an old,
long-forgotten system of physics. The theory, based
on hyperdimensional mathematics, provided a fundamental connection between the four forces of nature, an up-and-down link with invisible higher dimensions. Evidence indicated there were many
natural vortex points, centers of intense energy on
Earth, and even other celestial bodies in the solar
system.

Lakesh became convinced that some ancient peoples were aware of this, and could manipulate these
symmetrical Earth energies to open portals, not just
for linear travel like the gateways, but perhaps into
other realms of existence. He suspected the knowledge was suppressed over the centuries, an act of
repression he believed was the responsibility of the
Archons or the secret societies in their service. It
was an axiom of conspiracies that someone or something else always pulled the strings of willing or
ignorant puppets. He had expended many years trac-
ing those filaments back through convoluted and
manufactured histories to the puppet masters themselves.

To test his theory, Lakesh saw to the construction of a miniaturized version of a mat-trans unit, utilizing much of the same hardware and operating principles. He called it an interphaser, and like the gateways, the interphaser functioned by tapping into the quantum stream. The interphaser opened dimensional rifts as did the gateways, but instead of the rifts being pathways through linear space, he envisioned using the gaps as transit tunnels through the gaps in normal space-time.

The instrument was designed to interact with a natural vortex's quantum energy and create an intersection point, a discontinuous quantum jump. The device worked, but in ways he hadn't dreamed. Lakesh had always wanted to discuss the phenomenon with Balam, but the entity had refused to reveal any of his people's secrets outright. When Balam left his custody, he had despaired of ever learning anything more. Now it appeared he had a second chance.

Erica took his hand. "They're ready for you."

"Who?" he asked, resisting a moment, surprised by how strong she was. "Sam or Balam?"

She smiled seductively. "Come with me and find out."

Chapter 14

Reluctantly, Lakesh allowed himself to be led away from the map of the global energy grid. He figured he had studied it long enough. More than half an hour earlier, he, Sam and Erica had materialized in a gateway unit with rich, golden walls, as if ingots had been melted down and applied to the armaglass like molten paint. All of the official Cerberus gateway units mat-trans network were color-coded so authorized jumpers could tell at a glance into which redoubt they had materialized.

Despite the fact it seemed an inefficient method of differentiating one installation from another, only personnel holding color-coded security clearances were allowed to make use of the system. Inasmuch as their use was restricted to a select few of the units, it was fairly easy for them to memorize which color designated what redoubt.

Armaglass was manufactured in the last decades of the twentieth century from a special compound that combined the properties of steel and glass. It was used as walls in the jump chambers to confine quantum energy overspills. However, he couldn't recall if any Totality Concept-connected redoubt was color-coded a molten gold.

Outside, the chamber was a low-ceilinged corridor with stone-block walls. Lakesh had no idea where they were. When he asked if they were in Agartha, where Kane and Brigid had left Balam, neither of his companions gave him a definite answer. Regardless, he sensed they were deep underground, beneath inestimable tons of rock.

The location was of secondary importance as far as Lakesh was concerned. If Erica and Sam had wanted to kill him, they could've done so during the many hours he spent alone with them in the Cerberus redoubt. They certainly wouldn't have had to cajole, argue and finally plead with him to accompany them on a mat-trans jaunt.

Most of his questions about Balam, Sam's origins and particularly Erica's restored youth had been neatly deflected. Both people were adept at teasing him with hints and inferences about an undertaking that would forever change the nuke-scarred face of the planet. They wanted his involvement, but they refused to reveal anything but tantalizing scraps of information.

Lakesh couldn't help but be intrigued. He was suspicious of both of them, especially Erica, but she answered all of his questions about the inner workings of the Totality Concept and the personnel involved without hesitation. At length he accepted she was who she claimed to be, and he agreed to accompany them to their unnamed destination, where not only Balam awaited him, but where he would also find answers to his questions.

Over the strenuous and profane objections put forth by DeFore, Bry and even Banks, Lakesh entered a set of coordinates provided by Erica in the gateway's destination-lock computer, and away they went. He felt a little guilty about leaving Cerberus while the fates of Domi and Kane were still unknown, but both Erica and Sam vowed to return him in twelve hours. He believed them, and he didn't know why.

Although he experienced a strong physical attraction for the woman, he found it required a great deal of mental effort to refuse Sam anything or question anything he said. The boy possessed exceptionally strong powers of persuasion, and whether it was just charisma or something else, Lakesh was completely charmed by him. Actually, he was more than charmed—he trusted him and felt protective of him in a paternal way.

To his everlasting regret, Lakesh had never married or fathered children. The closest he came to producing offspring was when he rifled the ville's genetic records to find desirable qualifications in order to build a covert resistance movement against the baronies. He used the barons' own fixation with purity control against them. By his own confession, he was a physicist cast in the role of an archivist, pretending to be a geneticist, manipulating a political system that was still in a state of flux. Kane was one such example of that political and genetic manipulation, and the last thing Lakesh felt toward him was fatherly.

Erica van Sloan strode purposefully down the passageway, taking long-legged strides, her boot heels clacking in a steady rhythm against the stone floor. He shook his head a little remorsefully as he watched the sensuous twitch of her buttocks beneath the tight jodhpurs. She had a body built for sex, and if she was attempting to entice him with her restored youth and vitality, it was a cruel game.

Upon his revival from cryogenic sleep, Lakesh had undergone several operations in order to prolong his life and his usefulness to the Program of Unification. His brown, glaucoma-afflicted eyes were replaced with new blue ones, his leaky old heart exchanged for a sound new one and his lungs changed out. The joints in his knees weren't the same as those he had been born with, either. Though his wrinkled, liver-spotted skin made him look exceptionally old, his physiology was that of a fifty-year-old man's.

Erica stepped through an open doorway. Lakesh followed her and came to a halt, blinking owlishly at the furnishings of the room. It wasn't so much the lavish appointments that startled him as the sensation of stepping back in time several thousand years into a central clearinghouse of several ancient cultures.

A tall, round sandstone pillar bearing ornate carvings of birds and animal heads was bracketed by two large sculptures, one a feathered jaguar, and the other a serpent with wings. Silken tapestries depicting Asian ideographs hung from the walls. There were other tapestries, all bearing twisting geometric designs.

Suspended from the ceiling by thin steel wires was a huge gold disk in the form of the Re-Horakhte falcon. The upcurving wings were inlaid with colored glass. The sun disk atop the beaked head was a cabochon-cut carnelian.

Ceramic effigy jars and elegantly crafted vessels depicting animal-headed gods and goddesses from the Egyptian pantheon were stacked in neat pyramids. Arrayed on a long shelf on the opposite wall were a dozen small statuettes representing laborers in the Land of the Dead. Against the right wall was a granite twelve-foot-tall replica of the seated figure of Ramses III. It towered over a cluster of dark basalt blocks inscribed with deep rune markings.

A huge, gilt-framed mirror, at least ten feet tall and five wide, stood amid stacks of weaponry—swords, shields and lances. A spearhead with a single drop of blood on its nicked point rested on a table.

The center and corners of the floor were crammed with artifacts from every possible time, every culture—Incan, Mayan, Chinese, Egyptian and others Lakesh couldn't quickly identify. He wasn't even sure if he wanted to, since he had believed some the relics were pure myth, such as the mirror of Prester John and the Spear of Destiny.

Each and every item appeared to be in perfect condition. The huge room was an archaeologist's paradise. Lakesh struggled to comprehend the enormity of the collection and why it was here. Finally, he realized it was a representative sampling from every human culture ever influenced by the race he knew as Archons. Of course, what he knew of Balam's race was very little, but he did know they didn't refer to themselves as Archons, and certainly not as aliens.

Hundreds of years ago, when humanity dreamed of roaming the stars, speculation about the extraterrestrial life-forms they might encounter inevitably followed. The issue of interaction, of communication with aliens, had consumed a number of government think tanks for many decades. As Lakesh discovered in the waning years of the twentieth century, all of that hypothesizing was nothing but a diversion, a smoke screen to hide the truth. Humankind's interaction with a nonhuman species had begun at the dawn of Earth's history. That relationship and communication had continued unbroken for thousands of years, cloaked by ritual, religion and mystical traditions.

However, Lakesh did know that the Archons not only considered themselves human but native Terrans, since they existed on Earth as long as modern man, even if their forebears were extraterrestrial. According to information gathered over the past year or so, it seemed as if the source of the Archons lay with a reptilian race known in ancient Sumerian texts as the Annunaki.

Allegedly, they arrived on Earth before the dawn of humankind. They first battled with, then united with the Tuatha de Danaan. From this union was born the progenitors of the race that would eventually be called the Archons.

Lakesh looked around, trying to find Balam in the collection. For an instant, he thought he spotted him, then realized it was only a statue that closely resembled Balam. Standing in an erect position, less than five feet tall, the sculpture represented a humanoid creature with a slender, gracile build draped in robes. The features were sharp, the domed head disproportionately large and hairless. The eyes were huge, slanted and fathomless. Cradled in its six-fingered hands was what appeared to be a human infant.

Lakesh repressed a shudder, and nearly jumped straight up when he felt a light touch on his arm. He spun clumsily to see Sam beaming up at him. The boy looked to be about ten years of age with a smooth, alabaster complexion. His thick hair was pure warm silver, framing his full-cheeked face like the edges of a summertime cloud. His big, long-lashed eyes seemed to shift with all colors, and they were old eyes, at once wise and sad. His slender frame was draped in a robe of a soft, saffron hue.

Forcing an aggrieved note into his voice, he said, "You took ten years off my life, and at my age I can ill afford to squander even an hour of it."

Sam's cherubic smile broadened. "Perhaps we'll do something about that, Mohandas."

Like the first time he had heard it, the sound of the boy's voice touched off sweet vibrations somewhere deep inside of Lakesh. He was hungry to hear more of it. Still, he felt a distant unease at the comfortable way the boy called him by his first name, but he didn't comment on it. "Where is Balam?"

"You'll see him once you're convinced."

"Convinced of what, young man?" Lakesh demanded in his best authoritarian tone.

"Of who I am," Sam answered blandly. "Of the energies flowing through me."

Erica stepped up to Lakesh and caressed his deeply seamed cheek with cool, soft fingers. Teasingly, she said, "You've been consumed with curiosity about how Sam restored me, haven't you?"

"Among other things," Lakesh retorted gruffly. "Least of all why you refer to him as your son."

Erica chuckled. "First things first, Mohandas. Secrets must be revealed in the order of their importance."

"Secrets?"

"The first secret is energy," Sam stated. "It always has been, always will be. The science of moving it in precise harmony and in perfect balance, harmonizing it with other forms of energy.''

Lakesh bobbed his head in irritated impatience. ''You're not telling me anything I haven't spent my entire adult life studying.''

''Perhaps,'' Sam replied calmly. ''But studying and understanding all the principles and applications are often very different things.''

Lakesh bristled at the boy's patronizing tone. He drew on an untapped reservoir of strength, and managed to work himself up to a high state of annoyance, despite Sam's powers of persuasion. ''Demonstrate what you mean or I'm leaving.''

The corners of Sam's mouth turned down in a frown. ''You've come too far to dictate terms, Mohandas. I want you to understand what I am. I am an avatar.''

Chill fingers of dread stroked the buttons of Lakesh's spine. ''An avatar of what?''

''There must be an order to things. If war is necessary for that order to be established, then I am willing to wage it. But you must teach me certain things, make me more than I am.''

''I know nothing of war.''

''But you know deception, do you not? Is not all war based on deception, on misdirection and misinformation?''

Lakesh dredged his memory and came up with a quote from Sun Tzu. '''Use deception when you have not the power to win in open battle,'" he said quietly.

Sam nodded. "Exactly. You have followed that philosophy in your war against the baronies. I can learn much from you."

"And if you win your war, what kind of order do you intend to build?"

"One where the old humans and the new humans rally around me, the bridge between both, to help both coexist peacefully."

Lakesh gazed down into the boy's eyes of many colors and felt a little ill and frightened. He sensed the king's robes around the child even if he couldn't see them. But he also sensed Sam was either cursed or blessed with something outside the pale of normal humanity—or inhumanity. Hoarsely, he inquired, "Coexist under your single authority?"

Sam's frown deepened as if he were irritated by Lakesh stating the obvious. "Of course. I thought you understood that."

Lakesh exhaled a weary breath. "I understand, Sam. You're just another damn megalomaniac, another mutie with an attitude." He turned toward the door. "I don't know what powers you have, but it's obvious you lured me here under the pretense of a meeting with Balam. He's not and probably never has been here. You disappoint me."

Lakesh caught only a glimpse of Sam making a flicking hand gesture, then Erica van Sloan was on him, securing a hammerlock on his right arm and wrenching it up between his shoulder blades. She kicked the back of his knees, and his legs buckled. Crying out in pain and outrage, Lakesh collapsed. Only Erica's surprising strength prevented him from falling on his face. Into his ear, she murmured, "I'm sorry about this, Mohandas, but you'll thank me when it's over."

He struggled, but she cinched down even tighter on his captured arm. "When what is over?" he brayed.

Sam stepped toward him, pulling back the belled right sleeve of his robe. In a very soft, sympathetic tone, he said, "When I'm finished moving energy in precise harmony and perfect balance."

Sam spread his right hand wide and laid it against Lakesh's midriff. Once again he saw the faint pattern of scales between the fingers of his hand. From it seeped a tingling warmth. Ice seemed to melt against his body, and he felt painful, searing heat, like liquid fire, rippling through his veins and arteries. His heartbeat picked up in tempo, seeming to spread the heat through the rest of his body, a pulsing web of energy suffusing every separate cell and organ. He squeezed his eyes shut.

Lakesh's lungs gave a jerking, labored spasm as they sucked in air involuntarily, expanding so much in his chest he feared his ribs would break. His mouth opened and a scream came forth, but his voice wasn't reedy or strained. The cry was a full-bodied bellow of pain. He was aflame with it, the same kind of agony a man felt when circulation was suddenly restored to a numb limb. His back arched, and for the first time in more than fifty years, he felt a stirring in his loins. His entire metabolism seemed to awaken to furious life from a long slumber, as if it had been jump-started by a powerful battery.

The heat faded from his body, and he sagged within Erica's grip, panting and sweating. She released him, and he caught himself on his hands. Slowly, Lakesh opened his eyes. They burned slightly, feeling somewhat sticky, but his vision wasn't blurred or fogged. He tried to push himself up, but his body felt like a foreign thing, and it moved sluggishly.

Erica said softly, "Careful now, Mohandas. Take it easy at first."

Carefully, she helped him to his feet. His legs wobbled like those of a newborn foal's. When he raised a hand to wipe away the film of perspiration on his face, he realized two things more or less simultaneously—he wasn't wearing his glasses, but he could see his hand perfectly. By that perfect vision, he saw the flesh of his hand was smooth, the prominent veins having sunk back into firm flesh. The liver spots faded even as he watched.

Wildly, Lakesh stumbled over toward the huge mirror. He nearly fell twice, but Erica helped him along. He stood before it, stupefied into silence. The face reflected in its glossy surface bore little resemblance to the one that looked as if he had borrowed it from a cadaver. His hair, though still thin, wasn't ash-gray, but an iron color. It seemed to darken with every passing second. Uttering a wordless cry of wonder, Lakesh brought his hands up to his face, his fingertips exploring the smooth, unseamed cheeks.

A voice spoke from behind him, hoarse, faint and scratchy. "Now we will speak of the future, Mohandas Lakesh Singh."

The voice was familiar, and it sent cold prickles up and down his backbone. Slowly he turned, keeping his expression as neutral and composed as possible.

A figure stood beside Sam, dressed in a similar robe. Lakesh gazed without blinking at the high, domed cranium that narrowed to an elongated chin. The faint grayish-pink skin was stretched drum tight over a structure of facial bones that seemed all cheek and brow, with little in between but two great upslanting eyes like black pools. The slit of a mouth held the faintest suggestion of a smile.

"Yes, Balam," said Lakesh gravely. "We must speak of the future and my place in it."

Chapter 15

Lakesh was too dazed, too filled with incredulous wonder and joy to even inquire where Sam and Balam were leading him. With Erica van Sloan at his side, her arm linked with his, he could do little but smile foolishly as he walked down the corridor. He was keenly aware of Erica's firm breast pressing into his arm, and that awareness made him even less prone to ask questions that might be interpreted as impertinent at best and ungrateful at worst.

Balam's presence didn't evoke the visceral, xenophobic reaction it had during his long imprisonment in the Cerberus redoubt, but Lakesh wasn't comfortable in the entity's company, either. He had always conscientiously and consciously tried not to view Balam as a monster. An enemy, yes, but not an inhuman, soulless demon, despite the fact the creature patently wasn't part of humanity—at least humanity as he defined the term.

As if sensing his discomfiture, Erica leaned toward him and said in a breathy whisper, "I'd almost forgotten the pleasures of the flesh." Her tongue touched his ear. "But I'm remembering more every minute."

Lakesh shivered in pleasure but couldn't answer. The swelling in his groin became an embarrassing distraction. He heard even her faint whisper with sharp clarity without the use of his hearing aid. A bit more sternly than he intended, he sidemouthed to Erica, "Can you at least tell me where we are?"

She smiled wanly. "Would it make any difference?"

"How can I answer that question until you answer mine?" Lakesh tried not to sound stiff or disapproving, but Sam apparently caught the edge in his tone nonetheless.

Turning his head, he announced blithely, "China. We're in China. In what used to be known as the province of Xian."

Lakesh felt his mouth dropping open in dismay. "China?" he blurted incredulously. "Xian? Why there? I mean here? What's so special about—?"

His mouth suddenly seemed to fill with dust and he couldn't speak. Sam put his sudden realization into words. "Yes, Mohandas. We are within the structure once called the Great Pyramid of China."

Lakesh dredged through his memory. "As I recall, the Chinese authorities denied it even existed. It was reputedly larger than the pyramid of Giza."

Sam stated, "It was believed to have been part of the tomb of Shih Huang Ti. Originally, it was black on the north side, blue-gray on the east, red on the south and white on the west. The apex was painted yellow. The significance of the colors apparently had to do with the Taoist system of the five phases of existence.''

The hair stirred uneasily on Lakesh's arms, the new growth rose on the back of his neck. The pressure in his groin became less noticeable. He said, ''Archaeological excavations of the pyramid discovered magnificent jade objects and other gemstones. The pyramid is generally thought to have been built during the Hsia dynasty, though very little is known about the Hsias, either. Its emperors were allegedly the first authentic rulers of China following the semimythical Five Monarchs. The Hsia dynasty reigned from 2205 to 1767 B.C., and recorded Chinese history is considered to have begun with the Chou dynasty of 1122 B.C.''

Lakesh cleared his throat and added matter-of-factly, ''The purpose of the pyramid or tomb was never known, though Taoist tradition said it was built by the Celestials.''

Sam chortled, a childish musical laugh of genuine amusement. He surreptitiously pointed to Balam, who either ignored him or affected not to notice. ''Whoever they were. Others speculated it was a cardinal point in the world grid harmonics, a network of pyramids built at key places around the world to tap the Earth's natural geomantic energies. What you called *prana*.''

The passageway subtly changed. The floor became smoother and the square-cut blocks of stone on the walls gave to way smooth, seamless expanses. They glittered dully with inestimable flecks of all colors, providing a soft light. The ceiling was rounded like an arch, winding gently in an ever widening curve. The floor, gleaming to the eye like oiled slate, gave a solid footing.

The corridor suddenly opened into a vast domed space. Lakesh swept his eyes around it, seeing a natural cavern. The unfinished stone of its ceiling gleamed here and there with clusters of crystals and geodes.

The floor dipped in a gentle incline, and at the center, surrounded by a collar of interlocking silver slabs, was a pool. The inner rim was lined with an edging of crystal points that glowed with a dull iridescence. At first glance, the pool took up the entire chamber floor, except for a walkway around it, about five feet wide. Lakesh guessed the pool was about fifty feet in total circumference.

Lakesh couldn't be sure what lay in the pool, whether it was water or simply reflected light. He felt as if his eyes could penetrate it forever, but he couldn't see a bottom to it.

''The Heart of the Earth,'' Erica said quietly beside him.

As Lakesh stared about in wonder, he realized that not all of the crystals sparkled with the same intensity of light. Some glowed steadily, others flickered feebly, and still others were only multifaceted lumps of mineral. He realized that if all of them shone with the same light level, the interior of the cavern would have blazed as blindingly as a naked star.

"The Heart of the Earth," he repeated in a murmur.

Balam spoke for the first time since leaving the artifact chamber. "Yes," he said simply.

"But what is it?" Lakesh demanded, and he was disquieted when his voice didn't echo as it should have in the huge cavern.

"It might be called the essence of the world." Balam's voice was characteristically scratchy and strained, but it carried perfectly. He made a diffident gesture with his right hand, the six long fingers curling like the legs of a spider.

"Or," Sam spoke up, "it is a nexus point, a convergence of geomantic energy."

"Ley lines," Erica said. "A hub of Earth energies."

The surface of the pool began to pulse with a ghostly phosphorescence. Lakesh realized if he focused his vision directly on it, the luminescence seemed to fade, becoming like a dimly glowing mist. He could see it clearly only if he cast his gaze away from it at an oblique angle.

The mist began to swell out of the throat of the pool, bulging upward. A shimmering sphere the diameter of the rim slowly arose, like a hot-air balloon made of a semitransparent substance. Lakesh could almost but not quite see through it. His breath seized in his lungs, and he was distantly aware of stumbling back.

He backed away as far as he could as the ethereal-looking globe continued to rise from the pool. His flesh prickled with a pins-and-needles sensation, as if he were standing near a low-level electrical field.

In a serene, detached tone, Sam said, "This is the source of true power, Mohandas. It was known to vanished civilizations as the Earth Mother, the Gaia force or, as you phrased it, the world soul. Many human seekers of enlightenment, men of science, suspected its existence." He gestured with one hand. "Within it are contained the essential building blocks of the universe, the primal blocks of creation."

Lakesh stared unblinkingly as the sphere hovered at an equidistant point between the pool and the high domed ceiling. He saw that the crystals overhead pulsed with a purplish-black light that was beyond dark. He guessed the angle of tilt and the tuning of the facets against one another formed a balanced matrix, which drew out and suspended the energy globe.

After several attempts, he finally found his voice. "The universe was formed by an explosion of gases, plasma and matter. It was known as the Big Bang. Are you telling me that a collection of those proto-energies exists here in a temporal pocket?"

"Don't sound so skeptical," Erica said, her voice purring with amusement. "As a physicist, you know the basic building blocks of both matter and energy are no more than ripples in the quantum field. Everything, even hard matter, is only a stable pattern in the ripples.''

Lakesh nodded impatiently, straightening and taking a deep breath. ''Of course. On a subatomic scale, what appears to be a vacuum is really vibrating and shifting with particle and wavicle energy fluctuations. For example, a single cubic centimeter of space can, theoretically, contain the hard-matter energy equivalent of a thirty-megaton nuclear bomb.''

Sam nodded approvingly. ''The so-called quantum stream. It exists on a different plane of existence than our own reality. You and other scientists of the Totality Concept came to understand this, and with the aid of technology, managed to tap into it. All the spin-off researches of Overproject Whisper used the stream as a transit network between the physical here and there. And that included Operation Chronos's temporal dilator.''

Lakesh eyed the hovering sphere, noting how bands of muted color seemed to swirl over its surface. ''Am I to believe that I am standing before an encapsulated packet of the quantum field, captured like lightning in a bottle?''

''Or creation in a bottle,'' Erica remarked.

Lakesh threw her a slit-eyed stare. ''Explain.''

Sam gestured to the globe. ''The Heart contains the energies released in the first picoseconds following the Big Bang, channeling the matrix of proto-particles that swirled through the universe before physical, relativistic laws fully stabilized. It exists slightly out of phase with this dimension, with our space-time.''

Sam gestured with both hands, first linking then unlinking his fingers. ''From this central core extends a web of electromagnetic and geophysical energy that covers the entire planet. Nikola Tesla, of whom I'm sure you're aware, conceived of using this energy web as the basis for an entirely new principle of physics.''

Lakesh pursed his lips, swiftly reviewing what he knew about the twentieth-century maverick scientist. Arguably, he had been the greatest inventor who ever lived, and perhaps one of the most erratic. He said, ''If my memory hasn't failed me, Tesla experimented with something he called the 'teleforce,' a method and apparatus to produce energy manifestations in free air. In the late nineteenth century, Tesla built a transmitting tower on top of a Colorado mountain as an experiment to tap into the electromagnetic radiation of Earth to provide a free energy source.''

''Exactly,'' Erica declared. ''His intent was to use the Earth as a huge, resonant system. He called the geomagnetic grid terrestrial stationary waves. He tried to tap into the Heart of the Earth. He failed.''

''But,'' Lakesh said flatly, ''Balam's folk succeeded.''

Balam turned his huge dark eyes toward him. In

his whispery voice, he said, "My people had no need to tap into this energy source, Mohandas. We are part of it. And so are you. We realized it. Your kind never did."

Lakesh gazed steadily at the small figure, casting his eyes back and forth between him and Sam. There was very little resemblance except in height. Sam certainly didn't look like any of the hybrids he had ever seen, so he wondered at the link between the two. He understood the link could be invisible, a psychic or telepathic connection.

He knew Balam was anchored to the hybrid barons through some hyperspatial filaments of their mind energy, akin to the hive mind of certain insect species. When Baron Ragnar was assassinated, Balam had experienced an extreme reaction to the sudden absence of the baron's mind filament. Inasmuch as all of the Archon genetic material had derived from Balam, that connection wasn't particularly surprising.

Lakesh had learned that the DNA of Balam's folk was infinitely adaptable, malleable, its segments able to achieve a near seamless sequencing pattern with whatever biological material was spliced to it. In some ways, it acted like a virus, overwriting other genetic codes, picking and choosing the best human qualities to enhance. Their DNA could be tinkered with to create endless variations, could be adjusted and fine-tuned.

Apparently, Balam's race had done more than experiment with altering their genetic code, even in prehistory. Lakesh recollected what Kane had learned about Balam's race during his telepathic communication with him. After the global catastrophe that decimated their civilization, his race transformed itself to adapt to the new environment. Their muscle tissue became less dense, motor reflexes sharpened, optic capacities broadened. A new range of abilities was developed to allow them to survive on a planet whose magnetic fields had changed, whose weather was drastically unpredictable. Balam had imparted this piece of history to Kane, but Lakesh sourly reminded himself that almost none of the information Balam had conveyed could be proved empirically.

Balam's knowledge of hyperdimensional physics was proved, at least insofar as the mat-trans units were concerned, but Balam never revealed that the gateways could accomplish far more than linear travel from point to point along a quantum channel. Lakesh was still skeptical of Balam's version of the hidden history of Earth, but so far, he had encountered nothing that proved them to be false. Besides, Balam had removed with only a few words the threat of the Archon Directorate, though the myth remained.

"That's true," Lakesh said, not even trying to disguise the bitter anger in his voice. "We realized very little...particularly the fact that the nuclear holocaust would allow your kind to unify the Earth."

Balam met his gaze dispassionately, and Lakesh sensed the loneliness and pain radiating from him like an invisible aura. Regardless of his reasons, Balam and his kind had conspired against humanity for uncounted centuries. A natural cataclysm had decimated their civilization, so in turn they had orchestrated the nukecaust one to bring humankind in line with their concepts of unity.

"We did unify you," Balam said with no particular inflection. "And the Heart of the Earth has benefited from it. It has begun to heal."

"What?" Lakesh half snarled, his voice rising in pitch and volume. "How could the nuclear holocaust have possibly benefited anything, much less the Heart?"

Sam took it upon himself to respond. "Before the holocaust, Earth managed to support a population of six billion humans. That was far beyond the planet's apparent capacity to do so. The predark culture's scientific knowledge far outstripped its social and political development in less than three generations. Think about it, Mohandas—you were alive then. What was it like?"

Slowly, reluctantly, he answered, "The world suffered epidemics and plagues. It stewed and percolated in pollution, it bulged at the seams with people. There were entire cities—nations even—full of people aching for something useful to do with their lives. Governments and industries could have addressed these fundamental evils, but they saw no immediate profit in doing so.''

Softly, Sam intoned, ''They accepted the sad fact that civilization, on a global scale, was likely to fall apart, but rather than try to correct the slide, they prepared for the end. It was all part of the drive toward a one-world government, brought about by the culling of the planet's 'useless eaters.'''

Sam sighed heavily, as if grieving a lost love. ''A world population of intelligent, industrious and destructive creatures. They were capable of abstract concepts, of creating works of beauty, but they also destroyed the planet's natural resources without a thought given to the consequences. The Totality Concept technology was bestowed upon humankind as a gift, to help it evolve securely without paying the consequences, to restore the natural balance and harmonics of the Earth. That didn't happen.''

''No,'' Lakesh husked out, feeling his eyes sting with tears. ''It didn't.''

''Therefore,'' Sam continued, ''the nukecaust did not alter the balance at all. Instead, it set it straight.''

Lakesh looked at Balam again, and instead of a xenophobic cringing, he felt a shame, as if the guilt of the human race were laid on his shoulders.

The huge black eyes met Lakesh's gaze unblinkingly. Once again he experienced a sense of tragedy, not just for Balam's folk, but for the entire human race. Compared to Balam and his people, humanity was always arrogant and self-deluded, egocentrically imagining itself the first and future lord of Earth.

Squeezing his eyes shut and exhaling a shuddery breath, Lakesh asked, "What do you want of me? What is the future you have envisioned?"

"What it's always been, Mohandas," Erica said. "The agenda is what it always was."

Lakesh snorted. "Unification?" He glared at Sam, then at Balam. "As time has gone by, the world and humankind changed too much for your half-breed plenipotentiaries to rule with any degree of effectiveness. But your goal remains the same— the unification of the world under your control, with all nonessential and nonproductive humans eliminated."

Sam's smile broadened. "They pretty much have been, wouldn't you agree? But to complete the process, to achieve the final objective, cooperation is essential. Even if that cooperation is coerced. I know that seems like a contradiction. However, it will work if no one realizes they're being coerced."

Lakesh shook his head in angry frustration. "I don't understand what you mean."

"Ah." Sam nodded as if in sudden comprehension, but Lakesh knew he was being mocked. "You want an example, a visual aid—is that it?"

"That," Lakesh bit out coldly, "might help."

Sam gestured to the shimmering sphere. "Then look to the Heart."

Lakesh didn't move. He stubbornly thrust out his jaw. "Why?"

Erica's fingers bit into his arm. Urgently, she whispered, "Do it, Mohandas. Please. It's the only way for you to understand."

Slowly, reluctantly, Lakesh did as she said. He focused on the globe of light for what seemed like a long time. Nothing happened, then he became aware that the glow seemed to pulse and swim to the movement of his blood, to throb in rhythm with his heartbeat.

In piecemeal fashion, shapes and images began to form within the globe. When he tried to make sense of them, they became unconnected fragments, so he relaxed and watched them move and swirl and finally rush together, interlocking to form first a cylinder, then a square. He realized he was looking down at a ville, a fortress city, as if from a great height. Because the baronies were all standardized, he was unable to immediately identify it. Then he saw the silver windings of the Kanab River and realized he was looking at Cobaltville. The complex was visible in the light reflecting on the massive white pillar of the Admin Monolith.

He seemed to soar above the road leading up to the main gate. He studied the massive, pyramid-shaped "dragon's teeth" obstacles made of reinforced concrete that lined both sides of the path. Five feet high, each one weighed in the vicinity of one thousand pounds. They were designed to break the tracks or wheels of any assault vehicle trying to cross them.

A dozen yards before the main gate, stone bunkers flanked either side of the road. Within them were electrically controlled GEC miniguns, capable of firing 6000 5.56 mm rounds per minute. If the heavy-caliber blasters opened up, interlopers would be caught in the middle of a cross fire, and with no way to turn, literally chopped to pieces.

"How are you doing this?" he asked querulously. Even as he voiced the question, his mind supplied the most likely answer. If the energy sphere was indeed a manifestation of the electric and geomagnetic forces surrounding the Earth, and if Sam or Balam knew how to manipulate it, then they could use it as a way of transmitting and receiving images from afar.

"Hush," Erica said. "And watch."

Lakesh watched, noticing that the muddy streets of Cobaltville's Tartarus Pits were as bare of life as if a tornado had swept them clean. Then a fireball bloomed in the narrow twisting lanes. He flinched. Nature, even during its most outraged months following the nukecaust, never produced a hell equal to that which began pounding at the walls of Cobaltville. As if from a great distance, he heard a roar that grew steadily in volume, like the approach a huge wheeled machine.

He had the sensation of riding the wind currents above the ville, safely above the concussions of the high-explosive shells that punched huge smoking craters in the walls. Masonry tumbled from them to add to the incessant rumbling roar. Lakesh saw wheeled artillery pieces down by the riverbank, flame and smoke belching from their bores.

"What the hell is going on?" he demanded in a hushed tone. "Is this real?"

Sam's voice announced quietly, "It is very real, Mohandas. A new reality. Cobaltville is under siege by the combined forces of Barons Samarium and Mande. For the past ten days, they have been arraying their forces around the ville. Now, today, they launch their attack."

Lakesh could barely comprehend the concept of barons making war on their own. All he could do was stand and stare at the images of destruction swimming across the face of the sphere. In a series of staggered visions, he saw the entire siege from different perspectives. He realized all of the civilian population of the Enclaves had taken shelter in cellars beneath the residential towers, but the Pit dwellers were left to survive or die the bombardment on their own.

Cobaltville's armed defense was holed up in dugouts and trenches outside the bunkers, waiting wearily for the artillery barrage to lift—waiting and wondering whether they would be able to stem the attack, or even if they should make the attempt. All of them wore the black armor of Magistrates.

The close-packed troops of the enemy suddenly

poured up from the riverfront. Across the grassy fields they swept, moving as though they were pushed forward by a wind from hell. They rushed upon the barricade, and the first burst from the GEC minigun emplacments threw the ranks back in bloody confusion.

But the inexorable rush from the attackers in the rear vanguard pushed them forward. The troopers regrouped and blastermen split to either side, forming a wedge flanking their comrades. Though a hail of high-velocity rounds struck them and knocked them down, they kept coming, trampling over their dead or dying comrades. The Cobaltville Mags took refuge in the bunkers. They fought fiercely, but without hope, for they expected no mercy.

"I think we've seen enough," Sam said.

The bloody images flickered and faded, and the light exuded by the sphere dimmed. Lakesh knuckled his eyes. His mouth was dry and his temples throbbed. Blinking, he surveyed Sam, Balam and Erica van Sloan. All of them gazed at him expectantly, apparently waiting for him to speak.

At length, he did so in a low, hoarse tone. "That is an example of your cooperation and coercion. Another war."

"A war to end the tyranny of the barons," Sam replied smoothly.

"And to replace it with another form of tyranny. That of an imperator."

Erica shook her head in pity. "You don't understand, Mohandas. We wage war to end war."

He laughed sneeringly. "I've heard that before. All of you disappoint me, you in particular, Balam."

The ever-present smile on Sam's baby lips vanished. "This is the new order of the world. We wish—no, we *require*—your cooperation to bring it to fruition."

"Then why don't you coerce me?" he retorted. "Except I'd know I'm coerced and that's not part of your program, is it?"

"Finding incentives certainly is." Despite the childish timbre of his voice, Sam's tone sent little fingers of dread crawling up Lakesh's spine.

"What do you mean?" He instantly regretted asking the question.

"We can either offer you something of worth," Sam said, "or threaten to take it away." He gestured to the sphere again. "Look."

Lakesh slowly followed the boy's hand wave. The energy globe glowed and once more shapes slid across it. They coalesced into three figures and then acquired definite shape and form. Lakesh's heart began to pound uncontrollably when he recognized Kane, Brigid and Grant.

"We offer you a choice, Mohandas," Sam declared in a singsong croon. "You can either have these three people, or you can lose them. Which option most motivates you toward cooperation?"

Chapter 16

Baron Sharpe smiled at the naked human male and female, noting how cleverly the twisting double helix was superimposed over their bodies. His eyes flicked over the large, full-color illustrations tacked on the wall. Though faded and yellowed with age, the printed colors of the sequence of images were still vivid.

The next illustration depicted the corkscrewing strands of DNA molecules separating, then intertwining again to form a new chain configuration. Another image showed egg cells being opened by microscalpels so their dark nuclei could be replaced with new ones.

The final picture showed the male and female holding the hands of a baby standing between them. The baby possessed a very high forehead and domed cranium. From beneath pronounced brow arches was a pair of big, slanting, staring, eyes.

Smiling, Sharpe reached out and tickled the baby beneath its pointed chin. "Oochee-kootchee-coo," he murmured.

From the floor, Crawler uttered a throaty noise between a chuckle and a snort. Then he asked,

"How long do you propose to stay here, my lord? The installation is secured. Baron Cobalt is too busy dealing with the siege against his ville to return here and try to reclaim it."

"What's your hurry?" Baron Sharpe asked, turning from the illustrations that nearly ran the length of the chamber walls. "Don't you find the desert air invigorating?" He was still wearing the camouflage clothing he had adopted during the journey from California to Nevada.

"I might," Crawler responded, "if we ever got out into it. Instead we've been under the desert for the last week. I don't find stale, recycled air invigorating."

"Get used to it," Sharpe snapped. "We're liable to be in Dreamland for a long time."

Contained in the dry lake bed of Nellis Air Force Base was a vast installation that extended deep into the desert floor. Only a few of the buildings were aboveground. Area 51 was more than just a military installation; it served as an international base operated by a consortium from many countries. Now the plan was to have its operation overseen by a consortium of barons, which in turn would be overseen by the imperator.

The ancient Roman Empire was governed by a senate but ruled by an emperor, sometimes known as an imperator. This person served as the final arbiter in matters pertaining to government. Less than a month before, during a council of the barons in

Front Royal, Baron Cobalt put forth the proposal to establish a central ruling consortium. In effect, the barons would become viceroys, plenipotentiaries in their own territories. They were accustomed to acting as the viceroys of the Archon Directorate, so the actual proposal didn't offend them.

The barons were less in favor of the concept than Baron Cobalt's proclamation that he be recognized as the imperator. Their displeasure didn't last, since the proposal and title were adopted by another.

Sharpe, followed by Crawler scuttling along at knee level, walked out of the room and into the corridor. The face of the door held a small plaque that read Purity Control Orientation. He recalled the foundation of ville class distinctions was based on purity control.

Purity control was little more than a euphemism for eugenics, and this was determined by the Directorate, or so Sharpe and the other barons had believed. With access to the findings of the twentieth-century Human Genome Project, everyone selected to have full ville citizenship and be allowed to reproduce had first to meet strict criteria. One of the Totality Concept's subdivisions, Scenario Joshua, had its roots in the Genome Project.

The goal of this undertaking was to map human genomes to specific chromosomal functions and locations. The end result was in vitro genetic samples of the best of the best. In the vernacular of the time, it was purity control.

Everyone who enjoyed full ville citizenship was a descendant of the Genome Project. Sometimes, a particular gene carrying a desirable trait was grafted to an unrelated egg, or an undesirable gene removed. Despite many failures, when there was a success, it was replicated over and over, occasionally with variations. Even the baronial oligarchy was bred according to this system.

However, with the destruction of the Archuleta Mesa medical facility, without access to the ectogenesis techniques of fetal development outside the womb, the oligarchy and the entire hybrid race was in danger of extinction. Baron Cobalt occupied Area 51 with the spoken assumption of taking responsibility to sustain his race—but only if he was elevated to a position of high authority, even above his brother barons. It wasn't a matter of making an incursion into another baron's territory, since most of Nevada was an Outland flat zone, not a part of an official baronial territory, certainly not Baron Cobalt's.

Since Area 51's history was intertwined with rumors of alien involvement, Baron Cobalt had used its medical facilities as a substitute for those destroyed in New Mexico. Of course, he couldn't be sure if the aliens referred to in the predark conspiracy theorists were the Archons, but more than likely they were, inasmuch as the equipment that still existed was compatible with the hybrid metabolisms. In any event, Baron Cobalt reactivated the installation as a processing and treatment center, without having to rebuild from scratch, and transferred the human and hybrid personnel from the Dulce facility—those who had survived the catastrophe, at any rate.

Still and all, the medical treatments that addressed the congenital autoimmune system deficiencies of the hybrids weren't enough to insure the continued survival of the race. The necessary equipment and raw material to implement procreation had yet to be installed. Baron Cobalt had unilaterally decided that the conventional means of conception was the only option to keep the hybrid race alive.

Cobalt's command for the female hybrids to commit acts of miscegenation with human males was one thing, perhaps even forgivable under the circumstances. When he dangled the treatments before his fellow barons like a carrot on a stick rather than share them freely, war was the inevitable result.

Of course, barons had made war on one another before, but not since the institution of the Program of Unification. In decades past, the barons had warred against one another, each struggling for control and absolute power over territory. The barons who survived the wars of territorial expansion, and clawed out enclaves of civilization for themselves, were summoned to the ville of Front Royal in the foothills of the Shens by a mysterious black-clad emissary who went by the simple name of Thrush. They met with the baron of Front Royal in order to confer and discuss each ville's strengths and definite weaknesses, and perhaps by forming an alliance, the whole would become greater than the sum of its parts.

Front Royal was chosen for the historic summit because it was the most influential and peaceful ville on the eastern seaboard. Its current baron was the latest in a generations-long hierarchy, just like his fellow barons. He had expressed his desire to decisively end the reign of blood and anarchy. Front Royal was probably the most powerful of the baronies, despite the fact it never made raids into other territories or enslaved its people. The ville was well known and envied for its high standard of living.

The barons met with the diplomatic envoy, who outlined all the rewards that would be theirs if they put aside their differences, concentrated on their commonalties and united. Barons had united before, observing trade agreements and nonaggression pacts. What Thrush proposed was different. A new form of government would be institutionalized in the baronies, and all the villes would be standardized according to preexisting specifications.

The barons would be provided with all the materials needed to achieve these goals, including a vast treasure trove of predark technology as pristine as the day it was manufactured. Thrush wove a thoroughly spellbinding tale of a vast vault designed to protect everything stored in it from the ravages of time.

Not just a few boxes of ammo, he hastened to point out, or a couple of crates of guns or the odd wag, but literally tons of matériel—advanced weaponry, electronic equipment saved from electromagnetic pulses, even aircraft. All of it was in perfect operating condition. No longer would the individual barons be forced to cobble together electrical generators with spit and baling wire, or waste time with long periods of trial and error to figure out how to repair rusty engines. Moreover, they would be participating in a grand, radically new kind of social engineering.

After all, Thrush said the unification program was already mapped out, with all the methods in place, tools to be provided and timetables set. All the barons needed to do was to implement it. Of course, if they refused, then the Directorate would visit another holocaust upon the face of the Earth, annihilating every living thing upon it, and the Archons would take over anyway.

The most persuasive argument didn't appeal to the barons' fear—it played on their greed. As an added incentive, the Directorate vowed to make the barons the progenitors of dynasties that would rule forever, a form of immortality. They would live on in their descendants and they could never be overthrown from within or conquered from without.

Eventually, although the original projected timetable was skewed by several years, the united baronies were established, through propaganda and sheer naked force. The long-forgotten trust in any form of government was slowly reawakened, generations after the survivors of the nuclear war had lived through the deadly legacy of politics and the suicidal decisions made by elected officials.

The leaders of the powerful baronies offered a solution to the constant states of worry and fear— join the unification program and never worry or fear or think again. Humanity was responsible for the arrival of Judgment Day, and it had to accept that responsibility before a truly utopian age could be ushered in.

All humankind had to do to earn this utopia was to follow the rules, be obedient, and be fed and clothed. And accept the new order without question. For most of the men and women who lived in the villes and the surrounding territories, that was enough, more than enough. Dreams of peace and safety were at last being transformed into reality. Of course, fleeting dreams of personal freedom were lost in the exchange, but such abstract aspirations were nothing but childish illusions.

Over the following four generations, order was indeed restored to America, and the barons themselves represented the new order, as well as a new form of humanity. Only the barons themselves knew how different they were, not only from their human progenitors from whom they inherited their names and territories, but also from the humans they ruled.

The populations of the villes and Outlands co-

operated with baronial tyranny for several reasons—
the first and foremost was guilt. For the past three
generations, a belief was bred into the descendants
of the survivors of the apocalypse that when Judgment Day arrived, humanity was rightly punished
for its sins. The doctrines expressed by the baronies
was that humankind had to endure ongoing punishment before a utopian age could be ushered in.

The dogma encouraged people to tolerate, even
welcome, a world of unremitting hardship, because
humanity ruined the world and had to pay for its
sins. Therefore, the punishment they suffered was
richly deserved. Ultimately, the doctrines amounted
to extortion—believe and obey or question and die.

But no secret as complex and as wide-ranging as
that of the Archon Directorate could be completely
hidden. Rumors abounded about the Directorate and
the Totality Concept, even before the nukecaust,
though they were relegated to the status of conspiracy theories. During the century and a half following
skydark, some of the secrets were discovered. Humanity, what was left of it, was too scattered even
for the Directorate to control. The near annihilation
of the race hadn't extinguished the race's inborn
sense of curiosity, the drive to search in strange
places for strange things.

Many of those strange places were penetrated, the
strange things uncovered, but humankind was too
concerned with day-to-day survival to question the
whys and wherefores behind them. It required only

a generation to reduce the knowledge of strange places and things to mere rumors, and another generation to fanciful legends. Therefore, in order to prevent another apocalypse, maintaining the secrecy of the Directorate and its work was a sacred trust. It was a sworn and solemn duty, offered to very few, and thus was born the Trust.

Each of the nine villes had its own version of the Trust. Less than an organization, and more of a secret society, it was the only face-to-face contact allowed with the barons.

The Trust acted more or less as the protectors of the Directorate, and its oath revolved around a single theme—the presence of the Directorate could not be revealed to humanity. If their presence became known, if the technological marvels they had designed became accessible, if the truth behind the nukecaust filtered down to the people, then humankind would no doubt retaliate with a concerted effort to wipe them out—or the Directorate would be forced to visit another holocaust upon the face of the Earth, simply as a measure of self-preservation.

Over the past few months, especially after the Dulce disaster, the barons' steadfast belief in the Directorate had waned. Recently, a measure of their faith was restored to them, as well as a savior. The flames of war came in the imperator's wake, but all of the barons were certain it was a cleansing fire, and a stronger, more united society would arise from the ashes.

Of course, Baron Sharpe reflected with wry amusement, not only had war returned to the baronies, so had the so-called baron blasters. Baron Cobalt was the first victim of the rebellion, and it could all be traced back to the night Kane was inducted into the Cobaltville Trust.

As Sharpe understood it, Kane, whose father had been a member of the Trust, was recommended for recruitment by Salvo, his former Magistrate Division commander. Kane was informed that his father was a member of the Trust, and therefore he had to accept the tradition, the honor offered to him. Like his father, he would belong to the elite that literally ruled society in secret. Henceforth, like his father, he would work for the evolution of humankind.

Kane accepted the offer—and after that, everything went to Hell on a slide. Sharpe was never briefed on exactly what happened in the twenty-four hours following Kane's entrance into the Trust. He knew he escaped Cobaltville with Brigid Baptiste, a seditionist awaiting execution, and his partner of many years, Grant. Salvo was badly injured trying to stop the escape, and a few Magistrates were killed.

Kane reappeared only a day later when Baron Cobalt arrived at the Dulce facility for his annual medical treatment. Kane had attacked and humiliated him and escaped after killing a number of hybrids.

But all of that was just prologue. Only a few months later, Kane and Grant led a raiding party into the very heart of the Admin Monolith where they not only killed a pair of the Baronial Guard, but they also abducted Lakesh and Salvo.

Sharpe never learned the entire story of the raid and the abduction. The version put forth by Baron Cobalt explained some of it, but by no means all of it. Upon examination, there seemed no reason for the kidnapping of his fellow members of the Trust. In the intervening months, no ransom demands had been made in exchange for their return. It was as if the two men had fallen off the face of the Earth.

Reports of Kane, Grant and Baptiste sightings increased, coming in from all over. The obvious conclusion was they were using the forbidden mat-trans units to jump from sealed redoubt to sealed redoubt. A cooperative undertaking among the nine barons to inspect all of the installations in their territories resulted only in false trails—and violent attacks on two barons.

Fearing an uprising, Cobalt's fellow barons agreed to help him find the criminals. For the first few months it was as if Kane, Baptiste and Grant had vanished off the face of the Earth.

Not long after that, caravans of precious metals and ores were hijacked by frightfully well organized and armed raiders who struck, killed and disappeared. A Mag assault force dispatched to deal with the raiders had been completely annihilated. Although none of the few survivors of these attacks described anyone resembling Grant and Kane as being involved, the suspicion was definitely there.

And because their names figured prominently, they became figures of inspiration to the disenfranchised, to the outlanders. Their acts of terrorism triggered sporadic rebellions in the Outlands. They weren't organized uprisings, but their frequency was of a kind not seen in ninety years, since the days of the baron blasters.

Sharpe wasn't worried about becoming a victim of the insurgents, since he had already survived two face-to-face encounters with Kane. He knew he couldn't die, because Crawler had told him so.

Part of his legacy from his human great-grandfather was a small private zoo of creatures that had once crept and slithered and scuttled over the Deathlands. The monsters had been fruitful and multiplied over the decades and one of them was a doomie called Crawler.

It was more of a title than a name, bestowed upon him after his leg tendons had been severed. The psi-mutie had displayed a great cunning and propensity for escape from his compound, no doubt employing his mental talents to find the most opportune time and means to do so. After he had been crippled, his psi-powers availed him nothing, inasmuch as his movements were restricted to dragging himself around his cell by fingers and elbows.

Baron Sharpe visited Crawler one still, sultry summer midnight. He gazed in revulsion at the hu-

man face staring back at him from a wild, matted
tangle of gray beard and long, filthy hair. The baron
had no idea of Crawler's age, but he understood that
he was one of his ancestor's last acquisitions before
his mysterious disappearance, some ninety-odd
years before. He knew the doomie was very old, but
some muties possessed remarkable longevity.

Ignoring the thick wall of mingled stenches the
cell exuded, Baron Sharpe commanded Crawler to
approach him.

"I have a question," Baron Sharpe announced.
"About my death."

Wheezing whistles issued from Crawler's hair-
rimmed lips. For a moment, the baron thought the
mutie was undergoing an asthma attack and would
expire, but then he recognized the sound as laughter.

In a high, whispery voice, Crawler said, "That
question has no meaning, my lord baron. You have
died and crossed back. You no longer need fear
death, for it is behind you, not ahead of you."

Baron Sharpe was so delighted he came close to
bursting into tears of gratitude. His hopes had been
realized, his fear that he was mad proved groundless.
That very night, he ordered the release of Crawler
from his cage, saw that he was bathed, fed, shaved,
cropped and pampered. He installed him as a high
councilor, ignoring the outraged reactions of his personal staff.

And now, Crawler was the only creature he
trusted, even though he had tried to orchestrate his

murder at one point. After that, both of them realized they were linked in some fashion and knew that if one died, so would the other. The notion made no real sense and couldn't be tested without incurring lethal results, so they decided to trust each other implicitly from then on.

Baron Sharpe and Crawler traversed the corridor for a hundred yards, followed a dogleg to the right, then entered a multileveled man-made cavern. The dimensions were so vast the far end ran away into the dimness. The ceiling was at least three hundred feet above their heads, and dotted with bright stadium lights. It was far larger than the biggest chamber beneath the Archuleta Mesa.

Large containers were arranged in orderly fifty-foot-tall aisles, stretching as far as they could see. Gently sloping ramps led from level to level, broad flat passages for lift trucks and dollies to carry their loads. The ramps were the only method of getting from level to level.

A floor-mounted, narrow-gauge electric monorail track ran the entire length of the enormous chamber, to disappear in the darkness beyond wide open double doors. The vast chamber was a bustling beehive of activity, with forklifts moving to and fro laden with boxes, and the small shifter engines of the monorail train zipping back and forth.

Crawler commented blandly, "Soon you won't even miss the installation in New Mexico."

Baron Sharpe nodded distractedly. "Yes, it's gratifying to see how well it's coming along. It gives me hope.''

"Hope for what?" Crawler sounded genuinely puzzled.

Sharpe glanced down at him, frowning. "For the future, what else?"

Crawler nodded and a smirk played over his face. "I didn't know you cared about the future, my lord."

"Sometimes I do," Sharpe snapped. "This is one of those times."

A high, musical voice called out from behind him. "My lord baron?"

Sharpe turned around and saw a female hybrid approaching him. Her name was Quavell, and like all of her kind she was excessively slender and small of stature, less than five feet tall. Her compact, tiny-breasted form was encased in a silvery-gray, skin-tight bodysuit. Silky blond hair topped her high, domed skull.

The texture seemed to be a cross between feathery down and thread. Above prominent cheekbones, huge, upslanting eyes of a clear crystal blue regarded him in a silent appraisal. They gleamed with emotion, which was not characteristic of hybrids of any type, barons or not.

Quavell had served excellently as a spy within the complex during Baron Cobalt's brief occupation of Area 51. If not for the intelligence she provided and her organization of a fifth column among the installation's personnel, Dreamland would have never been wrested away from Cobalt and his forces.

Therefore, Sharpe was kindly disposed toward and greeted her with a warm smile. "Yes?"

To his mild surprise, she returned his smile and swayed before him like a reed in a breeze. It was ritualistic form of greeting between hybrids, the precise movements an instinctive show of respect and submission. "I thought you might like to see how the infants are responding to the treatments."

He nodded. "I would indeed. Take me to them, please. I'm very interested."

Crawler remained where he was as Baron Sharpe crossed the floor to a set of double-swing doors. As they entered a corridor, Baron Sharpe commented slyly, "I'm also interested in how you and the other participants responded to Kane's treatments."

Quavell's elfin face didn't so much as twitch in response. "It is a bit too soon to tell, my lord. If any of us conceived, we won't know for at least another month, perhaps longer." She paused, the corners of her small mouth quirking in an almost imperceptible smile. "As you know, attempting to conceive in such a fashion and with such a partner is unprecedented among our people."

Baron Sharpe wasn't certain if she was speaking sarcastically or being brutally blunt, but either way he didn't care much for the implications.

Chapter 17

The Dreamland complex was far too huge for even its most basic layout to be depicted on a map. Sharpe wasn't even sure how Baron Cobalt learned about its existence in the first place. He and the other barons presumed there had been data pertaining to it in the computer banks of the Cobaltville Historical Division.

Because of the installation's sprawling size, Baron Sharpe didn't even try to learn his way around except for a single section, and even that was the length of the entire Admin Monolith if it had been laid on its side. Quavell apparently knew their destination, so Sharpe followed her along a dimly lit corridor, past a number of computer-locked doors. He didn't know what lay behind them, and he didn't care.

The corridor opened into a square room nearly twenty by twenty yards across. The overhead lighting was as dim as the hallway, but Sharpe's hybridized eyes functioned best in a soft, dusky murk. The room was filled with rows of little plastic boxes, transparent cubes with no tops to them. Quavell stopped by one of them and bent down. She picked up a hybrid infant and laid its domed, nearly hairless cranium against her shoulder.

Sharpe surveyed the makeshift nursery, noting with approval that the infants no longer lay listlessly on their foam pads, and only a few were still connected to IV drips. Most of the tiny children raised their huge dark eyes to him. Still, even though the infants showed more strength than the last time he had seen them, before they were transferred from the ruin of the Archuleta Mesa complex, he saw over a dozen empty plastic cribs.

Rather than comment on it, he said, "They appear to be much improved. My congratulations."

Quavell inclined her head in a short gracious nod, and the infant in her arms uttered a cooing sound. "I am honored, but it was the combined resources of all the villes' medical sections that provided us with the raw organic material to reverse their deterioration. As it is, your congratulations may be premature. We have yet to stabilize every one of the survivors, and five of the weakest have expired in just the past seven days."

Sharpe sighed. "How many does that make of the two thousand in the incubation chambers in Dulce?"

"Only fifteen, my lord." Quavell spoke flatly with no particular inflection or emphasis.

"I suppose saving even those few at this juncture is an accomplishment. And once we have the cloning tanks installed and the blood-purification system up and running, we may be able to avert this crisis altogether, particularly if we begin the harvesting of new merchandise as soon as possible.''

Quavell didn't respond, and Sharpe caught the slight moue of distaste that tugged at her lips. Casually, he inquired, "Something disturbs you?"

She carefully placed the baby back in its plastic-walled crib. "No, my lord."

Baron Sharpe chuckled. "Yes, it does. You may speak freely to me. I am not as preoccupied with ceremony as my brethren. All of that 'bow, yield, kneel' nonsense closes out of town, if you catch my meaning."

She cocked her head at him puzzledly. "I'm afraid I don't, my lord baron."

He gestured dismissively with one long-fingered hand. "Never mind. Speak."

Quavell's lips seemed to tremble, as if on the verge of forming themselves into a frown. "Perhaps the quarterly harvests will no longer be necessary."

It was impossible for Baron Sharpe's eyes to widen, but he lifted one of his prominent brow arches. "Why would you say such a thing?"

Quavell laid her hands on her belly. "If any one of us were impregnated by Kane, and we carry a child to full term, the salvation of our race will lie within its hybridized genetic structures."

Sharpe fingered his pointed chin musingly. "Yes, that is certainly possible—if there are children that are healthy. If so, we should be able to synthesize biochemicals from their blood and cerebrospinal fluids to bolster our own autoimmune deficiencies.''

Because of those deficiencies, the barons lived insulated, isolated lives. The theatrical trappings many of them adopted not only added to their semidivine mystique, but protected them from contamination—both psychological and physical.

Although all the hybrids were extremely long-lived, cellular and metabolic deterioration was part and parcel of what they were—hybrids of human and Archon DNA. And even though they were a biological bridge between two races, the barons weren't precisely sure of the reasons behind the hybridization program. But Baron Sharpe wasn't so blinded by arrogance that the irony was lost on him—in order to rule humans, they were dependent on the biological material they provided.

Just like the caste system in place in the villes, the hybrids observed a similar one, although it had little to do with parentage. If the first phase of human evolution produced a package of adaptations for a particular and distinct way of life, the second phase was an effort to control that way of life by controlling the environment. The focus switched to a cultural evolution rather than a physical one.

The hybrids, at least to their way of thinking, represented the final phase of human evolution. They created wholesale, planned alterations in living organisms and were empowered to control not only their environment but the evolution of other species.

And the pinnacle of that evolutionary achievement were the barons, as high above hybrids like Quavell as the hybrids were above mere humans.

"That way, at least," Sharpe continued, "Kane will have balanced out his act of genocide to some extent." He smiled at Quavell warmly. "Your service was splendid during the retaking of this installation."

"Thank you," she replied. "But without Kane's actions to supplement my own, the entire venture would have failed."

Sharpe eyed her with a mixture of curiosity and humor. "You must have employed wiles hitherto unknown to me to sway him to our cause."

Stolidly, she declared, "Only the truth, my lord baron. Kane seemed genuinely moved by the plight of the children. As did his companion, the albino female. More than likely, she was the instrument in convincing him to help us. A pity she was killed."

Baron Sharpe knew that Kane and an albino woman had penetrated Area 51 and been captured. The girl, Domi, had been found by Quavell's little group of insurgents while Kane was sentenced by Baron Cobalt to what amounted to stud service.

During his two weeks of captivity, he was fed a steady diet of protein laced with a stimulant of the catecholamine group. It affected the renal blood supply, increasing cardiac output without increasing the need for cardiac oxygen consumption.

Combined with the food loaded with protein to

speed sperm production, the stimulant provided Kane with hours of high energy. Since he was forced to achieve erection and ejaculation six times a day every two days, his energy and sperm count had to be preternaturally high, even higher than was normal for him.

Baron Sharpe had learned from the Cobalt's people in the installation that Kane was supposed to be special, for a variety of biological reasons. Of course the main reason he was chosen to impregnate the female hybrids was simply due to the fact male hybrids were incapable of engaging in conventional acts of procreation, at least physically. Their organs of reproduction were so undeveloped as to be vestigial.

Kane wasn't the first human male to be pressed into service. There had been other men before him, but they had performed unsatisfactorily due to their terror of the hybrids. At first the females selected for the process donned wigs and wore cosmetics in order to appear more human to the trapped sperm donors. The men had to be strapped down and even after the application of an aphrodisiac gel, had difficulty maintaining an erection.

Such a problem wasn't something a hybrid, baron or no, was likely to ever experience. What made the barons so superior had nothing to do with the physical. The brains of the barons could absorb and process information with exceptional speed, and their cognitive abilities were nothing short of supernatural.

Almost from the moment the barons emerged from the incubation chambers, they possessed IQ's so far beyond the range of standard tests as to render them meaningless. They mastered language in a matter of weeks, speaking in whole sentences. All of Nature's design faults in the human brain were corrected, modified and improved, specifically the hypothalamus, which regulated the complex biochemical systems of the body

They could control all autonomous functions of their brains and bodies, even to the manufacture and release of chemicals and hormones. They could speed or slow their heartbeats, increase and decrease the amount of adrenaline in their bloodstreams.

They possessed complete control over that mysterious portion of the brain known as the limbic system, a portion that predark scientists had always known possessed great reserves of electromagnetic power and strength.

Physically, the barons were a beautiful people, almost too perfect to be real. Even their expressions were markedly similar—a vast pride, a diffident superiority, authority and even ruthlessness. They were the barons, and as such, they believed themselves to be the avatars of the new humans that would inherit the Earth.

But since they were bred for brilliance, all barons had emotional limitations placed upon their enor-

mous intellects. They were captives of their shared
Archon hive-mind heritage, the captive of a re-
morseless mind-set that didn't carry with it the simple comprehension of the importance to humans of
individual liberty.

Smug in their hybrid arrogance, the baronial oligarchy didn't understand the primal beast buried inside the human psyche, the beast that always gave
humans a fair chance of winning in the deadly game
of survival of the fittest.

Visceral emotions didn't play a large part in the
psychologies of the so-called new humans. Even
their bursts of passion were of the most rudimentary
kind. Although the tissue of their hybridized brains
was of the same organic matter as the human brain,
the millions of neurons operated a bit differently in
the processing of information. Therefore, their
thought processes were very structured, extremely
linear. When they experienced emotions, they only
did so in moments of stress, and then so intensely
they were almost consumed by them.

Baron Sharpe abruptly seemed to lose interest in
the conversation. "Yes, but both she and Kane are
only humans. Regardless of Kane's help, he is still
a criminal and must pay for his crimes."

Quavell hesitated before saying, "My lord, I
hoped he would be extended a modicum of mercy
in light of his aid to us."

"Oh, he will be," Sharpe retorted placidly. "Before he set out in pursuit of them, I instructed Ra-

mirez that if at all possible to kill Kane quickly and not to let him suffer...much, that is.''

His pale blue eyes turned as cold as the mountain meltwater they resembled. ''Surely you don't entertain feelings for him?''

Before Quavell could respond, Sharpe began speaking in a flint-hard voice, snapping out words in a staccato fashion. ''Allow me to remind you that if not for Kane's actions in Dulce, none of these horrific events would have come to pass. Due to him, the Archuleta Mesa complex was destroyed, and with it nearly an entire generation of our kind. He also was involved in the assassination of Baron Ragnar. And though I never cared for him personally, he was still a baron.''

Sharpe paused to inhale a breath. ''For what he did to me in Washington Hole, I bear him no malice. But when he declared war on the barons, he declared war on unity, and my own feelings are irrelevant, as should be yours. It is an official matter of policy. Do you understand me?''

Quavell had listened to Sharpe's tirade without a flicker of emotion. Her answer was a subdued monotone. ''I understand, my lord baron.''

Sharpe turned smartly on his heel. ''See that you continue to understand.''

As he marched out of the nursery, he sensed Quavell's unblinking stare fixed on the back of his head. The skin on his nape began to crawl. He felt anger in her stare, and an almost complete lack of respect. Without that respect, there was no fear and without fear, he realized darkly, the barons could no longer rule.

Chapter 18

They approached Thunder Isle at the tail end of a raging thunderstorm. Another storm front had moved back into the area by midafternoon, and Kane had tried to race it to the little island.

Dubois's sailboat rode the roaring breakers at the shoreline, rising and falling, rising again. Waves lapped over the sides, drenching Grant, Kane, Brigid and Dubois from head to foot, the salt spray stinging their eyes. Dubois kept the small craft on course, knowing how easily a swell could pile them up against a submerged boulder.

As they drew closer to the shore, the violent buffeting ebbed somewhat. Crooked fingers of lightning broke through the cloud cover, glinting on the rippling waves. The flashes showed a rocky beach, which was surrounded by thick growths of tall, slender palm trees and heavy underbrush. They also saw, canted on its port side, the landing boat from the CG-47.

Dubois skillfully steered the boat to the shallows near the rock-strewn beach. When the keel grated on stone, Kane climbed nimbly out, waded ashore and made the boat fast with a rope looped around the trunk of a palm. Grant and Brigid followed.

"How long do you want me to wait for you?" Dubois shouted.

His voice was barely audible over the rhythmic boom of the surf and roar of the deluge. Kane shouted back, "Your discretion. Give us a couple of hours at least."

Kane surveyed the shoreline. It looked innocuous enough, but what lay beyond the fence of palm trees was a complete mystery. He, Brigid and Grant entered the labyrinth of foliage. The men wore their suits of Magistrate body armor, and the rain made it gleam as if it had been rubbed down with oil. They constantly had to palm away droplets of water from the visors, and Kane supposed they were lucky it wasn't acid rain. Although Mag armor was treated to withstand prolonged exposure to toxins, a shower of acid rain, even if only a drizzle, wasn't something to take lightly.

Both men had been keenly aware of the sudden fear in Dubois's eyes when they boarded the boat sheathed in black polycarbonate and their visages concealed by the visored helmets. They were now symbols of awe, of fear. They looked bigger somehow. Strong, fierce, implacable.

When a man concealed his face and body beneath the black armor, he became a fearsome figure, the anonymity adding to the mystique. There was another reason behind the helmet, the exoskeleton, and it was a reason all Magistrates knew—once a man put on the armor, he symbolically surrendered his identity in order to serve a cause of greater import than a mere individual life.

Brigid herself still wore a partial suit of Tigers of Heaven armor, but she had dispensed with the helmet.

When the three of them volunteered to go after Ramirez and the escaped Magistrates, Shizuka hadn't objected, but she seemed loath to send any of her samurai with them. They didn't blame her particularly, since losses in the ranks had been high. Besides, though she didn't mention it, she obviously felt that the three outlanders should take care of their own. They more or less had led the invasion force to New Edo.

Also, there was a matter of local superstition to contend with. In the short time New Edo had been settled, a body of legends had sprung up about the little volcanic island they referred to as Thunder Isle. According to what they had been told by both Lord Takaun and Captain Kiyomasa, a cyclical phenomenon occurred on the island. The men described lightning that seemed to strike up, accompanied by sounds like thunder, even if the weather was clear.

They had no explanation for it, but they knew that on the heels of the phenomenon often came incursions of what the more impressionable people claimed were demons. The outlanders were shown the body of one such demon, killed only recently.

Brigid tentatively identified it as a Dryosaurus, a man-size dinosaur.

She was able to identify other artifacts found on the shores of Thunder Isle—a helmet from the era of the conquistadors, and stone spearhead that resembled a Folsom point, so named for Folsom, New Mexico, the archaeological site where the first one was found. It was evidence of a prehistoric culture many thousands of years old.

According to Takaun, the phenomenon had been very sporadic for the past five years, occurring only a few times. Recently a new cycle had begun, and it was happening with far greater regularity.

Brigid had studied the isle through a telescope, and witnessed a blaze of white light, far too bright to be a reflection. And if it had been, the reflecting surface had to be gigantic. She heard a thunderclap-like rumble in the distance, accompanying the flash.

Kiyomasa claimed that a few samurai had been sent over from time to time. Some found nothing, some never came back and some were found decapitated.

Brigid had been very intrigued by the story, but not so much that she didn't walk with extreme care through the undergrowth. The rain was very heavy, like sheets of shifting water, bowing down the vegetation and making the ground marshy underfoot. A stiff wind rattled the leaves and branches of trees. The sky was crowded with thunderclaps and lightning strokes.

Unhooking the Copperhead from the magnetic clip at his web belt, Kane clicked an ammo clip into place. As the clouds thickened, he activated his night sight mounted on the helmet. The image enhancer gathered all available light and made the most of it to provide him with one-color night vision, at least for twenty feet or so. Viewed through the treated visor, the jungle seemed to be lit by a lambent, ghostly glow. Where only black had been before, there were various shifting shades of gray.

"I'll take the point this time," he whispered. "Stay close."

The three people went carefully, doing their utmost to be stealthy, despite the vines snaring their ankles and the thorns snagging their armor. The footing was soft and marshy, and reeked with the rotten-egg odor of swamp gas. A steady wind rushed over the island. The tops of the trees moved violently, palm fronds rattling. The wind carried the pungent scent of decomposing vegetable matter.

Kane's eyes watched everything, studied the slightest motion in the dim jungle. He was especially on the lookout for trip wires or snares set by their quarry. He saw nothing, yet he had the feeling they were being watched. He was positive Ramirez expected pursuit by him and Grant.

Kane was so occupied looking for traps, he stepped into a depression and very nearly stumbled. Looking down, he saw deep parallel tracks that had squashed and flattened the vegetation on the jungle floor. The outside edges of the prints showed a pattern resembling splayed, three-toed feet. They were twice the length of Grant's big feet.

"What the hell made those tracks?" he demanded, raising his voice so Brigid could hear him over the incessant clatter of wind-whipped foliage.

She knelt to examine the prints more closely. "If you want an educated guess, I'd say a companion to the Dryosaurus."

"Another dinosaur?" Grant asked skeptically.

"It stands to reason if there's one such creature on this little island, there's bound to be another." She frowned at the print. "But this doesn't look the same as the feet on the Dryosaurus. The claws are much longer."

Kane snorted. "That's what I wanted to hear."

Brigid straightened and threw him a slightly patronizing smile. "Relax. That print looks to be at least a day and a half old. Whatever made it isn't in the vicinity."

"I'll relax when we're off this rock," he retorted stiffly.

Annoyance flickered briefly in Brigid's jade eyes, but it faded when he smiled in a slightly abashed fashion to let her know he meant no offense.

For a long time at the beginning of their relationship, it was very difficult for Kane and Brigid not to give offense to each other. Both people had their gifts. Most of what was important to people in the twenty-first century came easily to Kane—survival skills, prevailing in the face of adversity and cunning against enemies. But he could also be reckless, high-strung to the point of instability and given to fits of rage.

Brigid, on the other hand, was compulsively tidy and ordered, with a brilliant analytical mind. However, her clinical nature, the cool scientific detachment upon which she prided herself, sometimes blocked an understanding of the obvious human factor in any given situation.

Regardless of their contrasting personalities, Kane and Brigid worked very well as a team, playing on each other's strengths rather than contributing to their individual weaknesses.

The three of them moved on through the jungle. Wind-driven sheets of cold rain rushed down, mixed with tiny fragments of hail. Suddenly, Kane thought he heard the murmur of voices. He signaled for his comrades to come to a halt and strained his ears to hear over the constant pounding of the rain and the thrash of vegetation. He picked up snatches of conversation.

Male voices, more than two, he guessed. He gestured to Brigid and Grant to continue warily. When they reached a thinning fringe of undergrowth, they sank beneath the fronds of a palmetto scrub and peered out at the jungle beyond.

When lightning flared across the sky again, Kane saw four men wearing Mag armor, huddled beneath a canopy formed by the boughs of a tree. Since their faces were hidden by the visored helmets, Kane couldn't be sure if Ramirez was among them. Two of the men cradled Copperheads in their arms. A voice, as sharp as a whip crack, shouted something behind them.

Kane whirled, raising his Copperhead. He saw nothing, but he heard a series of staccato cracks and the palmetto fronds on his right were torn to tatters as half a dozen rounds ripped through them. Flying pieces of pulp stung the exposed portion of his face. Not really aiming, Kane swung his subgun to his shoulder and squeezed off five rounds. He caught a brief a glimpse of four armored figures scattering in all directions through the overgrowth.

Kane heaved himself to his feet, grabbing Brigid by the elbow and jerking her to her feet. She, Kane and Grant rushed back into the jungle at an oblique angle to both parties of Magistrates. They didn't bother with stealth; the storm was making so much noise, no one could have heard the blundering of a Dryosaur.

The three of them changed course, struggling through thorns and vines. They found a depression beneath a copse of brush and rolled into it, lying side by side. Kane didn't believe any of the Magistrates had seen them alter their course, but the men fired blindly into the jungle anyway, Sin Eaters and Copperheads both.

Bullets thudded through the air, knocking bark off trees and slashing through shrubs and branches.

Bushes bent and leaves fluttered. Kane realized that his earlier sensation of being expected was correct. The only edge he and Grant possessed was that in the thick bush, the Magistrates would have to proceed slowly or risk shooting one another. Their own Mag armor was the best protective coloration.

Brigid huddled next to him, trying to soften the frightened harshness of her breathing. The Colt Mustang in her hand trembled. They heard the sounds of men moving swiftly, if not noiselessly, through the foliage.

The rain slackened for a moment, then poured hard again. The storm's intensity showed no indication of ebbing any time soon. Water dripped from the leaves of the bush and down the backs of their necks.

A lightning bolt touched a tree nearby, the electricity crawling along its trunk like fingers of living fire. The flash was dazzling and the crack nearly deafening. In that brief blaze of light, they saw the dinosaur.

Chapter 19

Even the examination of the dead reptile in Lord Takaun's palace couldn't have prepared them for the monster they saw, made even more nightmarish by its momentary illumination by lightning.

The dinosaur was bipedal, ten to twelve feet tall. Grinning jaws bared rows of glistening yellow fangs. The saurian snout bore a pair of flared nostrils that seemed to dilate and twitch. The head, bigger than that of a horse, was set upon an extended scaled neck.

Huge cold eyes like those of a serpent's a hundred times magnified stared unwinkingly from beneath a pair of scaled knobby, protuberances. Two huge legs almost as big around as some of the palm trees they'd seen supported the massive, barrel-shaped body.

A long tail trailed out from behind, disappearing into the undergrowth. Its wet hide bore a pebblelike pattern of dark brown scales. Clawed forelegs were drawn up to its chest almost in an attitude of praying.

Brigid felt Kane shudder beside her. When the next flash of violet lightning flared, the creature was gone, as if it had never existed except in their imaginations. For a few seconds, Kane tried to convince himself that what'd he seen was only a gnarled tree trunk, its bark glistening with moisture and his mind supplying the fangs and talons. He failed to persuade himself and he whispered into Brigid's ear, "You saw that, right?"

Lips compressed in a tight white line she jerked her head in a nod.

Kane turned to Grant. "What about you?"

He nodded too and rumbled, "It didn't look like the same thing in Takaun's study."

"It wasn't," Brigid said lowly, a tremor of fear lurking at the back of her throat and making her voice quaver slightly. "It wasn't a Dryosaurus. What we just saw resembled artists' approximations of an Allosaur or a Velociraptor."

Bleakly, Grant whispered, "Something in the way you said that makes me think that if what we saw is either one of them, we're in trouble."

"We are," she retorted flatly. "If it gets on our trail."

"Which one is worse?" Kane murmured uneasily, his eyes scanning the dark, dripping vegetation.

Brigid shifted position on the wet ground. "Six of one. I think we'd better stay put for a while. It's on the prowl, and predatory reptiles are attracted by movement more than scent. We don't want it stalking us, so don't move."

Neither of the two men objected to her suggestion

although they were impatient to get moving. Although Kane and Brigid quarreled frequently, he had the utmost faith in her assessments of situations, especially when they were bizarre.

After fifteen minutes, the worst of the downpour had eased to a steady drizzle and the thunderclaps were no longer as frequent. Kane felt confident enough to stand. When the prolonged scream knifed through the stillness, he dropped back down again.

The terrible masculine scream seemed to go on unbearably, and then broke in gurgles and gasps. Interwoven with the shriek was grisly crunching, a series of cracks, like the breaking of distant branches, and then they heard the triple jackhammer roar of Sin Eaters on full-auto. A deep-throated bellow sprang up from the direction of the shots and screams. It beat at the air, and the trees seemed to quiver from it. The roar was filled with rage, triumph and death. Even when it faded away it seemed to echo still.

The shots and the screams seemed to stop simultaneously, and silence pressed down over the jungle again, an oppressive quiet as if a giant bell jar had been placed over the entire isle.

Grant, Brigid and Kane exchanged swift, grim glances, then rose to their feet, nape hairs tingling. Carefully, they began walking in the direction of the commotion, moving with as much stealth as possible. Both Kane and Grant reflexively strode heel-to-toe as they always did in a potential killzone.

Kane, once more assuming the point man's position, used his combat knife to slash branches and lianas blocking their way. Fourteen inches long, the heavy tungsten-steel blade was blued to mute all reflective highlights. The double-edged blade was honed to a razor-keen cutting edge.

In the wake of the storm, the humidity increased. The air was hot and steamy, and sweat gathered on all of them. Kane and Grant felt as if they were wearing bogs under their armor. The smell of decaying vegetation blended with that of exotic flowers blooming in gold and crimson against the dark green of the rain forest.

They came across a set of three-toed, claw-tipped tracks. The tracks were intermittent, but there were enough impressions to provide a trail to follow. They followed the tracks into the undergrowth. There was an eerie lack of insect or bird sounds. All they heard was the squish of the muddy earth beneath their boots.

The jungle was thick all around them, the deep green fronds, the heavy-leaved interlocking branches pressing in everywhere. Even the sunlight that filtered through the branches held a greenish tint. Still, combined with the beams of their Nighthawk microlights, there was sufficient illumination to follow the trail.

They entered a small clearing, and Kane started to walk across an open patch of ground. Then his point man's sixth sense rang an alarm, and he came to a full stop in midstride. He stopped so suddenly that Brigid bumped into him. She started to apologize, then the words clogged in her throat.

The black-helmeted, red-visored head of a Magistrate lay on the ground amid a puddle of crimson. The mouth gaped open in a rictus of slack-lipped horror and agony. The rear part of the helmet bore deep gouges, where teeth or claws had scored it. The ground was torn up for yards around, and even the boles of nearby palm trees were splashed with artless patterns of blood. The amber beam of his Nighthawk winked on brass cartridge cases scattered on the ground.

Kane swallowed the column of bile rising in his throat and husked out, "I guess that particular dinosaur won't be stalking us tonight, since he's already grabbed his evening meal."

Sounding half-strangled, Grant demanded, "How the fuck did dinosaurs get on this island in the first place?"

The question wasn't rhetorical, but directed toward Brigid. When she didn't respond, Kane said impatiently, "Usually you have a scientific theory or hypothesis for every phenomenon or anomaly, no matter how trivial. A dinosaur from the Cretaceous period running around biting men's heads off isn't a trifle."

She shot him a slit-eyed glare full of reproach. "Whatever theory I could offer wouldn't be very scientific."

"You're sure it's not some kind of mutie lizard?" Grant asked. "One that only looks like a dinosaur? Mebbe it swam here from a hellzone on the mainland."

Even Grant didn't sound as if he believed it. Hellzones were areas that were still hot due to lingering radioactivity or other hostile environmental features. Though fewer hellzones existed now as compared to a hundred years earlier, when almost the entire continent was a Deathlands, there were still a number of places where the geological or meteorological effects of the nuking prevented a full recovery.

Neither Kane nor Grant wanted to think about an animal, mutated or not, that possessed jaws powerful enough to bite through Kevlar and chew up a polycarbonate helmet. After examining the wet, marshy ground in the vicinity, Kane found impressions that he assumed were made by the Magistrates. He also saw broken twigs and stems in the undergrowth. He followed the path, keyed up and anxious. Veils of mist drifted in from the sea, looking like wraiths, tricking the eyes into believing their quarry stood where there were none but possibly disguising where they really were.

The sun dropped lower in the sky, and a sickly twilight deepened over the island. There was nothing to see but trees and undergrowth, not even insects or snakes. Yet Kane's point man's sense felt danger, and the feeling increased so it was almost tangible.

The close-set palm trunks were draped with loops of flowering lianas that hung like nooses. Soaked with sweat, Kane probed the greenery about them with alert eyes. He wasn't the only one who sensed an approaching threat. Brigid and Grant moved in silence, and even Brigid's poker face began to show apprehension. None of them could really identify the emotion they were feeling.

An hour later, they were still walking and night had fallen over the jungle save for a narrow band of sunset glow along the horizon, but the heat and humidity didn't abate. They noticed how the fronds of trees and leaves of shrubbery were stained and spotted with livid streaks of yellow. When they breathed through their noses, the sweet, fetid stench of decay was so thick it was almost sickening.

Breathing through their mouths was no improvement, since every inhalation of air tasted like a compost heap. Only Grant, whose nose had been broken three times in the past and was always poorly reset, didn't appear discomfited by the odor.

Then suddenly the vegetation and shrubbery dropped away as if the foliage dared not cross an invisible boundary. Beyond it spread a flat, sandy plain at least half a mile in diameter. Rising from the center of the dead zone was a dark, almost shapeless mass.

The clearing place seemed to mark a circle of demarcation across the ground. On the far sides of the circle grew thick, lush grasses and ferns. On the other side of the invisible boundary the grass was thin and brown, little more than stubble.

The dark mass took form out of the dimness. They went forward even more warily than before, blasters in hand, eyes searching every shadow. At first, they could make nothing of the black featureless shape that lifted out of the ground one-quarter of a mile before them. It was like a miniature mountain of black stone squatting in the center of the circle of dead vegetation.

As they strode closer, edging along the circle of defoliation, details emerged from the murk. It was a huge structure that lay partly in ruins. It looked like a fortress of some kind, but of a streamlined architectural type. Made of dark stone, it rose in a complex of pillars and overhanging buttresses. Roughly cubical, the building loomed above smaller structures like a squared-off mountain peak towering over foothills.

Kane said, "That doesn't look like a city, predark or otherwise."

"No, it doesn't," Brigid agreed. "Could be the ruins of an old military base."

Kane stared hard at the distant structures and replied, "It doesn't look like that, either."

Grant went to one knee, gingerly probing the ground with his gloved fingers. He murmured, "What could have caused this? Everything is green and growing on this side, but deader than hell on the other. Some kind of blight?"

Brigid eyed the complex of buildings and then the dead plain. "Some kind of radiation poisoning, I'd judge. You can see the energy pattern extending out from those buildings in a parabolic shape. I'd say the whole area is regularly subjected to short bursts of high-power microwave radiation. The bursts probably aren't over two seconds in duration."

She stared intently at the ruins and said, "There's got be a transmitter in there somewhere, set to let loose an HPM burst at a predetermined time. Of course, the burst literally cooks anything in its path."

"Harmful to us?" Kane asked.

"Maybe even lethal," she replied matter-of-factly, "if we're unlucky enough to be inside its effect radius when and if it kicks off again."

She gestured and Kane followed her arm wave with his eyes. Sprinkled across the barren and sere landscape were the browned skeletons of birds, their featherless wings outstretched as if they had dropped dead in midflight. Here and there were smaller collections of bones, like those of rats and other animals.

Grant unscabbarded his combat knife and tentatively stabbed the ground, working up a clot of dirt. It lifted out easily with no resistance. The blades of grass were lank and pale, the roots brown and dead.

"Cooked," he grunted.

"The bursts must be part of the phenomena Lord

Takaun and Kiyomasa told us about,'' Brigid said, her eyes surveying the defoliated area.

"Mebbe Ramirez and his Mags were caught in the last burst and cooked in their shells,'' Kane ventured hopefully. "Like crabs.''

"Nice thought,'' Grant replied dryly, straightening. "But we'd see their bodies.''

Kane inhaled a lungful of fetid air, exhaled it, spit and extended his right leg. He stepped over the line of demarcation and stood motionless for a moment. He exchanged a meaningful glance with his companions. "You can wait for me if you want.''

Grant growled deep in his chest and stepped over the line. Brigid followed a heartbeat later. They started walking, their feet stirring up bits of ash and powdery grit. They had walked only a few dozen yards when they came across the prints of many booted feet all of them with a familiar tread pattern. In a flat tone, Kane announced, "I guess we're still on the right track.''

Chapter 20

The nearer they got to the structures, the higher they loomed. They looked more massive than Brigid, Kane or Grant had expected. They were made of blocks of a dark, stained stone that reflected no trace of light. Some of the smaller buildings had eroded so much that they had fallen completely into ruin. Roofless arches reared from the ground, and a few storage buildings were scattered around the outer perimeter of the walls.

A broad blacktop avenue ran toward the main building. The asphalt had a peculiar ripple pattern to it, and weeds sprouted from splits in the surface. All three of them had seen the rippling effect before, out in the hellzones. It was a characteristic result of earthquakes triggered by nuclear-bomb shock waves.

Lampposts lined the road, most of them rusted through and leaning over at forty-five-degree angles. The avenue widened inside the walls, opening into a broad courtyard filled with great blocks of basalt and concrete that had fallen from the buildings. Secondary lanes stretched out in all directions, like the spokes of a wheel. Their eyes followed the spiderweb pattern of streets, and picked out what might have been offices and pedestrian walkways.

All along the streets empty husks of buildings stood like skeletal sentinels. One of the structures had collapsed entirely, folded in on itself like a house of dominos, with the fallen rear wall knocking down all the interior sections one by one.

Only the largest building, the Cube as Kane called it, showed little sign of wear. Its dark facade showed no windows, and when he looked at it he felt an inner cringing and an icy touch of fear. A subliminal aura of evil radiated from the structure.

"This layout is like the campus of a predark university or private institution," Brigid murmured. "Or it's some kind of industrial complex. But that's not likely."

"How come?" Grant asked. "The Western Isles were part of California, so mebbe this chunk held a school."

"Maybe," she admitted, but she didn't sound as if she really considered it possible.

On the far side of one of the secondary roads, they saw a section where the buildings weren't in ruins although ruined areas joined it. Obviously, all of it had once been part of the same complex. The three of them walked without speaking, very conscious of external stimuli—the tramping of their feet, the faint sigh of a damp breeze.

Kane's point man's instinct was conscious of something else. Though he couldn't put a name to it, his sixth sense rang a sudden, insistent alarm. He came to a halt, dropping into a crouch, swinging the bore of his subgun from left to right. He moved his head as a wolf did when catching a far-off sound or a faint scent. "Wait a second," he whispered urgently.

Brigid and Grant halted, eyeing him anxiously. "What?" Grant asked.

A thundering full-auto salvo stitched holes in the wall opposite their position, showering them with rock chips and fragments. Instantly, they took cover behind a low tumble of concrete. Kane peered over the top and glimpsed two black-armored figures brandishing Copperheads duck-walking between a line of ruins.

Grant triggered his Sin Eater in their direction, dousing the walls with a 9 mm barrage that sent them scuttling back. Another volley of autofire blazed from the direction in which they had come, steel-jacketed slugs snapping over their heads like the popping of whips. Weapons stuttered from both sides, short pencils of blasterfire lighting up the gloom of the alleys.

Kane looked toward Grant, who met his gaze expressionlessly. "The sons of bitches are trying to catch us in a cross fire. They'll be able to cut off our retreat," Kane warned.

Grant nodded. "Brigid, get moving. Stay low."

Brigid hesitated, but Kane told her curtly, "Get going. We'll cover you."

Setting herself, Brigid took a couple of deep breaths and sprang away from the rubble. She began a fast, crouching run, paralleling the main avenue, angling toward a split in the walls.

Grant glimpsed three figures fanning out two lanes over, dashing to intercept her. He triggered a long burst from the Sin Eater, red-hot Parabellum rounds chewing up the asphalt around the Magistrates. They scattered, diving out of sight.

Rising to their feet, Grant and Kane sprinted as fast as they could after Brigid. Four Mags moved from either side of the street to cut them off, two to a side, crouching in tight defensive postures. Their blasters began to stutter, and Grant stumbled from a triple-hammer blow against his right hip. The rounds didn't penetrate the tough polycarbonate exoskeleton, but the impacts nearly knocked him off his feet and sent him staggering to one side.

Gritting his teeth against the pain, Grant depressed the Sin Eater's trigger, dousing two of the men with a prolonged figure-eight stitch pattern, toppling both of them under a blazing barrage. He doubted they were dead, but the kinetic shock might have incapacitated them.

They began running again, Grant gasping in pain and exertion. They heard Brigid shout their names, and they swerved in the direction of her voice. Within a few yards, they realized Brigid was shouting an alarm, a warning. They only realized it when three Magistrates materialized out of the shadows of a ruined building and jumped them. The Mags were either low on ammunition or decided to outmuscle their adversaries rather than try to outshoot them. Long combat knives, mates to Kane's and Grant's own, sprouted from their fists.

Grant recognized Ramirez's voice as he snarled in a thin, aspirated voice, "Fuckin' traitors to unity!"

The man was a ville-bred zealot, but he was also a pro. His training was evident in the fast thrust he made toward Grant's face. Grant used the frame of his Sin Eater to parry the thrust with a clashing of steel and a small spurt of sparks. Even as he did so, another Mag slid up behind him and knocked his feet out from under him with a fast leg sweep. He fell heavily onto his back.

Kane slashed with his own knife across a man's neck, intending to open him up. The double-edged point caught and dragged in the Kevlar weave of the armor's bodysuit.

The material didn't part, and the man grappled with him, securing a wrist lock. They strained against each other, faces inches apart. The Mag kicked himself forward, the crown of his head connecting with a teeth-jarring, vision-blurring impact against Kane's chin.

Kane reeled backward, trying to maintain his balance. The third black-armored man surged over the ground in a flying, feet-first arc. His thick-soled boots slammed into Kane's chest, bowling him over.

Despite the armor, the force of the kick vibrated through the bones of his upper body, down to the small of his back. Kane didn't try to resist the shock of impact. He allowed himself to fall, reflexively slapping the ground to absorb the momentum and minimize the chances of having the wind knocked out of him. He continued rolling backward and got to his knees, his knife still in his fist. Flipping it up, he caught it by the blade with accustomed ease, finding the balance. Drawing his arm back, he threw the knife hard.

The blade spun once, then caught the Magistrate in the throat, sliding halfway to the hilt in a narrow exposed area between the high collar of the Kevlar undersheathing and the underjaw lock of his helmet. Shock twisted the man's mouth, and he fell to his knees, clutching convulsively at his throat. He made hoarse gagging noises.

Ramirez tried to stomp Grant's gun hand, but he levered his lower body up, arching his back. The thick treads of both boots pistoned out like horizontal pile drivers, smashing full into Ramirez's face. With a mushy snap of bone and cartilage, Ramirez's body careened backward.

At the same moment, Kane got to his feet and used the butt end of his Copperhead as a bludgeon, whacking a Magistrate across the torso, sending him staggering toward a wide opening between two sections of wall. Both he and Ramirez fled through it.

Grant rushed to his feet, his teeth bared in rage.

Ramirez's companion raised his voice in a shout, and a 3-round burst roared from Grant's blaster. All three bullets found a target. The man's cry of warning ended in a gargled grunt as the 9 mm blockbusters hammered him backward. He fell heavily and made no movement after.

For a second, there was no sound but the rolling echoes of the fusillade. Then, from around the bend in the wall came an outcry of startled voices. The thudding of many pairs of running feet reached them.

"Son of a *bitch!*" Kane snarled, snatching at a fresh clip for his subgun.

A contingent of Magistrates broke around the corner of the wall in a wedge formation. They came in a milling rush, at a dead run, firing as they charged even before they had acquired targets. They spread out across the area, some trying to cut their quarry off from a retreat.

Shots cracked and boomed. A bullet hissed past Grant's ear, and another skidded over his shoulder epaulet. He dived behind a stone support post, half-buried on one side, his finger pressing on the trigger of his Sin Eater. Three bullets took a Mag in the visor, punching him between the eyes.

Kane went to his knees behind the fallen column, and his two autoblasters began to roar in a smoothly synchronized rhythm. A pair of 9 mm slugs hit a Magistrate with a devastating one-two punch, knocking him completely off his feet, his Sin Eater blasting thunderously into the air.

A barrage of bullets spewed from four autoblasters, slamming into the pillar, gouging out fragments, but not penetrating it. Kane and Grant kept their heads down and kept firing. The thunder of the gunfire was deafening, magnified by the walls of the buildings.

A Magistrate raced directly for their position, swinging his stuttering Copperhead in left-to-right arcs, holding down the trigger. Grant shifted the barrel of his Sin Eater and let loose a burst. The black-armored man jerked and doubled over, falling face-down barely four feet from the stone column, rendered unconscious by the shock of the triple shots fired at such close quarters.

A round fired from a Sin Eater took Kane in the left shoulder and knocked him off balance. He fired his Copperhead in return, and two rounds penetrated the visor of the man who had shot him, slapping him off his feet, his limbs twisting and convulsing.

Kane dropped the subgun, feeling the numbness of the bullet's impact spreading from his shoulder into his arm nearly to his elbow. The armor had redistributed the kinetic shock, but some of the impact had leaked through.

He saw Grant, still laying down a left-to-right pattern of fire with his Sin Eater, fastball a metal egg with his left hand. Kane buried his face in his arms, bracing himself for the explosion.

The high-ex compounds detonated in a tremendous cracking blast, a blinding burst of dust and sand erupting from the ground. The sound of the explosion instantly bled into a grinding rumble of a stony mass shifting. The groaning grating sound overlapped the ringing echoes of the detonation, then overwhelmed it.

The grinding noise expanded into a rumbling roar. As Kane and Grant watched, a long section of a wall toppled forward in a crushing cascade of bouncing blocks and spurting dust. All the men were engulfed, buried by the tons of basalt and concrete.

Kane and Grant crawled quickly away, shielding their faces from ricocheting chunks of stone. After the rolling echo of the crash faded, there came a stunned silence, stitched through with a clicking of pebbles and faint moans. Grit-laden dust hung in the air like a blanket over the fallen mass of rock.

Fanning the dust away from his face, Kane asked hoarsely, "Think that did it?"

Grant coughed and wiped away a powdery film from his visor before answering, "I sure as hell hope so. The only way to find out for sure is to dig up these bastards and do a head count."

Kane nodded glumly. "We sure have been forced to kill a lot of Mags lately."

Grant pivoted on his heel and strode away. "Casualties of war."

Kane followed him a few seconds later, not in the least fooled by his friend's callous pronouncement.

Although Kane had come to terms with his exile, with his status as both outlander and traitor, he knew Grant still grappled with guilt. The peeling away of their Mag identities, the loss of their Mag purpose had been a painful process and hard to endure. Grant rarely spoke of it, but the man was always stoic in the face of physical and emotional pain—and he was particularly reticent about revealing his grief over Domi's death. And if he felt remorse over the killing of Magistrates, Kane knew his guilt about Domi was probably all-consuming.

The change in attitude that had come over her before their jump to Area 51 wasn't a positive one. Usually, Domi was forthright, forthcoming and very verbal. Kane had been on a number of missions with her, and she'd earned his trust and respect.

But she had become taciturn, even insulting, particularly toward Grant. The short fuse of her temper seemed to have shrunk to little more than a wick. It took only a tiny spark to light it into an explosion of homicidal anger. Right before he and Domi had jumped from Cerberus, Grant confided in him that he was the reason for Domi's confrontational attitude. For more than a year, she claimed she loved Grant, but he was always reluctant to return that emotion for reasons even he couldn't articulate.

Kane guessed Domi represented a kind of innocence to Grant, and he didn't want to taint it with sex—despite the fact she was no stranger to it before being smuggled into Cobaltville to serve as Guana

Teague's sex slave. He also figured Grant didn't want to do anything that might diminish the memory of Olivia, the only woman who'd ever truly claimed his heart.

So Grant always drew the line at physical intimacy with Domi, sometimes citing the age difference between them as the reason, even though not even Domi knew how old she was. Kane never found that argument defensible. Waiflike in appearance she might be, but Domi had proved time and again she was anything but a child.

She hadn't reacted like a child when she came across Grant and Shizuka, the female samurai, locked in a sweaty embrace. That Grant had even informed him of the incident was a matter of some surprise to Kane. Although they were friends, partners for more than a dozen years, the two men observed an unspoken agreement not to speak of personal matters unless specifically invited. Very rarely had Grant extended a specific invitation. Therefore, when he told Kane about Domi seeing him with Shizuka after the battle with Mags who had abducted the citizens of Port Morninglight, Kane's reaction was to be amused. The amusement didn't last long.

During their penetration of the Dreamland installation, Domi's change in behavior had become actually frightening. What little self-restraint Domi practiced in the past was completely discarded. Without Grant as the mitigating influence, the authority figure, she was unleashing all of her bottled-up passions, turning them from love to violence.

Kane mentally shook himself, trying to drive memories of his last real conversation with Domi from his mind. When they were reunited after being separated in Dreamland, he had been astonished by yet another profound change that had come over her. He consciously decided it was past time to either stop thinking about Domi or talk it all through with Grant and Brigid. When he had initially expressed his inability to accept the girl's death with Brigid, he told her that since Domi's body hadn't been seen, he felt there was a slim possibility she had survived. Brigid's response, which he felt was a trifle insensitive, had been short and to the point: "Is that what it'll take to convince you—a maimed corpse?"

Catching up with Grant, Kane said impatiently, "Let's find Brigid and get the hell out of here."

"We don't know if Ramirez is buried or not," Grant retorted.

"So what? Leave him for the dinosaurs."

Grant thrust out his jaw truculently. "I promised Shizuka we wouldn't leave a single Mag to seed. We can't risk a single one of them escaping and making a report to Baron Snakefish."

"We'll bust up the boat before we leave," Kane argued. "I don't want to hang around here any longer than we have to, just in case there's another pulse of microwave radiation."

Grant opened his mouth to voice an objection. Then, from the direction of the Cube came a flat, hand-clapping report. Both men knew it was made by Brigid's Colt Mustang.

Chapter 21

Kane's heart hammered in his chest, and blood thundered in his ears. He sprinted around and through the maze of collapsed walls, outdistancing Grant as he approached the looming edifice of the Cube. Two more shots split the silence, followed by a voice yelling something indistinct. The voice was undeniably that of a man, and the gunshots were undeniably those from a Sin Eater.

Gritting his teeth, Kane forced more speed into his pumping legs. His mind supplied a variety of frightening scenarios, all of which involved Brigid being either pinned down by vengeful Magistrates or already dead at their hands.

The very concept of her being dead always shook him in a such a profound way. He shied away from examining the feelings, except that he knew on a gut level that he had failed to keep her from being killed before.

From the very first time he met her, he was affected by the energy Brigid radiated, a force intangible yet one that triggered a melancholy longing in his soul. That strange, sad longing only deepened after a bout of jump sickness both of them suffered during a mat-trans jump to Russia. The main symptoms of jump sickness were vivid, almost-real hallucinations.

His own hallucinations seemed and felt like glimpses from past lives. He saw himself, and he saw Baptiste and Grant, and though they didn't look like themselves, he recognized them, knew them.

He and Brigid had shared at least one hallucination, but both knew on a visceral, primal level that it hadn't been gateway-triggered delirium, but a revelation that they were joined by chains of fate, their destinies linked. Images from that vision spun in the depths of his memory. He saw Baptiste, a beautiful captive dragged at the stirrup of a Norman lord's horse. Men in chain-mail armor laughed and jeered above her, and long black tongues of whips licked out with hisses and cracks. Callused hands fondled her breasts, forced themselves between her legs.

Kane saw a man rushing from a hedgerow lining the road. He was thin and hollow cheeked, perhaps nineteen or twenty years old. His gray-blue eyes burned with rage. He knew the youth was himself, and Brigid called out to him, shouting for him to go back.

He knocked men aside to reach her and a spiked mace rose above his head, poised there for a breathless second, then dropped straight down with skull-shattering force.

In all of those fleeting images, he had recognized Grant and Baptiste and all the bodies that had carried their souls throughout the changing ages. Always, in the bloody scenes of strife, their spirits were together, living and battling and dying, being reborn and somehow always finding one another again.

They never spoke of it, though Kane often wondered if that spiritual bond was the primary reason he had sacrificed everything he had attained as a Magistrate to save her from execution. The possibility confused him, made him feel defensive and insecure. That insecurity was one reason he always addressed her as Baptiste, almost never by her first name, so as to maintain a certain formal distance between them. But that distance shrank every day.

Long months before, during an op to the British Isles, when Kane had protested to Morrigan the blind Irish telepath that there was nothing between him and Brigid, the Irish telepath had laughed at him. Brigid was his *anam-chara*, Morrigan had claimed.

In ancient Gaelic, Kane learned, *anam-chara* meant "soul friend."

He wasn't sure what that meant, but he knew he always felt comfortable with Brigid Baptiste, despite their many quarrels. He was at ease with her in a way that was similar yet markedly different than his relationship with Grant. He found her intelligence, her iron resolve, her wellspring of compassion and the way she had always refused to be intimidated by him not just stimulating, but inspiring. She was a

complete person, her heart, mind and spirit balanced
and demanding of respect.

Kane found the thought of losing that person too
horrifying to contemplate, not just because of the
vacuum she would leave in the Cerberus personnel,
but because of the void her absence would leave in
his soul. The memory of the kiss he'd given her
when they'd taken the jump back in time to the eve
of the nukecaust drifted across his mind. It was no
surprise that he should remember the kiss, but the
intensity of emotion associated with it shook him.

He also recalled with startling clarity what the
Sister Fand of the third lost Earth had whispered to
him about Brigid Baptiste: ''The lady is your saving
grace. Trust the bond that belongs between you. The
gift of the *anam-chara* is strong. She protects you
from damnation—she is your credential.''

In the dark hours between midnight and dawn,
Kane had often wondered that if he lost Brigid, lost
his credential, would he become a damned soul,
cruel, merciless, and without any purpose in life,
except to killing?

Kane skirted a great heap of broken stone and
debris, and spied a single doorway in the featureless
face of the Cube. There wasn't a door, only a
twisted, blackened metal frame hanging askew on
sprung hinges.

He gave the big plastic sign bolted to the wall to
the right of the doorway only a single glance as he
kicked the frame out of his way. The words were

still legible despite two centuries of chem storms, fallout and weathering. It bore a familiar warning: Entry To This Facility Strictly Forbidden To All Personnel Below B12 Clearance. Below it he glimpsed an unfamiliar symbol, that of a stylized hourglass.

He entered a large lobby. The floor was thickly layered with concrete dust. The walls were black-speckled marble and showed ugly crisscrossing cracks. A litter of office furniture was half-covered by broken ceiling tiles.

A big reception desk occupied the far wall, and it was nearly buried by plaster and metal electrical conduits. On the left side of the room, a hallway stretched away, lined on both sides with wooden doors. On his right, he saw a glass-and-chrome door, leading to a murky semidarkness. Though the heavy glass panes bore cracks, it was still intact and slightly ajar.

Kane loped to it, shouldering it open, the unlubricated hinges screeching. The echoes of the metal squealing against metal rolled down the broad corridor, and were smothered by the sound of full autofire. Streaks of orange flame stabbed through the gloom.

The stuttering hail of bullets ripped toward him, starting low and going high. Kane felt a numbing blow across his right hip as he threw himself against the wall.

Extending both blasters, Kane pressed the triggers, smearing the shadows with flickering tongues of fire. The Copperhead sprayed a steady stream of bullets with a sound like the prolonged ripping of canvas. Little flares flashed sparks on the sides of the tub as bullets ricocheted from the steel.

Kane knew that sustained bursts of full-auto only wasted ammunition, but his focus was on driving the Magistrate to cover, not scoring lethal hits. Though he emptied both of his weapons, he achieved his objective—the Mag shouted, "Enough! I've had enough!"

Kane recognized Ramirez's voice. "Throw down your blasters," he commanded.

Within a couple of seconds, a holstered Sin Eater and a Copperhead were tossed from around the corner. "Take off your helmet and move out so I can see you," Kane snapped.

Grant came pounding into the building at that point, and Kane spared him only a swift over-the-shoulder glance. The big man was winded and gulped air noisily. He pushed open the door, making sure to stand to one side. "Who've you got?" he managed to ask hoarsely.

"Your old friend from Snakefish," Kane replied. "Ramirez."

"Where's Brigid?"

"That's what I'm about to find out." Kane raised his voice. "Come out, Ramirez."

"No," the man replied. "You'll shoot me in the

head." He didn't sound fearful of the possibility, only annoyed by it.

"You smarmy little son of a bitch," Grant snarled, still breathing heavily. "I'd just as soon chuck a gren at you as talk to you. Now come on out or I'll do it on general principles alone."

Slowly, Ramirez stepped around the corner, his hands linked at the back of his head. He walked toward them carefully with a measured, deliberate tread. "Where's Brigid?" Kane asked.

Although it was hard for the Magistrate to shrug with his elbows crooked and extended he managed a fair approximation. "How I should I know?"

Trying to maintain a grip on his anger, Kane said, "We heard her blaster, then we heard yours. She's in here somewhere."

"Mebbe so," Ramirez grunted in a nasal, snuffling voice. Crimson flowed from his nostrils, coating his lower face. His lower lip was puffy and split. "But I haven't seen her."

When he reached a point of six feet from Kane, Ramirez slowed his pace. "You can stop now," Kane told him.

The Mag kept coming. "Why?"

"Because if you don't, I *will* shoot you in the head."

Ramirez chuckled snidely. "No, you won't. I counted your rounds. You fired both your blasters dry."

As soon as the last word left his lips, Ramirez's

right leg whipped up in a swift, spinning crescent kick. The side of his boot knocked the Copperhead out of Kane's hand, sending it clattering against the far wall. Almost in the same fluid motion, Ramirez brought his arms down from behind his head. A combat knife was in his right hand, and he lunged for Kane's throat.

Kane sidestepped, and before Ramirez could recover his balance, he pivoted, driving his elbow sharply against the man's belly. But Ramirez backstepped, and the blow didn't land effectively.

It was still hard enough to hurt, and Ramirez was taken by surprise. Then, as Kane clubbed at him with his Sin Eater, Ramirez jumped back and completely evaded the blow. Kane moved in cautiously, trying to get the Mag to strike. He wanted to grab the younger man's wrist and wrest the knife away, but Ramirez was wary. He gripped the knife solidly with its double-edged point held upward, ready to slash at the first opportunity.

Grant lifted his Sin Eater and said with weary exasperation. "Let me just shoot him so we can get out of here."

Kane shook his head. "He wants to take at least one of us with him. I'll give him a chance to get the job done."

Ramirez's lips quirked in a smirk. "Thanks."

Kane feinted, but Ramirez didn't rise to the bait. He advanced slowly, his teeth bared. He thrust with the blade toward Kane's shoulder and missed. Instead of dropping back, Kane took a swift sidestep toward the Mag. The motion disconcerted Ramirez, who didn't have the time to get his knife in position for another attack, and he struck out with his free hand. Kane leaned away from the clumsy blow, and in the instant that Ramirez had used to throw a punch, Kane's right hand shot out and closed around his wrist. He pivoted at the same time on the ball of his right foot.

He pulled Ramirez forward, hooking his left arm over the smaller man's shoulder. Keeping his weight on the pivot foot, he extended his left leg between Ramirez's feet. The Mag fell heavily to the floor but held his grip on the combat knife, and Kane maintained a viselike grip on his wrist.

Yanking the knife wrist upward, Kane slammed a knee into his chin, then brought the Mag's elbow across his knee with such force that he screamed with pain. He tried to scramble forward to relieve the pressure on his arm.

Kane twisted his arm, and Ramirez was forced to turn in the same direction or risk having his shoulder dislocated. Kane raised his foot and brought the heavy-treaded boot sole down on his adversary's wrist. He put all his weight into his heel and Ramirez screamed again. His fingers opened around the handle of the knife.

Leaning down, Kane grasped Ramirez by the hair and straightened, jerking the man to his feet. Measuring the man off, he drew back his left arm and threw his fist with every ounce of his weight and strength behind it.

The blow caught Ramirez on the point of his chin with the sharp sound of a whipcrack. The shock of impact jarred along the bone of Kane's wrist and into his shoulder socket.

Ramirez's head snapped up and back. His eyes rolled up, and he lurched backward. He collapsed onto his back like a wet sack of sand. Trying not to let the sharp pain in his knuckles show on his face, Kane kicked the knife aside.

Stepping forward, Grant nudged his unconscious body with a foot and said in disgust, "That's just great. Now we'll have to wait until the little prick wakes up to find Brigid."

"No, you won't." Brigid's voice floated from somewhere above them.

Both men cursed and skipped around, leading with their blasters, their hearts racing. They saw nothing but the interconnecting rectangles of ceiling tiles.

"Sorry," Brigid said, her amused voice wafting from nowhere. Her voice, finely projected, sounded as if she spoke from thin air right beside them.

Eyes darting to and fro, Kane scanned the ceiling and demanded angrily, "Where the hell are you?" Then, as a afterthought he added, "Are you all right?"

"I'm not hurt if that's what you mean. Ramirez chased me a little ways, and we took pot shots at each other. I got away from him and locked him out."

"Locked him out of where?" Grant rasped with a great deal of asperity.

"I'm apparently in a security office. All the vid cameras are functioning and so are the comms. Just keep walking down the hall."

"Why?" Grant snapped. "All the Mags are neutralized, Ramirez is out cold, so there's no reason to stay."

A hard edge was evident in Brigid's retort. "I think there is. Just do as I ask for once."

Kane exchanged a glance with Grant, who glowered at him, then he shrugged and started off down the corridor. He ejected his Sin Eater's spent clip and thumbed in a new one. They passed through a narrow door and went silently along an ill-lit corridor. The dim blue glow of the occasional neon light provided the only illumination.

Kane looked back over his shoulder and saw the moonlight vanish as they rounded a corner. Presently, after many baffling turns, the corridor began to slant downward. At the same time, the hollow echoing voice of Brigid reverberated from in front of them. "Just keep coming."

Within another few yards, the two men reached a heavy metal door without a knob or a latch. Machinery clanked, and with a prolonged hiss of pneumatics the door slid to the right. They entered a room dominated by a huge flat-screen vid monitor.

The screen was divided into twelve square sections, each one showing a different black-and-white view from a variety of perspectives.

Brigid stood beside the wall display, the flickering light casting eerie shadows on the planes of her face. Her brow was furrowed either in consternation or fascination.

Kane looked around and asked wonderingly, "The power is still on in here?"

"More than that," Brigid answered. "I believe this place was occupied until recently."

Kane came to her side. "How recently?"

She smiled enigmatically and pointed to one of the squares that held the image of a wardroom or a galley. "*Very* recently." A plate lay on a nearby table, as well as silverware and a large coffee mug. There appeared to be a partially eaten meal on the plate.

Grant squinted at it and grunted. "Hell, that could have been there for a hundred years…two hundred even."

Brigid arched a sardonic eyebrow in his direction and put her finger above the mug. "And you say *my* eyes are bad?"

Grant and Kane gazed at the screen and discerned a faint cloud of steam rising from the cup. Kane's skin prickled with gooseflesh. "The coffee's still hot. Who was drinking it?"

"Who indeed." Brigid's response was a laconic drawl.

"Where'd they go?" Grant asked.

Brigid shrugged. "They probably hid themselves when they heard the firefight. And there's more—look."

Kane and Grant followed Brigid's pointing finger. The view seemed to be from inside a small chamber. It was circular, perhaps ten feet in diameter, with an eight-foot-high ceiling. The chamber was six sided, all the walls of the same smoke-tinted armaglass. The floor was patterned with interlocking, hexagonal raised metallic disks. The pattern was repeated in the ceiling.

Galvanized, Kane exclaimed, "A jump chamber! We can jump back to Cerberus without having to travel cross-country to the unit in the Sierra Nevadas."

"My thought exactly," Brigid said with satisfaction.

Grant shifted his feet uncomfortably. "You mean now—just jump back to Cerberus without telling anybody?"

Kane eyed him closely. "We can give word to Dubois if he's still around."

Grant didn't seem enamored of the idea, and both Brigid and Kane guessed he wasn't too anxious to leave Shizuka, much less without a goodbye. However, he wasn't about to put those objections into words.

"Let's find it first," Brigid said, indicating a door at the far end of the room. "That may lead to it."

The three people walked to the door, and to their surprise it opened automatically at their approach. As they stepped into a narrow accessway beyond, sensors in the walls reacted to their motion signature and overhead neon strips flashed on, shedding a wavery illumination.

Kane uttered a low whistle of surprise and glanced around apprehensively. "Damn considerate," he murmured.

As they walked down the passageway, they became aware of a low hum of sound ahead of them, almost like the vibrations of a gong that had been struck. Presently, a brighter light glimmered in the murk just beyond a tall arch, and the hum at the edges of their hearing became a continuous whine. The air seemed to shiver with the sound.

The archway led onto a railed catwalk overlooking a vast chamber, shaped like a hollow hexagon, and far larger than looked possible from the outside. A dim glow shone from the high, flat ceiling, two faint columns of light beaming from twin fixtures, both the size of wag tires. Massive wedge-shaped ribs of metal supported the roof.

The shafts of luminescence fell upon a huge forked pylon made of some burnished metal that projected up from a sunken concave area in the center of the chamber. The two horns of the pylon curved up and around, facing each other. Mounted on the tips of each prong were spheres that looked as if they had been sculpted from multifaceted quartz crystals. Skeins of electricity danced with sizzling pops between them.

Kane guessed it was at least twenty feet tall, with ten feet between the forking branches. Extending outward from the base of the pylon at ever decreasing angles into the low shadows was a taut network of fiber-optic filaments. They disappeared into sleeve sockets that perforated the plates of dully gleaming alloy sheathing the floor. Many of them were buckled here and there, bulging but not showing splits.

The catwalk led to a central control complex. Instrument consoles with glass-covered gauges and computer terminals lined the walls. The banks of computers chittered like a flock of startled birds, and drive units hummed purposefully.

The right-hand wall was completely covered by armaglass, running the entire twenty-yard length of the room. On the far side of it they saw the jump chamber.

Electronic equipment and machinery rose from plinths and podia, and none of the three of them had any idea of its function or purpose. Overhead lights gleamed on alloys, glass coverings, the CPUs. Chairs rose from the floor before each console. Kane counted ten chairs.

Covering four walls were crystal-fronted vid screens. Blinding light shone from some of the screens; others showed only whorls of color. As they passed the screens on the way to the gateway unit,

Grant suddenly froze in midstride, and a sound Kane had never heard before issued from between his lips—a gargling cry of commingled wonder and shock.

Both Brigid and Kane followed his transfixed gaze to a monitor screen. Neither of them made a sound when they saw what had frozen Grant into immobility, but only because their vocal cords were paralyzed. Despite the high aerial perspective, they recognized the scene instantly.

They saw the hangar at Area 51, the last, desperate seconds of the battle when Ramirez and his Mags turned on Grant and Brigid. Kane saw himself preparing to throw the implode gren with bullets kicking up sand and concrete all around him.

A stray slug caught him in the arm and despite his armor sent him staggering, the gren falling from his hand and rolling across the concrete toward the elevator cupola.

Domi darted out from the cupola, scooped up the gren in one hand and cocked her arm back to throw it at the vehicle. Grant rushed toward her, and though there was no sound, they saw his mouth working as he bellowed at her to drop the gren.

Then her diminutive form was completely engulfed by a brilliant blaze of white light. Frozen in place, Kane and Grant watched as the tremendous suction created by the implosion yanked their bodies forward in headlong, clumsy somersaults. Then the scene broke up in jagged lines and pixels before re-forming to replay itself again.

Grant was the first to speak, a ragged snarl of anguish. "What the fuck is this? How can this be?"

Kane had no answer, standing in stupefied shock, barely able to breathe, much less speak. He figured Brigid had no response, either, so he could barely restrain his surprise when he heard her blurt, in a half gasp, "Operation Chronos!"

Kane and Grant turned to regard her with wide eyes. They all knew Operation Chronos had been a subdivision of the Totality Concept's Overproject Whisper, as had Project Cerberus. However, unlike Cerberus, they had always assumed nothing re-mained of its researches, either failures or successes. Before they could compose themselves sufficiently to question Brigid, she began speaking with a ma-chine-gun rapidity, her words almost tumbling over one another in their haste to leave her mouth.

"This place must have been a research center, affiliated with the Totality Concept. What we have here is a version—maybe a prototype, maybe a de-bugged one—of the Operation Chronos temporal di-lator!"

She dragged in a shuddery breath, her eyes glint-ing like emeralds. "We know Operation Chronos reached a point where they were able to inject re-mote vid probes into past time lines, and I think this is what we're seeing here—a visual log of the battle at Area 51, the seconds preceding Domi's disappearance.''

It took Kane a moment to comprehend her choice of words. "You said disappearance, not death.''

"What are you trying to say, goddammit?'' Grant growled.

Brigid ran her hands through her mane of hair. "Kane, your instincts were right when they told you Domi wasn't dead. She wasn't killed in the implosion—she was time-trawled!''

Chapter 22

Grant whirled to face Brigid so quickly and violently that she involuntarily flinched from him. "You don't know that!" His voice rose to a snarling pitch of angry pain. "*How* could you know that?"

Kane almost snapped at Grant to back off and calm down, but adrenaline was speeding through his own system, making his stomach muscles cramp and his hands tremble.

Brigid understood the reasons for Grant's agitation and didn't respond in kind. As if she were trying to soothe an upset child, she said, "I admit it's supposition at this point, but it'll be simple enough to test the theory. We know time travel is possible. Remember what Lakesh told us about Operation Chronos and its experiments? He said they forced temporal breaches or dilations in the chronon structure.

"The purpose of Chronos was to find a way to enter probability gaps between one interval of time and another. Inasmuch as Cerberus utilized quantum events to reduce organic and inorganic material to digital information and transmit it through hyperdimensional space, Chronos was built on that same principle to peep into other time lines and even trawl living matter from the past, and perhaps the future. That's obviously what's been going on here…it's the only reasonable explanation for the extinct life-forms and the relics of past ages.''

"Yeah," Grant commented grimly. "I also remember Lakesh saying Operation Chronos had triggered a probability-wave dysfunction when they disrupted the chronon structure. He claimed they created an alternate-future scenario for humanity, and that led up to the nukecaust itself. So mebbe we shouldn't fool around with this stuff."

"I don't think we can make the world any worse than it is," Brigid replied dryly. She studied the machinery and the instrument boards. "Apparently, whoever activated all of this zeroed in on us with vid probes, like we did when we tested the Omega Path program."

"Yeah, but why?" Kane asked. "Who would be observing us?"

"I don't know," she answered stolidly. "I have enough things to speculate about right now." She didn't smile when she said it.

Grant visibly struggled to compose himself, squaring his shoulders and clearing his throat. "So you're saying Domi was snatched—trawled—right at the instant when the gren went off?"

Brigid nodded. "That's what it looks like."

Sweeping a hand toward the repeating sequence of Domi vanishing in the blaze of the gren's detonation, but avoiding looking at it, Grant demanded, "Then where the hell is she?"

Two vertical lines of deep concentration appeared on either side of Brigid's nose. She sat in the nearest chair, running her fingers lightly over the multitude of readout gauges, blinking buttons and keyboards without touching them. In a low, musing voice, as if she were talking to herself, she intoned, "The quantum interphase matter confinement channels are on-line with the chronon wave guide. The wave function and state vectors are all in sync—the coordinates have already been programmed and locked in...it's only waiting the final sequence to initiate retrieval."

"Retrieval?" Kane echoed, his voice harsh with skepticism. "Retrieve her from where? Or rather when—that particular day, that very second?"

Brigid absently combed nervous fingers through her hair. "No. In my estimation, she's already been retrieved but not yet rematerialized. The trawling process hasn't been completed. She's in a state of nonexistence, reduced to her basic energy form, not too different from a gateway's quincunx effect."

Both men had picked up enough techno-vernacular in the past year or so to understand that the quincunx effect referred to a nanosecond of time when lower dimensional space was phased into a higher dimension.

"This all guesswork," Grant declared suspiciously. "You can't change the past by pushing a few buttons."

She swiveled in the chair to stare directly into his face. "What's the nature of time anyway, Grant?" she challenged. "Can you describe it to me when the most advanced physicists of the predark world barely understood it? Before the nukecaust, modern science was just beginning to perceive that subatomic particles and quantum events made no distinction between space and time.

"The laws of physics are fixed only by our perception. According to Lakesh, that was the major problem both Project Cerberus and Operation Chronos personnel constantly grappled with. Another was computing the precise temporal transfer points. Cerberus moved things from place to place. Chronos had to deal with moving things from place to place and time to time.

"In certain circumstances, photons—the particles of which light is made—could apparently jump between two points separated by a barrier in what appears to be zero time. The process, known as tunneling, was even used to make some of the most sensitive electron microscopes.

"If the very existence of time depends on the presence of space, then time is only a variable, not an absolute. Therefore, you can have more than one event horizon, which means you can have more than one outcome from an event—"

Kane lifted a hand to stem a further floodtide of

scientific principle. "Nobody's arguing with you on this point. You're way smarter than we are, all right? We settled that a long time ago. But there are still a couple of areas we need to explore."

"Like what?" Brigid wanted to know.

Uneasily, Kane glanced from the control panels to the pylon to the vid screens. "First of all is the microwave pulse. It's obvious whenever this temporal dilator thing is turned on it sends out the burst."

Brigid nodded toward the armaglass barrier. "We should be safe from it behind the shielding. You know enough of the properties of armaglass to know that it goes opaque when exposed to certain levels and wavelengths of radiation. That's one of the reasons it's used in the mat-trans gateways, to block energy overspills."

"Fine," Kane retorted brusquely. "One area dealt with. That leaves us with the second—who the hell set up all of this for us? How do we know this isn't bait to trick us into pushing a button and blowing us and maybe this whole region of the Cific to atoms?"

"Who would do that?" Grant demanded.

Kane shrugged. "I can think of a couple of past sparring partners who might have the know-how, but they're dead—I hope. But you can't deny this entire arrangement is just a little too convenient for us to accept at face value."

"Whoever set this up offered us two choices,"

Brigid declared tersely. "We do nothing and Domi is lost to us forever. Or we can engage the final sequence, and at least initiate a chance to have her returned. I personally think that's worth taking the risk of blowing ourselves up...but then that's me."

She waited for Grant and Kane to respond. The uncomfortable silence seemed to stretch on for hours. Then Grant bit out, "That's me, too. Do it."

Kane didn't realize he hadn't been breathing until Grant spoke, and he released his pent-up breath in a relieved sigh. "Me, too. Do it, Baptiste."

Brigid turned her chair to the console, and her fingers flew over the keyboard like a concert pianist's. She hit a final button with a dramatic flourish. "Now we'll see what—"

The throbbing vibration that had been at the edges of their hearing and awareness since they entered the huge chamber abruptly climbed in scale and pitch, becoming almost painful. Sparks that were more energy than light flashed through the facets of the prisms, sizzling fingers of it darting from one sphere to the other and back again.

The crackling display of electricity between the forks of the pylon increased until a virtual ribbon of blue current seemed to stretch from one to the other.

The air between the prongs began to waver with a blurry shimmer like heat waves rising off sun-baked asphalt. For an instant, they glimpsed a swirling movement in the air such as the ripples made in water when a fish swam close to the surface. Tiny glittering specks, like motes of diamond dust, appeared within the area of distortion. They spun, then whirled faster and faster, turning into a funnel cloud, like a tornado made of gold-and-silver confetti.

A powerful wind built. A bone-jarring crack of thunder compressed their eardrums. The funnel cloud peeled back on itself as vivid bursts of color poured out from within it. A shape began to materialize, sliding into sharp focus.

All of their ears were struck by a continuous blast of sound, as if a thunderstorm of unparalleled fury were breaking loose inside the building. A deafening, concussive blast cannonaded from the pylon, then a consecutive series of brutal, overlapping shock waves crashed into the armaglass barrier. They could feel the pounding, like invisible breakers crashing into a seawall.

Waves of dazzling white flame and variegated lightnings streaked and blazed. The entire control complex vibrated like a heavy surf, pounding relentlessly against their eardrums and bones. From the curving prongs spit sharp bolts of lightning, which whipped and hissed along the network of wires like serpents made of blue plasma.

Their surroundings became like the negative of a pix, white on black with all the colors bleached out. Crooked fingers of energy continued to stab between the prongs, forming a cat's cradle of red lightnings. They watched with awe and dread as thousands of crackling threads of light coalesced in the center of the forks.

Gushing lines of energy formed a luminous cloud between the prongs, and almost faster than the eye could perceive, the cloud grew more dense and definite of outline. The shimmer built to a blinding borealis.

Then a star seemed to go nova, bringing a millisecond of eye-searing brilliance. The funnel cloud burst apart in fragments, as if a giant mirror shattered, and the shards flew out in all directions.

Amid the flying, glittering splinters, a small body plummeted out of the heart of darkness and fell heavily to the platform. The body wore a black, bulky combat vest, which contrasted sharply with her porcelain-hued skin and bone-white hair.

The three of them watched in shocked silence as Domi pushed herself to all fours on trembling arms and vomited.

Chapter 23

Brigid reached Domi first, sliding down a metal ladder that extended from the catwalk to the floor below. From the prongs of the pylon came a throbbing, insistent vibration. The very air was like a heavy surf, pounding relentlessly against eardrums and bones.

She knelt beside Domi as the girl continued to spew until her stomach was empty. All around, the whine of machinery climbed up out of the audible range, straining to hit an ultrasonic note. Brigid had no idea what was happening, but she knew it wasn't right. She felt the feathery touch of energy as if she were breasting invisible waves of static electricity.

The bright flares of plasma continued to leap and carom from the pair of crystal prisms on the pylon's prongs. Little flames, gold and orange and greenish blue, created a shimmering nimbus all up and down their lengths.

Domi dragged the back of her hand over her mouth and looked around, dazed and uncomprehending. In a querulous, little-girl voice she asked, "We take out Mags? We get 'em?"

Kane went to her side and pulled her to her feet.

His vision swam and blurred with tears. Domi tottered dizzily, sagging into his arms. His relief was so overwhelming he couldn't speak, but he doubted Domi could hear him over the shuddering vibrations anyway. Casting a glance over his shoulder, he saw Grant standing by the foot of the ladder, as motionless as a statue.

The quartz spheres continued to crackle and spark, spitting arcs of energy in random corkscrewing patterns. One passed by Brigid's cheek, fanning it with a hot, tingling shock. The spiral sprang up to caress the armaglass barrier, leaving a smoldering scorch mark.

Turning to Kane, she shouted, "This thing isn't down-cycling! It's running out of control—we need to get out of here before it releases another radiation pulse!"

The floor suddenly heaved beneath their feet, the metal plates squealing, rivets popping loose with the sound of gunshots. Kane, Brigid and Domi reeled. The outlander girl would have fallen, but Grant reached her with one long-legged bound. In one motion, he hoisted her into his arms like a child and started climbing back up the ladder, pulling himself and her along by one arm.

Light lanced from the prongs of the pylon, two coruscating fountains of fiery sparks that shed glowing droplets of molten silver. Brigid and Kane recoiled, shielding their faces. The smell of hot metal and ozone filled their nostrils.

"What the fuck is going on?" Kane bellowed.

"Some kind of feedback pulse!" Brigid's voice was shrill and frightened. "Like another energy signature intercepted and interfered with the output here."

They scaled the ladder quickly as fire filled the chamber below them, a solid wall of blue flame that became a pure white light so bright they couldn't even look at it directly. When they reached the catwalk, they dashed for the mat-trans unit. Grant was already halfway there, Domi limp in his arms, her head wobbling in rhythm to his footfalls. As they passed the control consoles, they saw the needles on the power gauges flicking back and forth like metronomes setting crazed rhythms. The indicator lights flashed erratically. Switching stations clicked. A console squirted a shower of sparks that smelled like scorched roses.

They piled into the jump chamber. Brigid paused by the keypad control to tap in the destination-lock code to the Cerberus unit. Pulling the metal handle affixed to the center of the armaglass door, Kane sealed the chamber. The sec lock clicked and the automatic transit process began. All of them understood, in theory, that the mat-trans units required a dizzying number of maddeningly intricate electronic procedures, all occurring within milliseconds of one another, to minimize the margins for error. The actual conversion process was automated for this reason, sequenced by an array of computers and microprocessors. Though they accepted at face value that the machines worked, it still seemed like magic to Brigid, Kane and Grant.

The disks above and below them exuded a silvery glow and wraiths of white mist formed on the ceiling and floor. Tiny static discharges, like miniature lightning bolts, flared in the vapor. As if from a great distance came a whine, which quickly grew in pitch to a drone, then to a howl like a gale-force wind.

Behind the armaglass walls, bursts of color flared and flashed. The characteristic hurricane howl of the gateway cycling through a dematerialization was drowned out by the hammering.

Then a force struck all four people with a tremendous impact, knocking them into oblivion.

THE UNIVERSE EXPLODED in a blaze of unidentifiable colors and images. Kane had the sensation of falling forever into a bottomless abyss. A nightmare vision of distorted space, of tangled geometrical shapes so crazed and complex, it was impossible for his mind to absorb them.

A never-ending stream of brilliant spheres passed by him. He retained a measure of consciousness, and for some reason he knew each sphere was a separate universe, a separate reality. Universes upon universes, realities upon realities, bobbing in the cosmic quantum stream like bubbles. He hurtled between them, following a complicated, twisting course, yet at the same time it seemed as if he were flying in a straight line.

He had felt frightened and trapped before, but never had he felt so crushed and helpless and impotent as now, and his mind recoiled from the effort to comprehend this welter of insanity, this streaming rush of extradimensional space. He knew he was hurtling headlong into a cluster of madness. One of the bright spheres loomed up ahead of him, and he tried to swerve away from it, around it—

Then only darkness surrounded him, the utter blackness of complete nothingness, of the empty spaces between the stars. The void boiled in his mind like a caldron of pitch the size of the universe itself. Then, small slits of light appeared, gray and distant. He became aware of his body again.

Kane opened his eyes, and the first thing he saw was the sun moving across a cloudless sky of purest, cleanest azure. It seemed to hover, then cross the sky in fits and starts. Pain came next and then smell, a stink of burned grease, of scorched oil clogging his nostrils and coating his tongue.

He felt a pounding as of rock hammers against the sides of his head. His awareness slowly returned, in bits and pieces and in no particular order. He heard a strange bass hum, as of a musical note refusing to fade. He tasted blood mixed in with the chemical stink and realized it slid from his nostrils.

The numbness in his limbs receded, and Kane felt a deep boring pain in the middle of his back and the center of his chest. With aching muscles, he heaved himself up on his elbows. Uncomprehending, he stared at the film of oil ashes covering his armor. His stomach heaved and twisted as he bit back a groan of pain.

That groan was echoed from his left, and he hitched around, though it made his head spin. His sight was impaired due to the black smears on his helmet's visor, but he saw Brigid, Grant and Domi lying sprawled on what appeared to be interconnecting flagstones. All of them looked as if they had been cleaning chimneys with their bodies. A layer of soot and ashes covered them from head to toe.

Kane turned over, lurching to his hands and knees. He stayed where he was, panting for breath. With effort, he undid the underjaw locking guard of his helmet and tugged it off over his head. He looked around, his vision still blurred. He realized he and his friends lay on the brow of a grassy hill overlooking a thickly wooded valley roughly a mile across. A river flowed through it, the foaming blue waters cascading down a gentle fall to the west. The area didn't look familiar, certainly not like the Bitterroot Range where the Cerberus redoubt was hidden. With a surge of unreasoning panic, he suddenly realized they weren't even in a gateway chamber, much less in the redoubt.

He turned his head slightly to see more of his surroundings. Then he froze, at first squinting, then staring with ever widening eyes at the vast, pyramidal structure shouldering the blue sky.

It was composed of countless fitted blocks of
stone, the top perfectly flat. Bright sunlight played
along the white facade of the monstrous monolith.
At its base, he saw tiny dark moving specks and a
couple of larger moving specks. He finally identified
them as men and vehicles.

Kane tried to estimate the pyramid's size by using
the men and vehicles as reference points. He could
only hazard a feeble guess—a fifty-story building
rising angularly from a twelve-acre base was the
best he could come up with.

He realized the pyramid was of such staggering
proportions as to make its true distance from him
difficult to gauge. He also realized he was so stupefied by what his eyes were seeing that he was in
a mild state of shock.

Kane had never really devoted too much thought
to how ancient peoples had constructed massive
megalithic structures. Even the mind-staggeringly
huge step pyramid he and his friends had seen on
Mars several months ago failed to rouse his curiosity.

But now he gaped openmouthed at the most enormous and finely engineered Terran structure he had
ever seen. It was almost too awesome to comprehend, and Kane had to consciously resist the impulse
to slap himself. As it was, he stared so long and so
hard without blinking in the blaze of sunlight, that

his eyes began to sting and water. He figured he and his friends were at least a quarter of a mile from the pyramid's base, yet the immensity of it completely filled his field of vision.

Slowly, painfully, he got to his feet, wavering like a reed in a stiff breeze. He took a tottering step, then another one, and his legs buckled. He sat down hard on Grant's midriff. With a wheezing curse, Grant jackknifed at the waist, causing Kane to fall over onto his right side. "Goddammit, get off me."

Kane gasped out an apology and tried to get to his hands and knees again. His brain felt as if it were turning pirouettes inside his skull. Domi and Brigid stirred slowly, lifting their heads, frowning at, then brushing at the layer of soot on their limbs. Domi looked like a negative image of herself, coated black from head to toe. Kane saw and smelled how the ends of both women's hair were slightly charred.

He scooted around to help Brigid sit up, and he nearly collapsed atop her. She pushed him away, looking into his face, then over at Domi and Grant. "Tar babies all. Bre'r Rabbit would flee from us screaming," she murmured.

Kane had no idea what she was talking about. He relegated her cryptic remark to post-jump delirium and didn't ask for clarification.

Domi blinked repeatedly, wrinkling her nose at the oil smell and the stink of burned hair. She turned her head toward Grant as he struggled to attain a sitting position.

"Did the gren do this to us?" she asked in bewilderment.

Grant fumbled with the lock on his helmet and finally managed to pull it off. The top half of his face was its normal deep brown complexion, while the lower part was as jet-black as his mustache. Domi stared at him, then giggled.

He glared at her. "What's so damn funny?"

She didn't answer and when Grant got a good look at Kane he figured out the source of her mirth. Domi stared around, muttering, "This doesn't look like Nevada to me—" She stopped giggling abruptly as if a volume knob had been turned to the Off position.

Brigid and Grant followed her gaze and shared similar reactions of stupefied silence when they saw the pyramid. In a hushed tone, Kane asked, "What is that? *Where* is that?"

Brigid tried to reply twice before whispering hoarsely, "I don't know. I've never seen anything like it."

Slowly, as if he were ninety years old, Kane climbed to his feet again. He stood swaying, his stomach lurching. When he was sure he wasn't going to be sick, he demanded, "What the hell happened to us? Why aren't we in a jump chamber?"

"That's what I want to know," Domi declared in her characteristic childlike piping voice. "First we were in that Dreamland place, then there was an explosion. Next thing I remember, I'm puking my guts out and then we're here.''

Brigid regarded her with a long, appraising stare. "You don't remember anything else?''

Domi narrowed her eyes. "What else is there to remember?''

"Nothing,'' Grant interposed, staggering to his feet. He gave both Brigid and Kane a meaningful stare as he said deliberately, "Nothing at all.''

He extended his hand to Domi, who after hesitating a couple of seconds, took it and allowed Grant to pull her effortlessly to her feet. "Are you all right?'' he asked, his voice a soft rumble. He didn't release her hand.

"Why shouldn't I be?'' Troubled, she glanced from his face to that of Brigid and Kane. "Why is everybody treating me like a jolt-brain? You act like you didn't expect to see me again.''

"No, that's not it,'' Grant said diffidently, letting go of her hand. He began to turn away again, then turned quickly, catching the girl's slim form in a crushing embrace. He pressed his cheek against the top of Domi's head. Squeezing his eyes shut, he whispered fiercely, "Thank God. Thank God.''

For a moment, a confused Domi tried to wriggle free, then slowly she put her arms around his waist. In ville society, with conditioning to place the wants of the many above the needs of the few, love among humans was the hardest bond to break. People were conditioned to believe that since all humans were intrinsically evil, to love each other was evil.

That was certainly one reason why Grant had been so reluctant to involve himself with Domi, but the actual, far deeper motivation was fear. He couldn't look at Domi's white skin and crimson eyes without the image of Olivia's café-au-lait face, deep brown eyes and black hair superimposing itself over the girl's features.

There had been women since Olivia, but no real passion and certainly no love. As a Magistrate, whenever he felt the need for sexual release, all he had to do was make a trans-comm call and a woman would be sent up to him. In the years since he had lost Olivia, he never spoke of her and did his best not to think of her. He had deliberately frozen the softer emotions within him.

Domi was a painful reminder of those emotions, although she was as different from Olivia physically and temperamentally as it was possible for a woman to be. An uninhibited, loving animal with no shame about her desires, Domi still resisted invitations from the other men in the redoubt. She wanted only him. And now Grant was beginning to come to terms with the fact he not only wanted her, but also he needed her.

Tears spilled from Brigid's eyes and cut twin runnels in the black film on her cheeks. She averted her gaze from Kane, who still offered her a hand. He pulled her up and they stumbled, holding on to each other to keep from falling down the hill.

"How did we end up here?" he asked. "Wherever here is?"

She shook her head, little flakes of ash flying from tresses and irritating Kane's eyes. "I can't even hazard the most extreme guess, Kane."

"Freeze!"

The shout, coming from behind them, caused Kane to heel around so quickly he felt twinges of pain in his neck tendons. His head reeled with vertigo, and caused amoebae-shaped floaters to swim over his eyes, so when he saw who had shouted, he wondered for a moment if he were hallucinating.

A squad of four men came up the crest of the hill, all of them identically clad in trim black uniforms made of a satiny material. They wore high black boots, ebony leggings and tailored tunics. Emblazoned on the left sleeve there was a familiar symbol—a red thick-walled pyramid enclosing and partially bisected by three elongated but reversed triangles. Small disks topped each one, lending them a resemblance to round-hilted daggers. All four of the Cerberus exiles recognized the patch as the unifying insignia of the Archon Directorate.

Kane's belly fluttered in a cold anger, but not really surprise.

He knew the symbol was supposed to represent some kind of pseudomystical triad functioning within a greater, all-embracing body. To him, all it represented was the co-opting and deliberately planned extinction of the human race.

The four men fanned out around the top of the hill and surrounded them. Two of the men looked Asian. The other pair were Occidental, but all four wielded slender SIG-AMT autorifles with a great deal of skill. Kane noticed how they instinctively kept out of the way of one another's blasters. None of them had any particular expression on their faces, not even curiosity, at the four people coated with soot as black as their uniforms.

One of the men, a man with a brown crew cut, said, "Disarm."

Kane and Grant didn't move, both of them weighing the odds. As if reading their thoughts, the two Asians shifted the barrels of their weapons to Domi and Brigid. Grimacing, Kane unbuckled his Sin Eater and dropped it at his feet. A heartbeat later, Grant followed suit.

"Now that we've been so cooperative," Kane said pleasantly, "can you tell us where we are?"

"Just stand there." The crew-cut man's tone was neutral, but he bit out the words as if he begrudged Kane every syllable.

The rising and falling drone of an engine, overlaid by a mechanical clank and clatter, reached their ears. Kane turned slowly, pausing in case one of the armed men objected. When they didn't, his friends did the same, gazing down the slope in the direction of the sound.

Shading his hands with his eyes, Kane saw a cloud of dust approaching the hill from the western corner of the pyramid.

"Here comes somebody who might be inclined to answer our questions," Brigid murmured.

"That's a Sandcat," Domi declared confidently.

Kane, Brigid and Grant squinted at the distant boxlike shape kicking up a plume of dust, but they couldn't pick out details. However, they knew the outlander girl's eyesight was acute to the point of being uncanny.

Within half a minute, the vehicle drew closer, and with a rising sense of anxiety and surprise, they saw Domi's identification was correct. The wag was a Sandcat, an all-terrain wag used primarily by the Magistrate Divisions of the villes.

The Sandcat slowly crawled up the face of the hill, the clank and clatter of its metal treads sounding strangely subdued, as did the growl of the 750-horsepower engine. Its gray armored hull plowed through the rippling grass like the blunt prow of a ship.

Like most everything in use by the baronies, the Sandcat was based on an existing predark framework. Designed as a Fast Attack Vehicle for a ground war that was never fought, the Sandcat's low-slung, blocky chassis was supported by a pair of flat, retractable tracks.

The gun turret, concealed within an armored bubble topside, held a pair of USMG-73 heavy machine guns. The hull's armor was composed of a ceramic-armaglass bond, which served as protection from not only projectiles, but went opaque when exposed to energy-based weapons, such as particle-beam emitters.

The vehicle topped the crest of the hill, and everyone moved back out of its way. Although he looked, Kane couldn't see who was driving it through the ob port. The Sandcat came to a clattering halt, and the engine was keyed off. The gull-wing doors on either side opened, and three figures climbed out onto the hilltop, but the four captives had eyes only for the man sliding from the pilot's seat.

A middle-aged man with tousled gray hair and an olive complexion tugged at the hem of his shiny black tunic and swept them with a jittery smile. In Lakesh's voice, he said, "Welcome to China, children."

Chapter 24

In the weeks since the disappearance of Kane and Domi and the many days that had passed since Grant and Brigid Baptiste left the Cerberus installation in search of them, Lakesh found to his consternation that he experienced a great deal of difficulty adjusting to the absence of the four people. Despite the fact Cerberus had functioned longer without them than with them, they had become the focal points around which all the events seemed to revolve. Of course, he reminded himself, the redoubt hadn't functioned as much more than a hideout, a bolt-hole for the various exiles from the baronies.

Only with the arrival of Kane, Grant, Brigid and Domi had the Cerberus resistance movement initiated action of any sort. The people Lakesh had recruited to staff Cerberus were primarily academics, tech heads, specialists in a variety of fields. Farrell, like Cotta and Bry, received training in cybernetics, and Wegmann was an engineer. All of them had led structured, sheltered lives in their respective villes. Until their arrival, the Cerberus resistance movement had consisted of little more than intelligence gathering.

Kane and Grant acted on that intel, performing as the enforcement arm of Cerberus. In that capacity, they had not only scored a number of victories against the barons, but also contended with other threats. There had been casualties since their recruitment—Adrian and Davis in Mongolia, Cotta in the Antarctic and Beth-Li Rouch right within the vanadium walls of the installation itself. All the deaths were unexpected, all sad, even Beth-Li's.

The prospect that Kane and Domi might be added to the casualty list was more than sad; it would be devastating. Lakesh had been too frightened by the possibility even to feel sad about it. If they were killed, if Grant and Brigid perished in the attempt to discover the fates of Kane and Domi, the work of Cerberus would end. He knew he wouldn't have the heart to recruit more people to compose—as Kane wryly put it—the enforcement arm of the operation. And even if he had the heart, his access to qualified people was exceptionally limited now that he was an exile himself.

So when Lakesh saw Brigid, Domi, Grant and Kane all bizarrely blackened but apparently whole and substantially uninjured, his knees went momentarily weak with relief. Only when he saw the surprise and suspicion gleaming in the four people's eyes did he realize he wasn't the doddering, wizened pedant they knew as Lakesh.

"It is me," he said reassuringly. "It truly is. I've

had something of a—'' he groped for the proper term ''—makeover.''

Brigid and Kane had seen a younger version of Lakesh during their journey back to an alternate time line. Brigid had also seen pix of Lakesh when he was younger, so they at least saw the resemblance.

Brigid found her tongue first. ''I'd say it was more of a miracle than a makeover.''

Sam stepped forward, smiling his disarming cherubic smile. ''Not really. I merely reversed the deterioration in his cellular structure and increased his body's production of two antioxidant enzymes, catalase and superoxide dismutase. I also boosted up his alkyglycerol level to the point where I reversed the aging process.''

''So that's not a miracle?'' Kane asked, angling an eyebrow at the boy.

''Not if you know how to do it.'' Sam's smile broadened. ''My name is Sam. I brought you four here. I'm sorry, but it looks like the transit was a rough one.''

''*You* brought us here?'' Grant rumbled. ''How?''

''I opened up a localized wormhole,'' he replied blithely. ''Unfortunately, I didn't foresee interference from a secondary energy pattern. I'm afraid the electromagnetic discharge of the two patterns meeting and merging left all of you rather the worse for wear.''

Erica moved closer, hands on her flaring hips. She eyed them all boldly, but the gaze she flicked toward

Kane and Grant was frankly carnal. Kane met her stare. "And you are?"

"Erica is my name. I'm an old acquaintance of Mohandas, and Sam's mother."

Kane nodded as if he had expected her to say something along those lines. Striving for a tone of nonchalance, he said, "I'm just guessing here, mind you, but I'll bet Sam has a nickname. The imperator, right?"

Lakesh's eyebrows crawled toward his hairline in astonishment. "How could you have possibly known that?"

"I get around." He jerked his head toward Brigid, Domi and Grant. "We all do. My question for you, 'Mohandas,' is this—what the hell are you doing here?"

Sam piped up, "He is helping me, like I hope you four will help me."

"Help you to do what?" Brigid asked.

Sam smiled almost shyly and when he spoke again, his voice was different. Lakesh realized he was manipulating the timbre and pitch so the vibrations would resonant sympathetically to the inner ear and stimulate the neuroenergy system.

"To institute a new form of unification," he said in a voice so low and smooth it was almost a croon. "Reunification, actually. Not just to the villes, but to the world. It is a task that I was created to undertake and fulfill. As the hybrids were envisioned as the bridge between the old and new human, I symbolize what lies on the other side.''

Grant folded his arms over his sooty chest. ''From what we've been told, there may be some barons who aren't interested in what lies on the other side.''

Sam acknowledged the comment with a short nod. ''Reunification cannot succeed with dissension, no independent or individual agendas. This is a matter of survival and we're all in it together—humans, hybrids, barons and outlanders alike.''

Kane looked Lakesh up and down. ''And that's the uniform of reunification, right? It didn't take much to swing you to his side, did it?''

Lakesh ran a hand through his thick hair. ''It seemed the least I could do.''

''And what is the least you can do?'' Sam asked. ''Will you join our cause, apply your resources and gifts to reunifying the planet.''

''For the sake of argument, what if we decline?'' Grant asked gruffly.

Sam sighed sadly. ''For the sake of argument, I fear I cannot allow X factors such as yourselves to run free, unfettered. You would cause too much chaos.''

''Is that a threat?'' Brigid asked.

Sam shook his head. ''Not at all. It would be a grave regret.''

Lakesh didn't like the direction the conversation was going. He stepped between Sam and Brigid, lifting conciliatory hands. ''This is not the best time or place to discuss this. My friends are tired and, as you can see, in dire need of refreshing themselves. Let's go back to the pyramid and give ourselves time to think everything through.''

Kane narrowed his eyes, staring first at Lakesh, then at the pyramid. "What's in that place anyway?"

"More than you can imagine," Erica said stiffly. "It's the Heart of the Earth."

"It has every creature comfort…even a gateway unit," Lakesh interjected inanely.

He said it so casually, Kane knew he was making a point.

Sam waved to the Sandcat. "Please get aboard."

Kane, Domi, Brigid and Grant didn't move. Sam snapped his fingers toward a black-uniformed soldier. "I think they need a little persuasion."

The crew-cut man came up behind Brigid and gave her a shove with the frame of his blaster. Raising her boot, Brigid stamped down hard on the soldier's instep, raking the edge of the heel down his shin. It was a move she'd learned from Grant and Kane in Cerberus redoubt.

The man yelped in pained surprise. He was still yelping when Kane chopped him across the throat with the edge of his right hand. Sam squalled in shock and rushed out of the way of the combat. Erica swept him up in her arms.

Lakesh drove his knee into an Asian soldier's midriff. The breath left him in a whoosh, and the man doubled up. Lakesh kneed him in the forehead as hard as he could, knocking the man over on his side. Grant and Domi snatched the two remaining men by the collars of their tunics and slammed their faces into each other.

Grant and Kane snatched up their Sin Eaters. Without hesitation, the five people raced toward the Sandcat and flung themselves into it. Kane took the pilot's seat with Grant beside him. Domi climbed up into the caged gunner's saddle, bracing herself on the footrests.

Kane keyed the vehicle's 750-horsepower engine to rumbling life. At the same instant, he heard the bark of a blaster and a bullet passed uncomfortably close to the open ob port. He glanced back toward the soldiers and saw one of them with his SIG-AMT to his shoulder.

Kane looked to his right and saw the soldiers running toward the vehicle, unlimbering their rifles as they ran. Sam shouted at them, but they couldn't hear what he said. Regardless, he sounded very angry.

"To hell with the imperator," Kane grunted as he engaged first gear and tramped the accelerator to the floor.

The big wag shot away at a surprisingly high rate of speed, taking Kane completely by surprise as it hurtled over the uneven ground. He wrestled with the wheel as he looked for something like a road, but the whine of bullets passing close kept his foot pressing the pedal to the floor.

He found the rutted trail and gunned the cumbersome wag along it. A quick glance to the rear revealed that their pursuit was confused and already outdistanced.

Turning in his chair, he shouted to Lakesh, "You say there's a jump chamber in the pyramid?"

Lakesh leaned close. "Yes. I know how to reach it...but first we have to reach the pyramid."

"How did you get here in the first place?" Brigid said.

He smiled ruefully. "It's a long story, dearest Brigid. Probably as long as yours. But I'm so happy to see all of you I'm not too interested in the whys and wherefores at the moment."

The Sandcat roared down the hill. A checkpoint was coming up with a sentry hurrying out of the gatehouse. He just had time to wave frantically as the wag raced through the opening. Kane caught a glimpse of the sentry's startled face. He changed gears, pressing the vehicle over the rough track as fast as he dared.

He heard a chuckle beside him. Grant leaned out the window, staring behind them. "Something tickling you?" Kane asked.

Grant withdrew his head. "Actually, no. But I figure I'd better laugh or I'll do something else that will either embarrass me...or someone else."

The wag reached a cobblestoned road and Kane

turned onto it—just as they heard the droning chop
of a helicopter. A Deathbird flew the length of the
road. "Ah, shit!" he snarled. "That kid's got Birds,
too?"

"I fear so," Lakesh said dolefully. "He has a lot
of everything."

Painted a matte, nonreflective black, the helicopter's sleek, streamlined contours were interrupted by
only the two ventral stub wings. Each wing carried
a pod of sixteen 57 mm missiles. Both T700-701
turboshaft engines were equipped with noise baffles
so only the sound of the steel vanes slicing through
the air was audible.

Although it wasn't common knowledge except
among the handful of techs and mechanics, the
Deathbirds were very old, dating back to the days
right before skydark. They were modified AH-64
Apache attack gunships, and most of the ones in the
fleet had been reengineered and retrofitted dozens of
times.

The maximum speed of a Deathbird was 186
miles per hour, and its internal fuel range was three
hundred miles, so there was no chance of either out-
running or outdistancing it, even if they decided to
forego the gateway unit and cut across China. The
foreport of the black chopper was tinted a smoky
hue, so the pilot and the gunner were nearly invisible.

The jackhammering roar of the M-230 A-1 chain
gun in the chin turret sounded like stuttering thun-

derclaps. The hailstorm of slugs chewed up the grass to their left.

"Warning shots," Brigid stated.

"Or they're lousy marksmen," Grant grated. "I'm betting they're warning shots."

The Bird climbed and banked, turning in a tight circle so that it was overhead and a little behind them. It hurtled past, the downdraft blasting up clouds of grit and dust, which blew through the ob ports. Kane heard a short triburst from the turret MG as Domi fired after the aircraft.

Kane glanced at the speedometer. They were racing at more than seventy miles per hour. The big wag straddled the narrow road, bouncing violently as the tires struck ruts and potholes. At one point, the rear end fishtailed alarmingly as Kane took a curve.

The Deathbird was behind them again. Domi fired again to no effect. "No real chance of bringing the bloody thing down, I guess," Lakesh grunted angrily.

"You never know," Domi called down from the saddle. "Been in this situation before. Turned out all right." Under stress her abbreviated mode of outlander speech became more pronounced.

The chopper made another pass as they were on a straight stretch of road. For what seemed like an age, the aircraft was overhead and flying alongside. Kane glimpsed the muzzle-flash of the chain gun and heard bullets ricochet from the armored hull.

Then the Deathbird was hanging ahead of them and Domi fired a final, impotent burst at it. As the vehicle roared underneath it, the chain gun stuttered and a bullet came through the ob port, tearing through the floorboards close by Kane's right foot.

Kane tightened his hands on the wheel. If the chase kept up, the chopper would sooner or later disable the Sandcat. The pilot timed his passes to the straight stretches of road, flying slowly at treetop height and firing short bursts with each pass.

Kane changed tactics and slowed down as soon as the Bird came close. It swept by swiftly but another round tore through an ob port and buried itself in the upholstery. He heard the vanes whipping the air, but fortunately, the road cutting through the tree line was too narrow to allow the aircraft to descend to a lower altitude. The pyramid was tantalizingly, mockingly close now.

Flickering spear points of yellow flame danced briefly just beneath the chopper's nose. There came a rattling roar, and .50-caliber bullets knocked up great gouts of road behind the Sandcat. Kane jerked the wheel and swerved in a left-to-right zigzag.

Bullets slammed into the rear end as he steered the vehicle beneath an arch formed by the intertwining boughs of tall evergreen trees, where the Sandcat was temporarily hidden from the crew of the chopper. He heard the strong thrum of the engines and whirling blades as the helicopter hovered over the arch, then moved on.

Kane braked to a halt, coming to a snap, almost insane, decision. He put the Sandcat in neutral. "Everybody out!"

Surprisingly, everyone obeyed him without question. Kane walked along the side of the road and after a brief search, found a heavy lump of sandstone on the roadside, weighing around thirty pounds.

With the driver's-side door open, he stood beside the vehicle, hefted the stone and jammed it down on the gas pedal. As the engine roared, Kane carefully pressed down on the clutch and engaged the first gear.

Kane released the clutch and flung himself away from the Sandcat. The vehicle leaped forward, the rear tires barely missing the toe of his boots. It barreled out from beneath the tree arch, and the helicopter whirled, descended and zoomed in, its landing gear barely ten feet above the road.

The snout of the chain gun flickered with fire, and .50-caliber slugs punched a cross-stitch pattern in the road in front of and to the left of the vehicle. The Sandcat kept going, avoiding direct hits. The lines of impact scampered across the cobblestones, flinging rock chips and splinters in all directions.

With the rear of the chopper facing them, Kane, Brigid, Grant, Domi and Lakesh began running toward the pyramid, hoping to put considerable distance between them and the helicopter before its crew realized no one was driving the vehicle.

At the sound of the crash, Kane looked behind

him. The Sandcat had plowed into a tree, tipping it to the right. Its momentum might have carried it on over, but a storm of bullets striking the bodywork caused it to list, tilt, then crash onto its side.

The helicopter hung over it like the bird of death it was named after, strafing the body with steady bursts. One burst punctured the fuel tank, and its contents went up in a brilliant fireball.

The Deathbird wheeled away from the licking flames, and for an instant the entire area was illuminated by the orange-yellow flare. In that instant, the tinted, bubble-enclosed cockpit of the helicopter was facing the five people.

"So much for my brilliant improvisation," Kane said sourly.

"What do you suggest we do, friend Kane?" Lakesh asked.

"Only one thing we can do," he replied. "Run."

All of them began running again, along the tree line, at an oblique angle to the pyramid's nearest corner.

The Deathbird did a figure eight from east to west and made a roaring pass, driving down from the rear. Bullets exploded dirt all around them. They dropped flat just as the chopper roared overhead. It came so close to the pyramid that it banked sharply to port, the vanes nearly scoring stone blocks.

Rolling onto his back, Grant squeezed off three shots from his Sin Eater as the chopper ascended, correcting for the decreasing range. Between pants,

Kane said, "Let's find out if they're suckers for decoys."

Ignoring the angry shouts from Brigid and Grant, Kane leaped to his feet, ran broken-field style across the open courtyard surrounding the base of the pyramid.

The Deathbird's pilot straightened and leveled off, but by then Kane was nearly to the structure's corner. The chain gun spat lead and noise and flame again. Bullets kicked up dirt in waist-high fountains two yards behind him.

Kane dived headlong toward the pyramid and rolled. The Deathbird roared overhead, the landing gear nearly scraping the ground at the far edges of his hearing, he heard Grant's Sin Eater roaring at full-auto. The chopper heeled to starboard and struggled to ascend out of range of the blasterfire.

The whirling blades sliced into the side of the pyramid, digging out pounds of stone in dust-filled eruptions. Sparks showered as steel struck stone, and the main rotors snapped with a painfully high-pitched, musical chime.

In a lurching sideslip, the Deathbird seemed to bounce away from the pyramid. The main rotor assembly continued to spin with broken, jagged stems. The craft cannonaded port-first against the pyramid's face.

The Deathbird was swallowed by a billowing, red-orange ball as the high-ex warheads in its stub wings detonated on impact. A roaring ball of red-yellow flame mushroomed out from the ruptured fuel tank. Kane recoiled as the hard hot wall of air, pushed forward by the thundering explosion, slapped his face. Debris rained to the ground, pieces of half-slagged and smoldering metal mixed in with blackened chunks of stone.

Kane rose unsteadily to his feet and backed away from the conflagration. Grant, Domi, Brigid and Lakesh raced up to him. He was still dazed and for a second didn't recognize Lakesh.

"We're very close to it now. Let's get inside— quickly!" Lakesh urged.

The entrance to the pyramid wasn't particularly grand or gaudy. It was a simple rectangle seemingly punched into its facade. Kane was only dimly aware of running down a dark passageway, his footsteps echoing like the beat of distant drums.

Then he saw the gateway unit, with its armaglass walls glistening like molten gold. Lakesh punched in the destination-lock code on the keypad. Grant slammed the door behind them, and the jump mechanism was triggered.

The metal disks in the floor and ceiling of the mat-trans chamber shimmered, the glow slowly intensifying, like condensed fire. A fine mist gathered and wafted down from overhead. A vibrating hum arose, climbing rapidly to a high-pitched whine.

Voices began to shout outside the chamber, and fists pounded on the armaglass. Grant squeezed Domi's shoulder reassuringly. She eyed him strangely at first, and then realized he wasn't trying to reassure her but himself that she was still alive.

Grant pulled her close to him and whispered, "Never again."

Domi whispered back, "Never again what?"

Grant didn't answer. As he entered the darkness, he clasped Domi's hand in his, feeling the solid warmth of her touch, and closed his eyes. He knew her hand would still be there when he opened them again.

OUTLANDERS®

FROM THE CREATOR OF

DEATH LANDS®

AMERICA'S POST-HOLOCAUST HISTORY CONTINUES....

OUTLANDERS®

Take
2 explosive books
plus a
mystery bonus
FREE

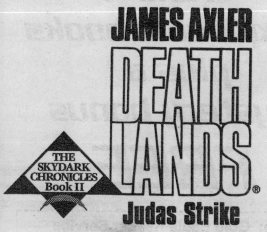